ABOUT THE AUTHOR

By day, PAUL DAVID HOLLAND teaches Latin, Classics and History of Art in a school deep in the Cotswolds, despite having begun his career as a teacher of Modern Languages. His degree in French and German led to a love of travelling around Europe, including a year living and working in Modena, Italy, and eventually to a series of posts in some of England's loveliest schools. However, the creative urge has always been strong, leading to the publication of two satirical novels based on the fictional world of St. Cretien's College, as well as the mystery thriller *Paean*, all of which include illustrations by the author himself. As a keen and prolific artist, he has also exhibited in a number of shows and exhibitions, with works specialising in architecture and urban landscapes.

Caligula Keith is Paul David Holland's fourth published novel, to be followed soon by a number of works based on ancient myth, fantasy and prehistory, as well as the non-fiction and educational works, *A Half-Life of Travel* and *Joining the Dots.*

ALSO BY THIS AUTHOR

St. Cretien's College, Vol. I

St. Cretien's College, Vol. II

Paean

Prometheus *

Joining the Dots *

A Half-life of Travel *

Atlantiad, Vol I *

Atlantiad, Vol II *

(to be published soon)*

CALIGULA KEITH

First published in 2022

ISBN: 9798842022311

www.pauldavidholland.co.uk

CALIGULA KEITH

PAUL DAVID HOLLAND

CALIGULA KEITH

PROLOGUE

Jam boner, jam boner, jam boner…

On and on it goes. Where it is exactly, he just cannot tell. Not quite inside his head, it's around him somehow. Bouncing off the walls of the bathroom, with each repeated tilt of the head.

Jam boner, jam boner…

What does it mean? Maybe it's a message. If it is, he'll understand it someday soon, and when he does, when he finally makes sense of this elaborate, convoluted plot, all hell will break loose. And when he finds out who is behind it all, woe betide them.

Someone will have to pay.

CHAPTER ONE

From the gently curved arch of concrete and railings spanning the six lanes of fast-moving metal, a shape, which was clearly a head above a white shirt, rose then fell.

From the dashboard, as it conveys us hurtling along the fast lane, the world appears as if through a gauze, a filter of dislocated reality; we career along fixed ley lines through condensed space and strangely compressed time, until we arrive as if by some inexplicable magic at a destination, having simply stared ahead, monitoring a great, glass screen filled with light and images of others journeying alongside. Nothing normally disturbs this trance-like existence of two or three hours, nothing impinges from the sides – at least we hope it won't… Any kind of untoward event would almost certainly spell the end of the journey in every sense.

Which is why the shock was palpable, a physical jolt, when Keith Hartman saw what he saw. The sight of a portly, grey-haired man falling headlong from a footbridge onto the opposite carriageway, and disappearing into the flood of oncoming, bank-holiday traffic had the air of unreality about it. Seeing him plummet bodily through an airy emptiness towards the silent splash of impact, it was as if he were watching it all unfold at the tail-end of a disturbing dream.

An image, real and unreal, projected onto the retina, a flood of information and activity, to which a response must be made.

'Shit! *Shit!* Did you see that?'

'See what?'

'My god, he actually fucking fell. He actually fell right off the bridge!'

'Who did?' Keith's girlfriend turned around in the passenger seat and, sure enough, she could see for herself the sudden bunching of red brake-lights, the manic flickering of hazard-lights; he saw that she sensed a thrilling flutter of panic at the now audible, dull thudding of collisions. A thick, acrid plume of black smoke was now rising into the gathering distance as their own car pushed on regardless.

'Didn't you see it? He fell straight off that footbridge back there. Oh my god, oh how bloody awful. A guy falling off a bridge! And...'

'And what?'

'Nothing. It doesn't matter.' Keith stopped himself.

'You're right,' she replied, shocked now. 'Something must have happened. The traffic's going mad.'

Keith glanced sideways at his girlfriend sitting there beside him.

Something must have happened.

How bloody typical of Karen, this non-committal response which, at its heart, indicated her lack of belief. Of course it had happened, did she think he was making it all up? Was he fabricating his life into something more exciting?

Never really happy to accept what he told her, always just one step behind, and stubbornly reluctant to catch up and walk in step with him... Why could she not just believe him in the first place? Why did she have to have this constant filter of doubt whenever things happened?

And it was bound to get worse. That's how divorces must take root, he mused, almost cheerfully, as the tarmac sped on under the wheels of their jointly-financed *Renault Mégane.*

Keith decided it was best not to mention to her the other thing he had seen as the man had been falling off the bridge. It just wasn't worth the trouble; for the moment he was still shaken, and within him a silent knot of horror kept him from saying any more.

Behind them, a sudden and shocking death was creating havoc on the M4.

Ahead were the slip roads and junctions that led eventually to his parents' house, that rarely visited relic of his long-abandoned youth. Then would come the stilted and shifting conversations which betrayed the ever-widening gap between their ages, their aims, their aspirations.

But for now Keith was driving away from the strange events gathering around the broken corpse lying on a bloodied patch of tarmac far behind him.

Chapter Two

Carter Henry was a tall man, over six foot, wiry and cadaverous, with sunken eyes and cheeks making him look for all the world like an extra from a horror film. It was not as though his appearance alone was what dictated Keith's attitude towards him, but there was no denying it affected his demeanour somewhat. Whenever Carter put his head around the door or rose ominously from behind the partition that divided their workspace, Keith would rarely suppress a shiver, and have to look away momentarily. There are some people we encounter who cannot be visually embraced without at least the briefest of pauses, though Keith liked to tell himself this was more to do with the inward personality that was manifested in their outward appearances; that old adage that one grew to look like one was. But Carter's habit was also to approach every situation with the earnest intensity of a man doing battle with a crisis, and this only served to accentuate the lines that time had wrapped around his balding head. As a result of this annoying, serious bent, Keith tended to steel himself with an inaudible intake of breath whenever Carter appeared with his latest *crise*.

It was, however, Keith, who for once was suffering a mild crisis as he stood slowly to address Carter, sitting opposite him at his own screen. Here he was, in the middle of a Wednesday afternoon's normal routine, sifting through the applications and deleted visas he dealt with on a daily basis; here he was, managing the tedious administration he had worked up through the Civil Service for, when suddenly something did not seem altogether right.

'This is wrong, I'm sure,' he ventured, poring again over the words of the report he had to attach to a form declaring an accidental death. He lifted his glasses to read more closely the words somebody had written, as if this would change what he had just read. 'Look at this, would you, Carter? I can't let this one go…'

Carter took it and read the information for himself: 'What's wrong? Looks fine to me. *Adeleke Olatunji… Nigerian national… accidental death… suspected suicide…* Go on, what's wrong?'

Keith looked again at the date, and frowned.

'This is so weird. Hang on, let me just get a quick look at a satellite map or something. Maybe I'm wrong.'

He brought up onto the screen the clear, sleek lines of the internet's twenty-first century Britain, speckled with labels and green national parks, and homed in stage by stage to what he was looking for.

'Yes, bloody hell, I thought so… Look at this!'

By this time Carter was on his feet too, and stood behind Keith's shoulder, looking at an unfamiliar area of southern England.

'See the date on this death certificate?' said Keith.

'Monday the second of May. So what?'

'It's my mum's birthday.'

'And what has your mother's birthday got to do with a dead Nigerian?'

'I saw this happen, we were on our way to visit my parents, I remember it happening. It was here, as it says on the form, look, from exactly this bridge. I was driving right under this very bridge at the time.'

Carter glanced across at his colleague, then over at the map on the screen: 'Goodness. You actually witnessed it, then? Fancy that…'

'And the point is, he wasn't black.'

'I don't get it.'

'The guy I saw falling off the bridge was not black. In no way was he Nigerian. And with a name like that, let's see…' Keith took back the form from Carter's lowered hand. 'Adeleke Olatunji is not going to be a middle-aged guy with white hair, is he?'

'And that's what he was, was he? You definitely saw a white-skinned man?'

'Bloody hell, absolutely I did! I'd swear on it, really.' Keith was suddenly filled with a fizzing desire to make sense of this strange inconsistency, and clicked on the screen to open a new tab. Typing in: *M4 accident 02.05.19 traffic jam road closure*, there now appeared on the screen a whole list of news pages for him to peruse, some local, some national, BBC and the like.

'Carter, do me a favour, would you? Could you bring up any files we have on this Olatunji fellow? Especially the immigration and justice files. Have a look under your commissions lists too, if you would. Let's see where and why it is he is registered with us, shall we… This is so weird, it really is.'

Carter shuffled awkwardly. 'Well, to be honest, I'm not sure that's really within…'

Keith turned and looked straight at him.

'Oh come on, Carter! What the hell are you saying? Look, here we are responsible for making sure the right reports go off to the right people for the right reasons; what else would Her Majesty's Civil Service be expected to do in such a case, if not follow it up? Let's see what you've got!'

With that, Carter went back round to his desk, started clicking, and within minutes he said: 'Ah! I see…'

'Go on!'

'Well, it appears he was, er, let's see: *Olatunji… 2008… refugee status after arriving in Southampton… illegal immigrant… limited visa granted in 2012… petty crime… Hackney… Tower Hamlets… Limehouse… then community service for minor theft… aggravated bodily harm, common assault, eighteen months…* interesting; seems like he goes off the radar after 2016 completely, but it looks as if he is suspected of heading back off to Nigeria, possible terrorism links… He's still kept on lists we're sharing with their government, but apparently: … *killed in a raid in the north-east of the country late last year.*'

'And look here,' said Keith, craning over his own screen. '*Westbound lane M4, completely closed... massive tailbacks... three dead and fourteen injured... suicide throwing himself off local footbridge...*

'But no real mention or description of the victim, none at all. Look, even the follow-up articles and reports. This is so strange. And then, five months later at the inquest, the families are told that an unnamed man of Nigerian descent was *the suicide whose actions on that day led to the tragic events.*

'Christ,' continued Keith, 'it must have been carnage on the day. May bank holiday, and all those cars. It was a real bloody pile-up, I remember seeing it starting to crunch up in my wing mirror. But quite why nobody noticed at the scene that the guy himself was white, and not black, well I just don't know...'

'Must have just been a messy tangle of bodies,' suggested Carter.

'Maybe, maybe. But...'

'But what?'

'Well, it doesn't add up, does it? We've still got a missing or dead Nigerian's name and details being used to sign off somebody's apparent suicide.'

'Apparent?' noted Carter.

'Just keeping my mind open.'

'We should report this as an anomaly as soon as possible, though.'

'Absolutely, yes. Hang on, though, let me make sure first. I'll have a bit more of a hunt-round this evening, and see if I can't fish out anything else.'

Carter leaned back in his chair. 'Why would anyone be trying to cover up how a Nigerian terrorist died? After all, he's not our problem any more, is he!'

'Maybe not, but think about it another way... Why are they using a dead man's identity to cover up another man's death on the motorway? No-one's going to cry over the Nigerian's demise, are they? So the real question is: who was the man who fell from the bridge, and why would the authorities want to keep his real identity from getting out?'

Carter stifled a laugh. 'You're thinking about this too much!'

'Am I? Maybe,' conceded Keith, and likewise leaned back on his chair, mimicking Carter's posture. 'It just seemed all so vivid at the time. It was only a few months ago, to be honest, and yet I can still see it all so clearly. Maybe you're right, though…'

'I tell you what, I'll keep looking into it myself, if that makes you feel any better. I'll have a word or two with Upstairs, if you like?'

Keith recoiled. 'You sure that's a good idea? It's all making me wonder whether I really did see what I saw. To bring in the big guns at this point, well that would be raising the stakes quite a bit…'

'As you like, fellah! You do a bit more digging on your side, and I'll ask a few more questions on the hush-hush, and get into a few more files. We'll see if anything comes up, shall we?' Carter was being awfully decent about this, Keith thought, and he decided to let him rummage around a little; after all, it would be good to get another angle on the whole thing, and maybe that might set his memory straight about what he actually saw.

'Fine. Cheers. I guess it can't do any harm, can it?'

'Of course not. And anyway, if we come up against state secrets and MoD smokescreens, they've always got the Official Secrets Act and what have you! I mean, you know what those chaps are like if anybody's fingers get too close to their flies! Just think of all those satellite images they doctor and patch over. It's happening all the time.'

'Thanks, Carter.' Keith moved on to the next form, and processed it with no interference at all from either his memory or his imagination.

But suddenly on that day there had been such a brilliant flash of inconsistency in what he was looking at, that a crack had irrevocably opened up in the fabric of the everyday, a sharp, jagged fissure had ripped across his life, and Keith Hartman's existence would now never be the same again.

It was very soon time to finish his work for the day, and after putting everything into its usual, ordered piles, Keith pulled on his jacket, and headed for the door.

'All the best, then, see you tomorrow!'

'You will,' called back Carter, predictably.

Keith paused. 'Ah, no… Actually, no you won't. Is it Wednesday today?'

'All day.'

'Ah, well. Listen, I meant to say earlier that I have a slightly embarrassing event to attend tomorrow. I'd almost forgotten all about it myself, to be honest. Hope you don't mind, I think I mentioned it to HR ages ago, but I've got a blasted driving speed awareness course to go to. Sorry.'

'Ha!' laughed Carter. 'You enjoy it. I hear they're great fun. And the more fun they are, remember, the quicker the time goes.'

Keith left and headed past the burly security men, between the buffers, then through the glass revolving doors, and out into the early summer sunshine stoking the heat down here in the unshadowed streets of Whitehall. With a sudden spring in his step, he headed out over St. James' Park and Green Park towards the Underground station and the Piccadilly Line.

Passing the now ubiquitous protesters who had gathered on various street corners along his route, brandishing signs and placards, he found himself standing on the platform feeling the rising wind as the next train approached. Fifty-five minutes or so, depending on the trains, plus a ten minute walk, and he knew he'd be back home. First Green Park station, then Hyde Park Corner, then Knightsbridge… And on and on, all the way to Uxbridge, through the swathes of suburbs.

The journey this sunny evening was a quiet, almost reflective experience. After the intensity of the office today, the riddles thrown up by his discovery and the questions left unanswered, Keith found there was something cathartic, something biting and purging about sitting on the train and watching these suburbs pass him by.

What secrets they must harbour, what hidden truths lurk behind the curtains, defended from prying eyes by the protecting rows of meaningless ornaments on window sills, pendants hanging like lucky talismans from the handles, the backs of dressing-table mirrors squatting, like unseeing, unhearing bouncers up at first-floor windows. Keith let his mind wander – it was something he could never stop from happening – into bedrooms hanging with erotic prints, fluffy handcuffs, whips, maybe even chains and whole theatres of sordid, messy play-acting, scenes steaming with brutal submission. What horrors might there be out there, just in this single moment's field of vision, he wondered, as he looked out onto the lines of roofs and stubby chimneys, the back lawns and featherboard fencing… He smiled, knowing he could never know. That was the sublime pact with Suburbia, and he was willing to be a happy signatory to this.

Chapter Three

It was the end of a long Wednesday. Work had been particularly tiresome all day.

Keith opened his front door and ventured within.

'Hello? Darling?' he called out. 'Are you home?'

'Hi! I'm in the kitchen.' A warm smell of cooking filled Keith's nostrils.

He lay his briefcase in the usual place, the *docking port*, he called it, a slim trestle table half-way down the hall, on which sat the landline phone and a spare key for the car. On this table all his work-related troubles, concerns and issues were mentally left behind. Although Keith always brought his briefcase home with him, if it ever made it past this point, then Karen knew something serious had to be looked at before bed.

He found her in her apron with her hands caked in flour, and with traces of various foodstuffs around her fringe, where she had wiped her long, blond hair away from her face.

'Cooking up something special for this evening?' he asked.

'Honey, you know full well what's happening, don't you?' she asked, turning away disapprovingly. 'Or have you forgotten again?'

'Forgotten what?' He paused for a moment before saying anything else that might incriminate him. Then: 'Samantha? I mean, Sam Taylor? Oh, yes of course, sorry…'

'Ah, you *had* forgotten. Well thanks a lot.' Karen turned away, muttered something barely audible about load-bearing trusses, and wiped her flour-smeared forearm across the beads of sweat on her forehead, before turning back to face Keith: 'Well I hope you don't make as much of a fool of yourself as you did last time.'

'A fool? What do you mean?... That's a tad unfair, isn't it?'

'A *tad* unfair? Well, I suppose you had the excuse that you were drunk. Doesn't quite allow for the amount of gawping, though, does it.'

'I'd had a few... Gawping?'

'Eyes on her legs the whole time.'

'Oh come on...' Keith rolled his eyes with laboured innocence in order to hide a certain coy recognition.

'I don't know why we've got her coming round again,' continued Karen. 'That's me being naïve, thinking it was nice to have somebody different in our lives, someone I could get to know, too.'

'Yes, that is nice, it is,' pleaded Keith. 'It *is* nice. I just don't remember it being as bad as all that, I have to say. She was good company, and I enjoyed seeing her after so long.'

'You can say that again!'

'What exactly did I do, then? I certainly didn't mean to cause you any offence.'

'You remember I was trying to describe the trip we're planning to France.'

'And?'

'You were pathetic. Goggle-eyed and boyish. For god's sake, I know you once had a thing for her.'

'Hang on. That makes it all sound a bit school-crush, frankly. We did once go out.'

'Don't I know...'

'Honey, it was ages ago. Years. Why bring all this up? I don't have any feelings any more. She was a fling when we were working together. Not exactly a *thing*, though. Just a passing, er...'

He closed his eyes, partly in delicious remembrance. He had enjoyed a short, flirtation-filled fling with the smoky-eyed brunette, well-known, in the office they had shared many years before, for her high-heels and pencil skirts, her coquettish retorts and her Christmas party tricks. Samantha Taylor! 'Anyway, come on... I wasn't that bad, honey! I said at the time you overreacted, and now here we go again raking it all up, for goodness sake.' Keith stepped right up to her and put his arms around her. 'Hi, honey, I'm home,' he murmured into her floury ear.

'Hello darling,' she conceded, as she turned her lips to touch his. A silly fling, of course, but one which Keith remembered fondly for the fun they'd had, for the excitement of dating a colleague at work without anyone else's knowledge, and for the butterflies that had fluttered so pleasurably whenever they'd had to keep up the pretence of continued professional dealings. They were working together in the junior office in East London, while they were doing a diplomatic training course.

The sex had been fun too, but the whole affair had been short-lived, and was all the sweeter for it, thought Keith, who had presumed there was little future in a rising civil servant being together with an aspiring policewoman soon to be transferred to Kent. They split with lots of smiles and unfulfilled promises to keep in touch.

But that was exactly what they were doing now, surely. It was Samantha, in fact, who had got in touch first, with Karen, saying she'd now been posted nearer to West London, asking whether they would care to meet up, etc.

It was in fact through Samantha's cousin or nephew or friend that Keith had first been introduced to Karen, now his girlfriend of two or so years.

She was a little younger than Keith. Karen had quickly fallen for his charms and from there into his bed. They began to share days out in North London and beyond. As their time together pushed on into the summer months they found themselves spending days and nights heading off into the centre of the capital. Karen was uncomplicated and strangely shy, though deserving of deeper exploration, thought Keith. Her own field had been English literature, and she had even thought about becoming a teacher, but admitting in the end that she had no genuine love or interest in what she had studied, other than as a means to getting a good degree. Now she worked for a decent consultancy, managing a sub-office team, or some such, on the outskirts of Slough.

They had known fairly soon that they would move in together, and after seven months began renting a flat in Chertsey, before scrabbling together a deposit for their house at number forty-two. It was a fine, Victorian town house, the middle one of a tall, stone terrace of five, located in an otherwise unassuming street just outside the centre of Uxbridge – three storeys, communal attic, dainty flight of four steps up to the front door, a hallway with black and white diamond tiles running all the way to the foot of the stairs.

And now the friendship with Samantha had suddenly been resumed, with the three of them meeting a couple of times for drinks at a local pub. One afternoon in the spring she'd come to visit with her dull beau, when they had a barbeque with a few other friends…

And here was Samantha coming round again, presumably along with her squeeze… God, he hadn't had much going for him, poor thing. Keith heard an inner voice muttering its admonition deep within his head:

Keep your thoughts to yourself. Don't think too much about it all.

Anyway, she's spoken for, now, since she hitched up with that Rob, Robert, Bobby, Booby… God knows. A colleague from work. Some pen-pusher, or maybe even a bean-counter from the back office… Keith couldn't even remember quite what he looked like. A vague memory floated to the surface of a large-eyed, balding guy who talked about improvements on the Birmingham line and how they had affected his journey times when visiting his sister in Walsall.

Had he really been looking that much at her legs? Possibly. They were very fine legs, from what he remembered, all done up in filigree black tights and ankle-boots…

But it's not as though Karen wouldn't notice this time; in fact, she'd be even more sensitive to it if it happened again, especially after this timely reminder. Just lay off the legs, keep eyes firmly aimed at face and hair and lips – well, maybe not so much the lips. And don't stare, for god's sake don't stare. There's nothing worse than a gaze that lingers too long for comfort, one that's gone beyond the *I'm really interested in what you have to say*, and ventured thrillingly into the *see how the eyes roll coquettishly heavenwards*, and *watch the lips move, watch her perfect teeth bite smilingly on the lower lip* territory.

Keith decided it was now the moment to engage Karen with the story about the dead Nigerian.

She did not seem particularly impressed. It sounded weird, she agreed, but was not sure whether Keith had actually remembered rightly when he described the falling man as white and middle-aged. In the end, though, she was of the opinion that Carter would probably know what to do, and said it was probably best left to him.

'I'm not convinced it's much to worry about,' Karen ended up saying, much to Keith's disappointment. 'Darling, you're making a mountain out of a molehill, I reckon. These mistakes must happen all the time, especially when it concerns old data that has passed out of the country.'

Keith found he agreed, but now wondered expectantly what Samantha would make of it; maybe he would bring it up later. He was sure she'd have something more to say about it than Karen.

When the doorbell rang, its chimes loosely based on a theme by Mozart, Keith held deliberately back, pretending to be sorting something out behind the back door. He heard Karen head out towards the hall, greet Samantha, and as he came back into the main house he noted a brief smack of lips and cheeks as the two women exchanged niceties.

'Hello, you!' he charmed, as both parties met at the centre of the house. 'How are things?'

'Hello, darling! Well, thank-you, *very* well. Great to see you both again!' Samantha, looking somewhat dishevelled from the drive, but still as attractive as ever, stepped back slightly to address them both, diplomatically, so thought Keith. *Good girl!*

'Let's have your coat,' he offered, as he manoeuvred to take it from her shoulders, 'and let's get you a drink!' She slipped out of her light summer jacket and was led towards the kitchen, a vision of lithe straplessness. Keith's admiring eyes lingered for an unnoticed second before turning dutifully to the hooks in the understairs. Then he made his way to join the two women.

Karen looked meaningfully at him as he sat down with his chilled beer. 'Sam's no longer with Bob.'

And suddenly Keith realised he hadn't noticed she was alone! Of course, the scintillating Bob was not with her. Well, well, well.

'I'm ever so sorry I didn't warn you both.'

'Don't be silly, it's no problem, honest,' replied Karen soothingly.

'All the more for us!' said Keith, delighted with the cheerful cliché.

'It's just that it's been a bit of a tough few weeks, to be frank, and well, I just…'

Karen edged closer to Samantha on the sofa they were sharing. 'Really,' she said, putting an arm around her shoulder, 'It absolutely doesn't matter. Poor you.'

'What happened?' Keith heard himself blurt out.

Samantha laughed. 'Well, really, let's be honest, shall we? It was never really going to work, not in the long term. He was rather dull, to be fair. Lived for his weekend tennis, had very little else to talk about…'

'Apart from the delays on the Birmingham line,' ventured Keith, stopping himself before he said any more.

'I'm so sorry for you,' sighed Karen.

'And,' Samantha went on, 'well, to be honest with you, he was a bit of a belt-and-braces kinda guy, really.'

Keith's curiosity was piqued. 'Go on…'

'Just very cautious. Needlessly so. The final straw came when he came out of a disabled toilet, and told me he had noticed there was not only the lift-up, disabled locking handle thingy, but also a normal toilet sliding bolt. And apparently he used both while in there.'

'Oh dear,' mused Karen, sitting back on the sofa.

'As the toilet-bowl was so far away from the door, he was always afraid he could be caught with his trousers down, or doing whatever, and not have the time to stop someone from coming in. So he preferred to lock the door twice.'

Karen sat even further back. Keith leaned forward, and said:

'Was Rob disabled?'

'No,' affirmed Samantha. 'The point is… we just weren't right for each other, I guess.'

With that, Keith leaned forward, and asked, 'What else has been going on in your life, then?'

Relieved at the change of direction, Samantha visibly untensed her whole frame. 'Oh, this and that,' she smiled, and over the nibbles and then the dining table, the conversation relaxed into tales of sailing and theatre visits.

Keith had always admired her, and he was enjoying listening to her now. She was always alive with ideas, he felt. 'How's work, anyway?' he asked.

'As ever, really. Lots of neighbour disputes at the moment with traveller communities. Borders and boundaries… god, it does get back to that a lot of the time.'

'We've got an awkward one just near us,' said Keith.

'Oh, I did see the orange curtains and the flags in the upstairs windows,' agreed Samantha.

'No, not them on that side,' retorted Keith. 'They're fine, though they do a lot of protesting in the town centre.'

'Who doesn't, these days? Which side are they on?'

'Who do you think? Big-time Europe-supporters. Which is fine, we're all in a mess at the minute… As long as they keep the music down when they have a really late party. And the cannabis doesn't waft through the walls too strongly–' He paused, realising who he was talking to.

Karen helped him out. 'No, it's the other side, though not the ones right next door. Ray and Kathleen are great, he's really into his Civil War re-enactment fandangos. But the old chap at number forty-four, he is beginning to get on our nerves.'

'He'll get his comeuppance,' mused Keith. 'People like that always do.'

Samantha was interested: 'What's he been doing?'

Karen explained. 'Silly, annoying things, just stuff to annoy you, you know what I mean? Nothing you could complain about, but not very neighbourly.'

'You know what, honey?' interjected Keith, 'When I went out last night to get the drinks from the offie, he was outside, tutting again about our car.'

'Because it's half in front of his house? But there was no other space when I got back last night.'

'It's not like it's blocking a drive, is it?'

'He never seems happy that we moved in here…' mused Karen.

'Best to ignore that sort of behaviour,' suggested Samantha. 'It often goes away when it doesn't get any attention; otherwise, antagonism tends to make it worse…'

'He's not happy that we're not married, that's what it is. Older generation, old-fashioned ideas.'

Karen laughed. 'What was it he called you last week?'

'Well, I don't know that he was talking to me, actually, but he was muttering about me sweeping the path early on the Saturday morning, and –'

'Go on, what was it he called you?'

'A popinjay.'

Karen laughed loudly – a little too enthusiastically, thought Keith. Samantha joined in. He didn't mind that. Samantha laughing was a good thing.

'Anyway,' he continued, 'as far as I'm concerned, he's just a pain in the arse, a meddling old fool who doesn't like the cut of my jib.'

'The cut of *our* jib,' Karen corrected him. 'I'm positive he called me a drunk, that time I came back carrying a crate of beer and wine for the barbecue we had in the summer.'

You know he keeps reptiles and all sorts in there, by the way, did you?'

'Really?'

'And insects and spiders.' Keith grimaced. He scratched the side of his collar involuntarily, at the mere mention of such pets. 'The old bugger has made our time here quite difficult on occasions. Bloody interfering, awkward old sod, he can be thoroughly unpleasant when he wants: Car parked right up against ours, so that we had to ask him to move it when we needed to get out last month, do you remember?

And rubbish bins put in the way of our entrance to prove a point; and only a couple of days ago some hardly veiled comments about the number of empties left out for recycling; letting his dog shit in front of our gate; poking his nose over the wall, looking into our lounge…'

Samantha laughed. Keith too broke into a laugh, pouring himself a glass of wine now, and topping up Samantha's. Karen disappeared into the kitchen, and at her voice a minute later Keith too jumped up, to go out and help. When they reemerged, carrying plates and dishes of vegetables and steaming hot lamb, the three of them set about helping themselves and tucking in.

'Had one or two funny characters recently,' said Samantha, and began to allude to some interesting cases she'd been working on in recent months. There was the one with the old university professor who had finally bumped off his wife, having come to the conclusion that he would no longer love her again; also the flasher who had attached a spy camera to his bits, in order to capture the reactions of the girls he exposed himself to – not dreadfully successful, that one, as it had pointed towards the ground most of the time. But Keith was most interested in the vigilante group identifying local paedophiles and confronting them in carefully-laid ambushes.

'What right have we got,' he asked, 'to tell them that's wrong, if they're acting in the common good? I mean, surely they are doing us a service, aren't they, if they're taking a few more of these perverts out of normal society? You haven't got the manpower or the time to pursue paedos in the same way as they have, what with all your financial constraints.'

'But it's still *our* job, not theirs,' retorted Samantha. 'We've been trained – they haven't.'

'Does that matter?'

Karen rounded on her boyfriend with a smile. 'You know, I think you quite admire them!'

'Maybe I do. So what?'

As the main course was cleared away, and as Karen brought the individually ramekined desserts through, Samantha joined in: 'Have you got your Batman costume ready for nightfall? Don't you think maybe you're taking neighbourhood watch to extremes?'

'Oh my god!' giggled Karen. 'So that's why the crime rate around here has fallen so much in the last few months! It's you, Keith! You're protecting us from all the bandits and robbers and paedophiles!'

'Very funny. I am just saying I can see why people go down that route, that's all. People get very territorial, especially about justice. Maybe this is just one way the more extreme-minded get it out of their system.'

'Would you become a vigilante, then?' asked Samantha, seriously.

Keith shifted in his chair. 'No, I don't think I would, I don't think it's my thing, really. But I tell you what,' he continued, draining his wine glass and pouring another generous one, before topping up the others: 'I'll tell you something for nothing; and that is, if I were on my own, if it was just me, I reckon I would be much more of an activist against all the unfairness out there in the world!'

The other two laughed, and Keith joined in. Then Karen asked politely, 'So you're planning for when I'm gone?'

'No, not exactly… Well - '

'And is that when I've left you, or when you've murdered me?'

'Maybe for when you've died,' said Keith, and then immediately regretted it.

'Really? Are you really?' demanded Karen. She scrunched up her eyes and nose. 'And when do you envisage that, exactly?' As Keith muttered something under his breath, she turned away, visibly knocked aback. 'I can't believe you're saying that.'

'It's not like it sounds. It's not like I enjoy being on my own. I'm sure I'd hate it, that's exactly my point. But I can't say I haven't thought about it, darling – surely everybody does, don't they? Surely you have, haven't you?'

'No, I damn well haven't,' retorted Karen, with a note of serious annoyance in her voice now.

Keith then decided this was a cause worth pursuing. 'It always struck me a bit like all those poor fellows before the First World War.' The two women looked at each other, expressionless. 'You know, all that innocence and all. They'd been desperate for the mould to be broken, and yet when it actually came, they didn't know how to deal with it. I guess it would be the same, once you've been left alone after all this time, having been with someone – so I have just thought about what I might do to fill in the emptiness. That's all, love,' he continued, touching her upper arm, which was immediately withdrawn. 'I wouldn't want life to be like that, but if I were on my own again, I know I would try to make the most of it.'

'By becoming a vigilante, chasing paedophiles? Brilliant…'

'No. I don't know what I'd do. But I'd do it well.'

'And currently, by being alive, I'm stopping you from fulfilling your true, golden potential? Thanks, honey. Lovely to hear. Thanks a lot.'

Samantha raised her eyes from the place-mat she'd been investigating so intently for the past few minutes, and suggested they all change the subject.

Expertly failing to change the subject entirely, she looked at Keith pointedly. 'What you've got to know is that trained police officers do a lot more than just fly around dealing with the big problems. Only last week, in Sutton town centre I had to deal with a woman, who – well, you wouldn't believe how low she'd got. She had an old, battered pushchair, full of bottles of cider and booze, and god knows what else. Absolutely out of her mind with worry. Not all that old, mind you, and yet clearly homeless, no family to speak of, no hope… Just went on and on about her life-chances, threatening to kill herself, then turning all violent against the shoppers who'd paused to look. Come on, Mr. Batman; you reckon you could deal with that? That's not about the vigilante lifestyle – that's about street life, that's about dealing with the abject awfulness and poverty of someone's broken life.'

'Yes,' said Keith. 'You're right. I shouldn't have raised it, to be honest. Sorry.' Then speaking to Karen's turned shoulder, he said, 'Sorry, honey.' With that, he began to clear away some of the detritus ready for coffee. As he piled the plates and cutlery together, he added, 'Hey, did we ever tell you how we had to rescue an old chap from being arrested for going the wrong way up a one-way street?'

'No! What happened?' Samantha giggled.

Karen jumped in: 'He was on a mobility scooter thingy.'

'And he was zooming up Regent Street, desperate to get into town,' added Keith, suddenly feeling elated, having grabbed everyone's attention back to more interesting things. He had salvaged the situation enough even for Karen to have re-engaged with the conversation; things had swiftly taken a turn for the better!

Then, as they sat around with coffee and nibbling on some fine chocolates which Karen in complete silence had helped him to find at the back of a cupboard, he continued: 'There's an old boy lives somewhere near here, who comes by only once a week, on a Sunday morning, dragging along behind him some sort of metal trolley thing with something heavy on it. All covered, all tied up with elastic hooks, but god knows what it is or where he's going.'

'To church?' suggested Samantha, deliberately playful.

'Are you kidding? What the hell would he be taking to church?'

Karen interjected: 'We've wondered if it's a corpse.'

'Of course you have,' smiled Samantha. 'Because you don't realise how boring a police officer's life really is, do you!'

'You must have some moments of high drama.'

'Yeah, but nothing like you imagine. Normally busting some crack-head or knocking down his door in the early hours.'

Keith smirked. 'Would you like to come round one Sunday morning and intercept him as he walks by?'

'OK!'

'No, seriously!' said Keith. 'I'm being serious! Why wouldn't you? After all, he does cause a bit of a public nuisance when he trundles past – the wheels scrape away and always disturb us. That's why we've looked out and seen him so often, and realised that he always comes past at the same time. If you were to confront him in your uniform, he'd have to show you what he's dragging round with him, waking up the neighbourhood every week.'

'What time does he come by?'

'Are you going to come?' asked Keith excitedly. 'It might be his dead wife in there!' Realising how he'd veered onto already delicate territory, Keith stopped talking and gathered up the plates from the chocolates, taking them off to the kitchen.

Now Karen leaned forwards too, and also smirked at Samantha. 'You're enjoying this, aren't you? A bit of intrigue for you?'

'Why not? It's fun!'

'Makes a change from petty shoplifting and speeding traps, does it?'

Samantha smiled. 'Oh no, it's always good to catch a speedster!'

In the kitchen, they heard Keith put the plates noisily down onto the sideboard.

'Damn! Bloody fuck it!'

Samantha thought she'd stepped over some mark or other. But, coming back into the dining room, Keith had his hand to his head, and said, 'You've just reminded me of what I've got to do tomorrow. Can't believe I forgot it.'

Karen looked up quizzically. 'What's up?'

'Speed awareness course. A whole day's course on speeding. Bloody hell. It'd completely slipped my mind earlier on today, too. What a waste of a day. Shit, I really could have done without that. Bugger it!'

Samantha sniggered. Karen looked furious.

'Where is it?'

'In bloody Bracknell. Can't believe it… Shit!'

With this final bombshell to inflict further calamity upon an already fragile dinner party, the evening was swiftly wrapped up. Keith could not imagine how it might have been worse. Samantha dispatched herself within a seemly twenty minutes, and Karen and Keith did some of the washing up in silence, before heading to bed.

At least, he thought, as he climbed between the sheets, he couldn't be accused of staring at Samantha this time. In fact, he was thinking more now about the driving course, and how early he'd have to get up in the morning in order to get there. But no way out of it now, these things have to be faced up to, and got through… As long as the worry doesn't get in the way of a good night's sleep.

Karen climbed in beside him. She remained stiff and silent.

'Not much fun, tonight, was she?' he ventured.

Still more silence.

'You still angry? I didn't mean to upset you.'

Finally, from beneath the duvet came a question: 'Are you sleeping with her?'

Keith sat upright and stared at his girlfriend.

'What? No, don't be ridiculous! Whatever made you think that?'

'Forget it. I'm tired. Sleep well. See you in the morning.'

CHAPTER FOUR

Keith's nights were generally disturbed somehow, whether by clicks and clacks around their old house, or by the voices of people passing below.

'You going straight back home from here?'

'Mandy was well hammered.'

'You can't talk. Look at you, man! You're shitfaced!'

'Call this shitfaced? Should of seen me yesterday. Out of it. Off my face, I tell you. Dude, you ain't never seen nothin' like it.'

Or snatches of a relationship in the grip of a drunken storm:

'What is your problem? Did you want me to hear that?'

'So it's me?'

'Who else would know?'

'Kacey.'

'Why Kacey of all people? Don't you think that is a totally unreasonable name to mention?'

'Why? Why shouldn't I mention her?'

'Because of what she did to us before? And what she's doing to Rich now. Shit, haven't you heard a single thing I've been saying?'

'Yes.'

'So why didn't you come and find me?'

'When?'

'When you saw that Peter had left.'

'Why did Peter leave? I didn't see him leave.'

'Well he wasn't there at the end, was he? Where exactly did you think he'd gone?'

'Did he arrive with Megan?'

'Are you kidding me?'

On and on these conversations would go, their protagonists and antagonists sometimes lingering within earshot as they found themselves increasingly entangled in their labyrinthine arguments; by this point even Keith could no longer work out who was telling the truth, and often his return to drifting slumber unleashed his own voices inside his head, and he found himself trapped within different, illogical conversations long after the real speakers outside had wandered off, taking their mutterings with them.

Other times he simply woke up from a dream and found he was suddenly too alert and buzzing with worries to get back to sleep, trying desperately to ignore the creaking boards and timbers that always seemed to disturb him at around the same time of night.

Tonight, perhaps in guilt at his thoughts earlier about Samantha, he was fully awake with his thoughts. Thoughts and thoughts. Whirling around inside his stupid head. Any attempt to control them, to bring them together into a single knot, a single thread, and then to find some mindful way of following that thread into a fog of slumber… any attempt at all seemed useless. Something would always pop into his mind without any warning, or a car would pass on the street, or someone would kick a can as they wandered back from some cool-cat party out in the centre of town.

Keith wondered whether his recent thoughts and urges about Samantha again were not just natural, male curiosity about how green other grass might be, or a lost opportunity, or actually part of a pattern, a need for someone new, something different. Girlfriends had come and gone. Keith knew what he liked, and what he wanted too. But the right one had never quite come along. The first proper one was Veronica, the dark-haired, angst-ridden temptress; her athleticism in the bedroom had quite put him off sex for a while, and instead highlighted actually how dull she was outside the bedroom.

Then came Magda, a German colleague he met on an international conference; she had been living in London for a while, and met most of Keith's criteria, including a sense of humour bordering on sadistic.

But something wasn't right with Magda, and on a clear, winter's day Keith caught himself looking intently at her face, her hair, her neck, and realised she was not attractive to him any more. The split with Magda made him feel a deep guilt, and he wondered uncomfortably for a long time whether he was unsuited to loving anyone else, was too demanding, too specific or simply too shallow. Perhaps his fastidiousness would forever be a permanent block to finding a soulmate and the everlasting happiness that apparently followed in their wake.

There had been Wendy, a suburban cutie who was over-fond of pedigree rabbits. And Saskia, a sporty type whose tedious interest in football and celebrity magazines unfortunately was not made up for by the mind-blowing sex games in which she involved Keith. And Miranda, whose parents were born-again Christians, and who herself seemed forever on the cusp of throwing her lot into some millennial preparation for the Endtimes; don't live too much now, she would say, let's wait until the world is remade after the Second Coming, when we can travel and visit places once they've been remade in the perfection of God's loving order. She lasted just two months, before she experienced her own, heartbreaking endtimes.

And then Samantha, the delectable Samantha…

Suddenly, from outside, came the aggressive thunder of massive engines, and the roar of several vehicles racing past the house.

A siren blared for a second's warning as they joined the main road nearby, then another, as two, three emergency vehicles raced past at full pelt. The shock of the noise and the urgency of their speed made both Keith and Karen sit up with a jolt.

'What in god's name is going on?' groaned Keith.

'Ambulances?' muttered Karen.

Keith got up and leaned out of the open window. 'Fire engines. Three of them. Oh I see, over there! They're heading across towards Henford, I think. I can see a glow, and quite a bit of smoke.'

On the horizon was a broad, bright smear, uplit from flames somewhere below, and rising from far away behind the houses on the edge of the estates, beyond the woods. This was where he remembered an old, maybe deserted, army base was to be found. He returned to the cool embrace of his bed, and finally drifted off into a troubled sleep.

CHAPTER FIVE

Jam boner... jam boner... jam boner...

How very strange. It shouldn't happen but it does.

Keith was standing, as every morning, in the shower, trying to wash off the sleep, while still enjoying the warmth of the hot water bustling about his body. It was the routine of his daily transition into wakefulness after the shock of the cold.

But he had been, over recent weeks, increasingly fascinated by the noise he heard as he pulled his clasped hands together over his head and back again, to wash out the shampoo. Of course, he knew it must be perfectly explicable as the echo of the running water within the confines of the shower unit, as the sound waves bounced irregularly around the tiny space, but there was no denying that his brain made it sound like: *jam boner... jam boner... jam boner...* again and again and again!

How weird, but how satisfying! Once you'd heard this, you couldn't undo it. Keith was fascinated and intrigued.

Only a few months before, he'd been sanding the floor of the bathroom, and with each stroke of the sander, all he could hear reverberating around the walls was: *sadie mascot... sadie mascot... sadie mascot...*

It was maddening but addictive.

Now here he was enjoying the same sound in the shower. And whatever *jam boner* might mean, it was likewise utterly satisfying. He rinsed his hair again, and then again. It was if he couldn't get enough of it. The sound of pigeons calling across the street was exactly the same first thing in the morning, when the still-dozing brain added an extra layer of inertia and imagination to their calls.

Dried and dressed, back he went to the bedroom. By this time, Karen was also getting up, stretching the aches out of her limbs as she climbed naked out of the bed. Admiring her body with a kiss, he sat down to put on his shoes.

'Good morning,' he said.

'Good morning.'

'All OK?'

'All OK.'

Keith kissed her goodbye as he grabbed his jacket from the back of the chair, and wished her a lovely day. She wished him luck for the speeding course and told him to have fun, which he promised he would.

Then he left their Victorian town house, the middle one of five, and closed the front door gently, bounced down the steps, and headed along the street towards their car. Within minutes he was on his way to Bracknell.

But as he drove, Keith could not help but go over once again the details of what was becoming an obsession for him: the strange case of the dead Nigerian.

He pulled over into a lay-by. Getting his phone out, Keith started writing a text message.

Sam. Hi. Sorry it was a bit fraught last night. Thanks for coming. Lovely to see you.

Send.

Then, without thinking, he started another: *Hey, you don't fancy meeting up later, do you? I have something to ask you about, something odd from work. After driving course?*

Send.

Almost sent it with *xxx*. Keith was glad he hadn't.

A meeting with Samantha… That would have to be dealt with carefully. Tonight, after returning later than expected from the course, he would naturally have to blame it on the volume of traffic blocking up the rush-hour roads. It would look awful to Karen, otherwise – unforgivably awful.

Moments later, he was jolted out of his thoughts by the unexpected buzz and vibration of his phone. It was a text. From Samantha. All too eagerly he opened it.

Hi, don't worry! Would love to meet. Where and when? xxx

Keith smiled.

Course just outside Bracknell. Nice cafe in centre called Live Wire. 5-ish? xxx

He'd work it out, the last thing he wanted was Karen thinking he was actually having an affair, even though the thought of it was evidently attractive to him. But all that would have to wait now, he realised, as he pulled back into the road and continued on his way. Turning off the main road into Bracknell, he made his way towards the venue where the course was to take place. It was nine o'clock.

Keith had secretly wanted to arrive in a furious whirlwind of antagonism. A self-immolating legend of defiance. Maybe even knocking over a couple of dustbins or boxes as he drew up…

In the event, of course, he didn't. As soon as he reached the drive into the car park where the course was to be held, Keith slowed his *Renault Mégane* to the speed of a Sunday driver on the hedge-lined lanes of Dorset, and crawled towards a free space between a *Nissan* and a *Subaru*; he edged into the slot with the care of a condemned man, turned off the engine and wearily undid his seatbelt. This was going to be a long day.

He found his way through clinically clean corridors into Conference Room number five, reticently greeted the peroxide-greying woman who attacked him with a chummy 'Hello there, how are you? It's Mr…?' He then went to find a place at one of the four round tables, on which were set a folder of relevant information, a jotting pad, a pen with the name of the *enforcement agency* (Bettadrive) printed on it, alongside bottled water and a packet of *Hobnobs*.

Keith sighed, and found a place between a mousey middled-aged man and a younger, plump woman with pink highlights and a single dreadlock-braid in her bobbed hair. The three of them all exchanged polite, but rueful smiles, like naughty children who know they are going to have a gentle-but-firm telling-off from their gentle-but-firm deputy headmaster. Slowly the place filled up with equally subdued faces.

'Hi guys!' began the man who was running the show. Along with his colleague, the woman who had got them all to sign their names at the entrance, he had edged to the front of the seminar room, and now gathered all their attention with his overly chummy *guys*, which, thought Keith, some people out there must still find endearing or somehow welcoming.

'Guys,' he continued, 'Thank-you all for coming.'

Keith thought he said this with the sanctimonious smugness of somebody who knows his audience is captive. Still, he decided, best give him a chance. There was a long time still to go…

'I think we'd better make a start, don't you?', There he was again, hinting at a level of choice that no-one in the room had. Keith shifted in his seat. 'We have to press on, so thank-you to you all for getting here on time. Now, as we've had your signatures, this, as I am sure you're aware from the small print, this signature commits you to finishing the course today, and, being an optimist myself, I don't see any reason why we shouldn't be able to sign you all off as having participated fully and actively in the day's course… Er, it's just that I do have to tell you legally that it is incumbent on us here, Sue and I, not to sign you off if we judge you not to have, well, not to have properly contributed, or to have abstained from it all.

'I think you know what I am saying, and so, without any further ado, let's put all this unpleasantness behind us, and get going, shall we? So, my name is Antony Duval, and I am Chief Executive Regional Training Officer, and this is Sue Parker, who I am going to hand you over to now. Thank-you!' He bowed, ever so slightly, as if accepting some imagined or expected applause.

Sue stepped forward, and started addressing the full room.

'Hi everyone! I hope I find you all well this lovely, summer morning! How are we all doing? My name is Sue Parker – well, hello there! I am the Senior Chief Executive and Consultant Training Officer for the South East, and, if you'll permit me to give you a bit of an idea of my CV and experience, I began working for Royal Berkshire County Council Transport and Roads Committee over fifteen years ago, when…'

Her long and unnecessary resumé was interrupted by the opening of the door, as a stocky latecomer burst in and noisily found his place. Antony Duval crept exaggeratedly over to him, lifting his feet higher from the ground than necessary, took his name, signed him off, and came back to where Sue was still going. Keith noticed that the newcomer wore a grimy T-shirt with the words *Country Monster!* written in large letters over some unrecognisable images, faded with washing. What was the meaning of *Country Monster!* wondered Keith. Was he a Country 'n' Western fan? Did it refer to his membership of the Young Farmers? Was it a wry reference to Hamlet? He chuckled silently to himself, as he considered the Country Monster's rotund, pink face, framed within a scruffy, ginger beard. Hats off to him, though, for coming looking like this; time was, when one would have put on at least a cheap suit and tie to come to this kind of affair. Still, everyone still seemed fairly obedient; maybe because they knew any excuse might be found to keep them trapped here longer than need be.

'So you see,' continued Sue, nasally and gratingly. 'You're here because you've all been caught transgressing the speed limit admittedly at a low level. You are, in effect, the lesser of evil-doers!' She laughed, and, looking around, Keith saw all the transgressors' faces smile politely. Then Sue said, very earnestly: 'I do need to confirm that nobody on today's course *was* convicted of doing a speed at more than fifty-five miles an hour?' She looked round with deliberate gravitas. 'Or was found to be over the alcohol limit?'

A hushed silence spread around the room, as people looked across at each other, perhaps hoping for a drama to relieve the tension. 'Good,' continued Sue, 'as there is a very different course for that group, very much away from here… a higher-level course.'

Keith thought he saw the hint of a wince pass over Antony Duval's face as Sue said this. So we really were the good guys, after all; the others were lucky they weren't being shot. Keith imagined them being dealt with on a course set in a gloomy room right across the other side of the building, maybe even underground, treated like grunting lepers, their course leaders covered head-to-toe in the sort of hazmat get-up you see in old footage from Chernobyl. God, he thought, there was as much guilt here as there was in the Catholic Church.

And so the day progressed. Interminably slowly, of course, but with various individuals' characters gradually bubbling to the surface, and even an occasional attempt at making a stand, a snide, very British form of sedition. At one point, a gentleman in an open-neck shirt and jacket, who had earlier resisted being chosen to volunteer to stick the correct labels onto the *speed donkey* set up at the front of the room, now suddenly responded to Antony's post-video comment that 'we are all guilty somewhere deep down for that mother's grief.'

'If I can call you up on that' called out the man, putting up his hand. 'That's a bit over-the-top, really, don't you think? I mean, I happened to be done for a minor infringement, on an open road at the dead of night. Don't reckon there was anyone wandering about at that time, especially not fourteen-year-old girls.'

'You'd be surprised,' started Antony.

'Yes I bloody would,' retorted Keith's new hero. 'In fact, I wonder whether it doesn't come down to the fact that we're here for the simple reason that there are some speed cameras set up specifically to make a profit for the fascist state.'

Whoops! He's said the *f*-word, thought Keith. Fantastic.

Antony looked hot under his smart, starched collar. 'I think that's a question for a different day, don't you? In fact, to be blunt, that's not why you're on this course, and I'm afraid we really can't begin to think like that, can we!' He looked desperately around: 'Any more questions on that point? Good, let's move on then…'

At another point, Country Monster put in a stellar performance, managing to misread every single road sign that was projected up onto the big screen; not only did he fail to recognise the *old people* sign for what it was, and declared the *no overtaking* sign to be about reminding French drivers to drive on the left, but when shown the octagonal *stop* sign, with the word *stop* in the middle of it, he still said: 'Give way.' Keith couldn't tell whether he was truly thick, or whether this was

Country Monster's way of subverting the whole course, and making his day less excruciating. With every misheard and misunderstood question, Keith admired him even more. When he admitted that he always got *maximum* and *minimum* mixed up, to a stifled communal giggle, Keith sat back in silent applause.

Another woman was particularly adept at bringing stories about her family into every exchange she had with Sue or Antony. About forty-five, she early on introduced herself as Sandra, and proceeded to weave her ten-year-old daughter (Sophie, or sometimes just Soph) into a convoluted story about doing a three-point turn behind the local Waitrose. Later, she mentioned her son (Gareth) who along with their dachshund (Willy) had been helping her to reverse-park into a space between two four-by-fours; Gareth had apparently been able to see the lamp-post better than she had, and thankfully she'd avoided disaster, especially at a time when she hadn't been feeling well. Finally, as a tour-de-force, within the space of one minute, Sandra revealed that she had never fully understood who gave way to whom on a roundabout, especially in rush-hour, hardly ever drove anyway, let her husband (Glen) do most of the driving, and was very skilled at holding the wheel while he took off his pullover.

Sue and Antony, presumably choosing to ignore this last detail, said only that we must all be very careful whether behind the wheel or not, and then moved on beyond Sandra's domestic concerns.

And on and on it all went. 'Twenty is plenty!' said Sue at one point, as they were all discussing in groups the right way to drive through urban areas.

'In fact,' interjected Antony, 'I would go so far as to say: *third for thirty!* There's no need to push it up to fourth, really, not when there might be *people* around.' Since Jacket Man's outburst, Antony had stopped making every victim prepubescent.

Tips thick and fast now came from both Sue and Antony, ranging from how to hold the steering wheel (Sandra even pushed her luck here, by asking whether this advice counted only from the driver's seat) to where best to begin accelerating as one came out of a village (Country Monster admitted having always thought that speed signs on country lanes were only advisory and put up by parish councils). One woman who had been quiet all morning started finding her voice during the afternoon, and a number of people on Keith's table began whispering that, as she had disappeared during the lunch break, maybe she'd gone for a cheeky drink. With every, '…and another thing!' his whole table sniggered like schoolchildren, until Sue had to call for a little respect for other people who wanted to contribute. Keith's neighbour ventured the suggestion that the woman was now getting right into the spirit, and his neighbour on the other side actually snorted. Antony looked across venomously. Keith sat back, eager to distance himself from the frivolity.

Finally, as the course drew towards its inevitable close, there was an atmosphere among all the participants of a shared experience, a collective suffering that they'd all gone through, in order to reach this point. Keith couldn't work out whether the genuinely well-meant advice and warnings proffered by Sue and Antony eventually outweighed the pent-up frustration he now felt after five hours of guilt-ridden lecturing; it almost made him want to get straight back in the car and go a little bit mad…

Let it be! he muttered to himself. A voice within him was telling him to behave. This was simply part of the price to be paid, especially for keeping your points. *Deal with it!*

A man who had spent most of the day within Keith's line of vision nodding and agreeing audibly with everything Antony and especially Sue had said, now went up to them to thank them loudly, and to say how much he'd benefited from it all. *Creep!* thought Keith. *Doing that makes us all feel obliged now.*

In the end, despite having a lifelong habit of thanking people at the very least for giving up their time, Keith didn't say anything; he left quietly, persuading himself that he'd been a paying customer, not only with his own time, thank-you very much, but also with the exorbitant fee he'd had to cough up for the privilege. Emerging blinking into the early evening, he made his way back to the car, and even managed to wave a goodbye to Sandra and Country Monster.

Then he caught sight of the piece of plastic-wrapped paper fluttering on his windscreen. No, surely not… He pulled off the brightly coloured document, and read it in disbelief: *Parking infringement – designated disabled space – fee due before 10th of…*

Unbe-fucking-lievable.

Tossing it onto the passenger seat, Keith climbed into his car, seeing the weathered wheelchair symbol on the tarmac as he reversed out of the parking bay. Cursing all the way out of the car park, he set off towards the centre of Bracknell.

The Live Wire it was called; a pokey, independently-run establishment, not quite cool enough to do completely away with the meaningless trinkets and car-boot junk that lined the high shelves around the pale yellow walls, but homely and inviting all the same. Two young women ran it with confident ease. When he had been here before, the blonde had always caught Keith's attention, her hair pulled back into a loose ponytail, strands skirting her neckline and down her mole-covered back. She always wore stylish dresses that set off her healthy skin colour to perfection. And she always smiled.

Keith entered and immediately spotted a chair on the further side not only with a view onto the street, but half-turned inwards to the café itself. He ordered a plain white coffee and took it over to the table.

The young couple sitting across from him were engaged in some lively chatter about tiles and colour combinations for their new kitchen. She favoured a retro-burgundy, he wanted slick, minimalistic white. She appeared to be winning the argument, though *he* had the look of longer-term strategy; Keith could imagine he would be using this as a bargaining chip for a later victory when they redecorated the back-room.

Behind the couple Keith could just make out two teenage girls. One had purple, plaited hair and a nose-ring, and was wearing black, grungy clothes seemingly designed to make her whole get-up look as awful as possible. The other was pretty and had torn jeans and a black top, sporting a tattoo of a skull and some Chinese writing which poked out from just under her short sleeve. This one was telling her friend about the previous night's encounter with some lad from a bar down the road who she had always fancied, but was not sure about now. There was a young lifetime's worth of tawdry experience in her words, a shabby parade of lustful lads, young and old, and an unknowing frustration, exasperation even, at the way her choices were leading her; ahead lay a longer lifetime of wrong choices, wrong men, suicidal days filled with thoughts of hopelessness, shackled eventually to a half-brute with three or four children running wild.

An old Chinese-looking couple entered and ordered teas and cake. They didn't speak to each other as they sat at a table near the window, but looked across each other's shoulders at nothing in particular. This pair had evidently been living here for many years – they counted out their change to pay without glancing twice at the coins they handed over, and when the waitress brought over the carrot cakes the man added an incongruous, but well-worn, *my love* to his thanks. They ate, they drank, they left, with him shuffling out first and not holding the door for her, as she struggled with the shopping trolley she dragged behind her stooped frame.

A taxi driver, clearly known to the servers, entered, brimming with banter and looking round expectantly, as if wanting his routine to be acknowledged and loved by all the customers. He winked cheekily at the Blonde as he carried his takeaway out to his car, validated and affirmed in himself for another day.

Where had Samantha got to? Keith ordered another coffee, and sat back to enjoy more comings and goings. The Blonde brought him his drink, and he enjoyed her fragrance as she leaned over him. He glanced at her lips without letting himself get caught, and savoured the shape of her legs as she left to go back behind the counter.

If he were free, if he wasn't already tied down to one person, wouldn't he do more than just look? Or even if he was; after all, plenty do, these days, probably always have done. Was he actually contemplating dating her? Dating was a bit too strong… Why start seeing somebody when you have just come out of a previous relationship?

Keith checked himself. A *previous* relationship?

The Blonde passed by again. Keith breathed in deeply and imagined her current life for a moment. Then he wondered how a fling with her might develop… He'd ask her out, she'd agree, flattered by the attention of a slightly older, more experienced man, especially one who was enigmatic, intriguing. She would take to him quickly, falling for his charms, they'd hang around together, she'd invite him back to hers, a small bedsit above a shop somewhere on the other side of town, they'd spend a torrid week of meeting up, going to the cinema, chatting online, nights and sultry afternoons would pass by in a haze of loved-up satisfaction.

Actually, she'd turn out to be a bore. A dolt. A dull youngster with nothing to say about the world, and maybe not even interested in anything worthwhile. More up-to-date with the latest soaps than engaged with…

With what? What exactly does a bland, humdrum civil servant expect of a fling?

A civil servant also obsessed with a conspiracy theory…

Keith had been an unassuming only child born to unassuming parents; this had marked out for Keith an unremarkable childhood in an ordinary Home Counties town. Perhaps this is why he had unwittingly fostered such an active imagination and a desire to get beyond the education which was provided for a swathe of unambitious, middle-class kids; eventually Keith had gone to university to study politics.

He had tried for Oxbridge but didn't make it in the end, and settled instead for one of those universities filled with students who felt they should be somewhere else, brandishing their resentful indignation like a badly hidden grudge. This was good for Keith, who now would not suffer the sense of unworthiness at having access to something he hadn't deserved. Keith would henceforth feel he was a big fish in a pond small enough to cope with; and, although he did not realise it, he began to cloak himself in the same righteous injustice as his cleverer peers.

The degree, when it came was the culmination of three years' studying, partying, panicking and attending lectures on history and philosophical theories barely comprehensible even to Keith; and it was a surprisingly decent Second. Delighted, Keith impulsively put to one side his plans to spend the next six months travelling the world. Instead, he now found himself actively following up the links he had half-abandoned for entry into the Civil Service.

His parents had been surprised. They had never seen their son so driven, or failed to recognise it nascent in his teenage years, as he had striven to flee their stifling household. But now it was all on show, a determination to use the tangible proof of his abilities that this degree had just confirmed for him. It was like boarding a ship he presumed had already sailed away. Phone calls, emails, visits to London, interviews, sharp suits and new glasses suddenly coalesced into a job offer, a fast-track route into Whitehall and in quick succession a flat in Streatham, gym membership and a new, top-of-the-range cycle, together with helmet, combination lock and reflective toe-clips.

The London life was almost complete, especially now he had settled down with Karen.

What more could Keith want? His career, his life were now fulfilled. He should be content. This could have been the moment when Keith might relax, sit back and reap the rewards of that drive he'd suddenly displayed so keenly on leaving university. But one thing still was not fulfilled, one area of his life simmered with latent possibilities which even Karen and career were not satisfying.

It went back to his childhood in all its bland tedium, its mindless, endless, unambitious acceptance of the ordinary.

It still shuddered and shook like an empty black hole at the centre of his existence.

Keith's *imagination* still needed to be fed.

'Hello again!' As she stood framed in the window, a delicious, shimmering light danced around Samantha's svelte figure. 'You were miles away!'

'I didn't see you come in at all, sorry. Sit down. Coffee?'

'Tea. Thanks.'

Keith went up to order, and as he came back to the table he savoured the sight of Samantha taking off her jacket to reveal elegant shoulders and neck half hidden by her long, dark hair, tied together in a loose bun.

'As I said in my text, I hope it wasn't too awkward round our place… We were a bit fraught, that's all.'

'So I saw.'

'Anyway…'

'Well, good to see you again.'

'You too. Mwaaah!' Keith leaned down to give the overdue peck on her cheek, which she duly rose towards slightly.

'How was your course?'

'Shit. A waste of a day. Angry-making and run by bureaucrats.'

'Well, at least I know how you stand on the matter,' she smiled back. 'Now, *Mr. Hartman*, what are you going to talk to me about? What is your deep, dark secret? I think you have quite a lot on your mind.'

Keith blanched, and wondered how she could have known… Then he remembered his text.

'Ah. The mystery. Yes.' He composed himself, took a deep breath, and continued: 'This is all very strange, so I wondered what you'd make of it.'

'I'm intrigued. I'm intrigued that you're intrigued.'

'A very strange turn of events, actually. Did I ever mention that awful accident we saw when we were off to visit my parents, when that chap jumped off the bridge and caused all that traffic pile-up?'

Samantha nodded in vague recognition.

'Well, weirdly, I came across the whole thing yesterday at work, and the man they described was, to say the least, nothing like the one we saw.'

'How do you mean?' Samantha was suddenly curious.

'According to the official death records, he was black.'

'And he wasn't?'

'No. I would swear it. I mentioned it to Karen, though she almost certainly wouldn't have remembered or even noticed it in the first place.'

Samantha leaned forward. 'Are you sure, though? Really?'

Keith nodded: 'He was white and middle-aged. I mentioned this to my immediate boss, too. He said he'd look into it.'

'Do you want me to check it out, too? I mean, it's easy enough for me to gain access to some of the documents, if you like?'

'Would you? That would be amazing!' Keith was delighted to have aroused such sudden excitement in Samantha. 'I'm not being weird about this, am I?'

'No, it might be worth looking into it, just in case something is up… You never know. And you are paid to spot any anomalies, after all. Why not send me the details of the dates and the place, and I shall see what I turn up.'

'That's great, thanks so much.'

'No worries. Anyway, it'll give me something to do while I'm on the course this weekend. I can access stuff from my laptop, and there'll be plenty of moments when I can be doing something else more interesting.'

'You're off on a course? Not a speeding awareness one?'

'Absolutely. I'm always pulling myself over for racing around town! Especially when I'm late for something. Mind you, I can just put the blue lights on, that normally works!' Samantha checked her phone. 'Right, I'd better be off. Piles of stuff to do tonight. I'm up early to miss the traffic.'

'Is it far?'

'Manchester.'

'Manchester?'

'A training course. Nothing very exciting. Few days away. Bit of a pain, really. Well, thanks for tea.'

'No, thanks for coming. And thanks for listening to my harebrained plots and conspiracies.' They both stood up. Keith walked her away from the table towards the door. 'Great to see you again. Really great…'

'Yeah, really cool to see you too. Both of you.'

As they passed the counter Keith smiled at the Blonde, but didn't dare to wink. Not yet.

Samantha nodded towards the end of the road: 'My car's this way. Goodbye, then.' They parted with another peck on the cheeks. Keith sprang off towards his own car, hoping that this time it was parked legally.

CHAPTER SIX

Under the bright blue of the summer sky, as Keith emerged from his station at Green Park into daylight again, he thought he saw London shining with more confidence than usual. The grey Portland stone and the white sash windows seemed to speak of a recently rediscovered comfort in the charm of the unchanging. Here in the post-Brexit capital, despite the daily marches, the angry protesters now camped permanently, it seemed, outside Parliament, the slogans and placards in every other front window, it was as if the city, never one for swagger or posturing, had picked up on its growing sense of self. In recent years, it was as if the place had finally turned its back on the grey and mournful post-war soul-searching. Any of those old films set in the 70s or even the 80s, like *The Long Good Friday* which he and Karen had watched again just recently, or some of the *Carry On* films, still had the unmistakable smack of austerity about them, and of a city seeking direction. And not just in the drabness of the buildings, the dreariness of newly raised concrete brutalism and the gaps still scarring the streets; but also in the clothes, and in the cars, too, which look as dated as if they had been designed and manufactured while the old king was still alive. The German *VW Beetle* has a timelessness that transfers well to the present day, even the *Citroën 2CV* can pull it off – but look at a British *Morris Minor*, and you're bang in the middle of rationing! Even the old *Austin Maxi* and the *Rover Princess* have more than a whiff of old Britain about them, without any of the tinge of nostalgia that the continentals can always muster.

Now, as he made his way through the West End towards his office in Whitehall, Keith could suddenly see more clearly than ever what made this place tick. It was the human scale of it all, the feeling that even in the middle of this great, grey patch on satellite maps, which seemed to squat toad-like over the south-east of the country, down here among the willows and duck ponds, the snack-bars and railing-bound lawns, there was a real *humanity* to it all.

Even the most grandiose parts, those huge Edwardian emblems of empire, and the more recent hi-tech towers in the City, even these could not hide the fact that just a few blocks behind them one often found the smaller-scale streets of the Victorian and Georgian buildings, only two or three storeys high and modest to the point of being bland. Yes, he thought, here was the proof of London's homeliness, its *ordinariness*. And here is why it could always afford to resist too much change for change's sake – because what goes around comes around, and somehow, for a while now, it had felt that London was beginning to relish again the very stiffness and awkwardness that it had tried so desperately to lose, ever since the Old World had become mired in troubles and wars.

Somehow London was cool again, but on its own terms this time, and this was always when the place was at its best!

This appealed to Keith Hartman. Change without change. Structural reform through incremental application of tried and tested methods.

Suddenly he had arrived at the revolving glass doors of his office building. Stepping through the security scanners, passing his rucksack across to bored, waiting hands, he made his way up to the room he shared with Carter.

Keith sat staring at his computer screen as it flickered slowly into life. He had come in a little earlier, so as to assuage some of his guilt at having had the Thursday off, which is why he was already at his desk when Carter came in, typically in a mild fluster.

'Hello, young man,' sighed Carter as he took his seat behind the low partition. 'Well, you did leave me with quite a lot to get on with yesterday, I can tell you!'

'Sorry,' muttered Keith, 'I felt absolutely awful leaving you in the lurch like that. I know there's a lot on at the moment.'

'I'm not talking about all that!' laughed Carter, staring across the room into the middle distance. 'No, I'm talking about the riddle of the sands you left me with. The Nigerian who fell off the motorway bridge? Or in fact didn't… Remember?'

Keith let out a sigh of relief. 'Oh, him. Go on, then, what have you found out?'

'Well, come round and take a look at this.' This was unusual; Carter normally came round to *his* desk. Keith had always presumed it was a territorial thing. He stood up, went round to Carter's side and leaned over his colleague, peering at the screen. It was still blue. In the middle of it was a space for him to write his password.

'Do you mind?' asked Carter. Carter's computer was as slow as its user.

'Sorry. I thought you'd…' Keith turned away. He'd been too eager to look. He turned back, but as he did so he spotted Carter's long fingers punching in the last three letters of his eight-letter code.

'Now, here we are…' muttered Carter. Keith pulled up a chair, knowing this might still take some time. The screen fizzed and flickered a couple of times, then Carter brought up the relevant files and websites he'd saved the day before. 'Look at this. The first thing I'd noticed was that there was indeed one witness report that referred to a middle-aged man as the one who had jumped off the bridge…'

Keith scrutinised the report swiftly, and it was true that one of the drivers who had been at the very front of the pile-up did mention a body he'd collided with, once it had bounced off the bonnet of the car in-front; *that* car had sustained major damage, and someone in it had died as a result. Keith noted the name of the witness: Leslie Trent had seen what he thought was a *middle-aged man.*

Keith read on: *Witness deeply traumatised by death of spouse. Do not contact.*

But other reports remained strangely vague about the appearance of the suicide victim. Another driver, from further back, seemed to have tried to administer first-aid. Rushing to help, Dr. Simon Hawes states that a number of the injured he tried to treat had opened their car doors and were spilling out onto the tarmac, some in a pretty bad state. There was not necessarily any way of knowing where certain bodies, dead or alive, had come from, but he makes the assumption that the black man he finds is the one who jumped. The police appeared to have worked with this.

'See?' exclaimed Keith triumphantly. 'It just doesn't add up, does it?'

'Guess not. Look here at this one, too.'

Keith read aloud: 'I saw the mess all around, there were bodies everywhere. I didn't know where to start. The black gentleman who had clearly jumped off the bridge was in pieces, literally all over the place. There were another two people crawling next to their cars and another older gentleman who was lying, dead I guess, on the central reservation. You couldn't move for people walking around. Two of the cars were on fire. Someone on the bridge, where the black man had jumped from, shouted down that he would come and help us, but I never did see him – not sure you could climb down to the motorway from there, it looked like a footbridge. Then myself and another couple of people tried to give first aid or make people comfortable. One of these was another doctor, apparently. By the time the first ambulances came, we'd counted about three or four definitely dead and a load more badly injured, about ten or eleven, or so.'

Carter sat back. 'Checked the second doctor's name out: Smythe, Daniel Smythe. Dr. Daniel Smythe, in fact. Turns out he's a former colleague of the aforementioned Dr. Simon Hawes – both studied at the same medical school, both used to work at the same research labs in Cambridge. Turns out, in fact, that they were both going to the same place that day, to some meeting or other in Bristol.'

'And yet he refers to his old friend as a *doctor, apparently*. As if he didn't know him!'

'Exactly…'

'Oh my god! It *is* a cover-up!' Keith sat back in his chair. 'What should we do?'

'I'm not sure. Maybe look into the chap who *did* see a middle-aged man drop. Leslie Trent. And perhaps we should bring in the two doctors?'

'Do we take it Upstairs?'

'Too soon. Let's dig around a bit more. Anyway, look here. I've found something else.' Carter leaned back too, with an air of smug satisfaction. Keith's curiosity was now well and truly piqued, and Carter knew it. 'I had a sniff around the lists of intakes at the local morgues, and all the bodies went to the same place: Dale's Funerary Services in Swindon, before being sent on to local funeral parlours, once their families were involved. All but one. One body didn't; in fact, it doesn't seem to have gone to any funeral parlour at all. No trace of any unidentified, white, middle-aged man being brought in from a motorway accident on the M4 on that day. And no trace, either, of a Nigerian, whether in one piece or several…'

'You tried all the funeral services in the area?'

'Within a twenty-five mile radius. And then in the places some of the deceased came from, too.'

Keith looked sideways at Carter. 'My god, you *have* been busy!'

'I said I'd have a rummage around, didn't I?'

Keith was now beside himself, filled with a boyish excitement. He could almost smell the whiff of adventure welling up within him. This really did feel like something waiting to be investigated.

Suddenly, it felt like they were treading around something that wasn't supposed to be tinkered with. Keith stood up and walked slowly round to his desk. Why was there a cover-up? Who *were* the two doctors, and why were they spinning the same story to the police? Yes, it must have been a confused scene, and that's what they must have been hoping for. But why? Had it all been timed to happen exactly as it did? It was certainly beginning to feel like it…

'There's something I haven't told anyone,' said Keith quietly. Carter looked up. 'You see, what that second doctor said about the man up on the bridge. That tallies with something else I saw that day.'

'What are you telling me?' asked Carter.

'I'm telling you there was somebody else up there with him on that bridge. And the older guy didn't fall off. I saw it – he was pushed!'

Now Carter sat still. He said nothing. Finally Keith wondered aloud:

'I reckon I need to do some more digging. Then I should take it Upstairs.'

Carter nodded. In the silence of the next few minutes both men turned at last to the day's lists of cases to work through, and for a while they had turned their minds away from the world of mad, twitching conspiracy, and were pushing their way on through piles of routine administration.

Suddenly, a *ping* indicated an outside email coming onto his phone. Keith flicked his mobile to life and looked at his inbox.

It was from Samantha!

Did he detect a flutter in his stomach? There was something, he thought…

He opened it. What he read didn't at first make sense; this was silly nonsense, surely – showtime dramatics! He read it through again:

Keith, hiya! This stuff's amazing! Thanks for sending me the details. Almost as if someone wants you to find all this out, isn't it! Made a few interesting phone calls to a good friend in the Thames Valley Police. Can't meet up with you at all over the next few days – am off to Manchester now for that course. Pity. Would have been good to have gone through some of this with you in person. Will have to wait! xxx

Even as he was re-reading this, another *ping* alerted him to more.

It was a second email from Samantha. This one was more enigmatic.

Keep digging. Careful who you talk to about this. Don't reply. Who lived between nineteen minutes to one. Isn't there a chicken crossing near you? xxx

Keith put it away, and thought long and hard about the message. Now *nothing* made any sense today, nothing at all. Perhaps he should ring her? Maybe even meet up with her in Manchester? Thrilling though the idea was for Keith, it would hardly be a thrilling experience trying to explain to Karen why he had gone.

Karen! He would talk to Karen about it. Then maybe Carter. Definitely…

The rest of the day passed without further incident. Carter and Keith battled on through their work, and only in the afternoon, as it was coming to the end of office hours did Keith say:

'Carter, thanks for looking into all that stuff for me. I appreciate it. It might be nothing, but I would like to get to the bottom of it, you know.'

'Not a problem, fellah! Always here to help. I'm working a bit late tonight, so you head off and sleep on the whole thing. I might carry on fishing around a bit, if I get the chance.'

'I'll have a good think about it all over the weekend. Try to piece it together…'

So it was that Keith arrived home that Friday evening with many more questions buzzing around his head than he normally had. Tonight his briefcase made it comfortably past the docking port, right past the dining room and into the kitchen.

'Hello honey.'

'Hi, darling!' Karen was in an altogether better mood, it seemed, than she had been in the past few days. And it was the end of the week, at last.

'Let's get out and have a drink!' suggested Keith. 'I have a few puzzles to run past you. Come on, grab your jacket – you've got to help me with this.' With that, they hastened out of the house, wandered arm-in-arm to their local, and as Keith set down the drinks – a pint of Old Droomer and a white wine spritzer – he put down beside them his phone, as well as the witness statements he had printed out earlier.

'Right! Here, let me explain…' he began, as he put all the evidence in front of Karen's baffled eyes. As he went through the various strands, he had to admit to himself that it did not amount to much. In fact, without Samantha's enigmatic emails, it was beginning to feel there was little more than a mix-up of identity in the heat of an awful, chaotic motorway accident.

As her texts and emails added so much to the mystery, Keith also had to deal with the simple fact that he had been in touch with

Samantha over the past few days. The café, the meeting the day before, all that could be held back, though; no point making waves, after all. As far as Karen was concerned, all they did was exchange niceties over their mobiles. He hoped Samantha's emails didn't make any reference to their meeting, for god's sake… He was sure they didn't.

Karen was looking at the strange message on his phone.

'What could she have meant by this? Was it code? Was she afraid something recognisable might have been picked up? What chicken was crossing near us? This is so weird…'

'And twenty-to-one? What is that? 'Twelve-forty… In the morning or in the afternoon?'

'Who could live just at one time?' asked Karen, 'unless it is a date, instead…'

'A year? 1240? OK, but who only lives for one year?'

'1240, let's check…' said Karen, flicking her finger around her mobile screen. She looked happy, engaged, thought Keith, like she hadn't seemed for a long time. Or like he hadn't happened to see her, to be precise. He was enjoying this, a sudden brightening of relations, a intrusion of sunlight into their lives.

'No luck,' she said. 'Nothing obvious here. Actually, it's 1241, isn't it… Nope, *nada*…'

'Hang on!' laughed Keith. Then: 'Ah! Yes, you've got it! What if it means the year twelve? As in AD. 12…'

'And it's 41.'

'So who lived between AD 12 and AD 41?'

Karen picked up her own phone, typed in the dates, and waited. Then the answer appeared. 'Here he is,' she said, delighted. 'Have a look!'

Keith took the phone from her hand and looked at the list of search suggestions that had popped up. There indeed he was, at the top of the list.

'AD. 12 – 41: The Roman Emperor Caligula.'

Chapter Seven

Crack!

What the hell *was* that? Every bloody night, in the middle of his already disturbed sleep, always in the dead of darkness…

'You all right, darling?' asks Karen, sleepy with the habit of asking him this. 'That noise again?'

'Too bloody right it was. Always wakes me up, always catches me out…'

'Well get back to sleep, darling. You know it's nothing. Just an old house, isn't it. Always creaking and cracking…'

She turns over, puts her back to his; 'Night-night,' she mutters, and shuffles herself off into deep sleep again. Within minutes, she is snoring lightly.

It's all right for her, though, she's always so unphased by anything like this. But Keith hears it every night, almost; and the other stuff… the creaks, the cracks, the footsteps.

God, sometimes it's like someone is living up there.

Chapter Eight

The chicken crossing came to him in the middle of the night, as he lay awake in the half-darkness, mulling over what *Caligula* might mean; did it even have anything to do with chickens crossing roads? Was Samantha just having a joke at his expense? And did that in itself mean anything, might it in fact mean she still had feelings for him, or even be wanting to reignite their fling? What would then have to be done about Karen? Or did she need to find out anyway... Perhaps she might even understand it – or maybe even encourage it? What might a threesome feel like?...

On and on it went, a whirring of nonsense and half-understood scenarios lurching and giggling around Keith's head.

Finally, just as he was properly beginning to drift off, and just as the images in his mind settled into a pattern of inexplicable events, doors opening into unexpected vistas, a walk along a childhood street, familiar animals elongating, suddenly Keith found he had somehow stumbled upon the answer. It did not surface again until the morning, though, when he awoke with the knowledge that something had been solved during the night, and had to search his memory to remind himself what it was.

Then it hit him.

He sat bolt upright.

'I've got it, by the way! Chicken crossing! I worked it out!'

Karen shifted around on her side of the bed with a surly slowness. 'Go on.'

'It is another way of saying something without mentioning it. My god, she really is making sure it doesn't get picked up in any email search.'

'Go on, then,' muttered Karen. 'Reveal all.'

'Chicken crossing is just a word-for-word way of saying the name of a place, which, of course, is *near here.* So *chicken* is *hen* and *crossing* is *ford.* Hen and ford… Henford!'

Karen sat up now. 'God, you're right. Henford! Where is that? Just down the road isn't it?'

'Exactly! It's, like, a kind of village suburb over there.' He gestured out towards the window. 'And there's an old military base right next door to it.'

'Well, let's go and look at it!' suggested Karen. 'Why not?'

Her enthusiasm surprised Keith, and delighted he agreed. Suddenly their minds felt alive with some nameless adventure, and they bounced out of bed and got dressed and breakfasted in no time. While Karen finished her makeup and sorted out a number of emails on her phone, Keith went downstairs, turned their computer on, and loaded up *Google Earth*, to have a quick look again at where they were heading, how best to get there, what routes to avoid, what state the place looked in… Come to think of it, he remembered, this was where he thought he had seen all those fire engines rushing off to, just a few nights before.

On the screen at his study desk in the spare bedroom, Keith brought up the familiar image of the great blue and green globe, homed in on their area, dragged their suburbs around a moment or two, before finding what he was looking for. There it was! It appeared deserted, he thought, and clearly hadn't been used for at least a decade. A patch of grid-line roads holding a cluster of plain, barrack roofs in place behind a boundary fence. The whole image, even from space, appeared scrubby and tussocky, disused and abandoned. To one side a line of smart, garden-bound suburban houses skimmed past a blocked-off entrance gate, while within the base there were a number of oblong buildings in rows, an area covered in tarpaulin, a faint H in a circle indicating a long-neglected helipad, and a blurry zone, at the far end of the site, set quite away from the entrance.

Keith wondered whether it was possible to go into the ground-level *street view*, to see how it looked near the entrance. Then he noticed, perplexed, that the virtual road lines extended right into the camp itself, so he dragged the little figure into the area, and what he saw completely threw him for a while.

The streetside view, as it resolved and hardened into focus, had all the appearance of a village of some sort. Houses stood all around. A manicured grassy area led over to a couple of old cottages. Ahead, pixellated figures waited under a bus shelter. Others were frozen as they crossed the road, shopping bags in their hands, pushing pushchairs and zimmer frames. Clicking and flicking the mouse, Keith easily pulled the scene around to check it out further. Sure enough, a whole instant captured by the camera revealed a parade of shops, a car approaching past some modern housing and a sign in front of a church: *Jesus Saves* or *What's Missing? UR*, or some such like…

This felt strange. Nothing in this correlated to what Keith knew was here in reality. Why was all this on the *street view*? How come he'd been redirected here?

Keith double-clicked along the street, the image blurred, then zoomed ahead. Sure enough, here it was, the same scene from some village or other. He didn't recognise the place, but it certainly wasn't what he would expect for this point on the satellite map. He went along a little further; all perfectly normal, the same, serene village scene… Except it wasn't normal. It wasn't right at all.

He came out of the *ground-level* view now, and moved his cursor along to what seemed like the entrance to the base. Now in he went again, onto streets he thought he should know.

This time it did look familiar. Here were the banks of large, hedge-hidden houses which lined the lane up to the base. He moved forwards in *street view*. Still the houses were there. Up ahead, where the road turned round a corner towards the camp, he spotted something. Moving forwards he found himself closer still. What was this? An army vehicle of some kind, khaki and heavy. Another double-click, another blurring race ahead, and there it was!

A large red cross on the side of the military vehicle, just as it was waiting to be let into the base, showed it to be an ambulance.

Now why on earth would there be *any* military vehicles, let alone an ambulance, waiting to gain entry to a base that had been closed for years?

Keith double-clicked on the gates to the base. The image blurred, sped towards him, and suddenly, there he was again in the imaginary village! No sign whatsoever of the abandoned barracks and pylons so clearly visible from the satellite photos. He was back in the place that had been superimposed onto this patch of land. Was he supposed to accept this?

Had the site now been redeveloped? Was there now a new, suburban village here? Maybe, thought Keith, but some of the buildings in this scene were old, so that didn't make sense either.

'Come and look at this, honey!' he called through the open door. Karen wandered in, stared closely at the screen, perplexed.

'That's weird,' she agreed. 'Doesn't add up at all…'

'Come on, then,' he said. 'Let's go and take a good look at this place, shall we…'

It was not far. A short, half-hour walk, and now here they were, walking along the same lanes Keith had earlier been travelling along virtually. Here were the houses, the high hedges. A few extensions might have been added since the images had been uploaded; a couple of walls had clearly been fixed or painted, but otherwise, here it all was, just as he had seen it. The houses fizzled out as the lane curved up towards the entrance to the base, where dense woods and thickets descended from a low rise. Into the dappled light caused by the summer foliage, a short lane turned off, and at the end stood high, rusting gates between tall, ivy-covered concrete posts. Barbed wire covered the top of the gates and ran off along high chicken wire into the undergrowth. This was the boundary of the base. Three heavy padlocks held the gates firmly shut.

'This way!' called Keith, spying a path trodden down by youths looking for somewhere to smoke and drink. They followed an overgrown track through nettles, which led along the boundary for some way, before coming to a tiny gap in the chicken-wire fence. Crouching down, Keith could just squeeze through. These youths were smoking and drinking at an ever younger age, he thought.

'Not sure I like this,' muttered Karen. 'We're clearly not supposed to be here.'

'It's looking fairly disused,' answered Keith. 'It wouldn't have a hole like this in the fence if it was still an active MoD base, now would it?'

'Suppose not.'

'Give me your hand then. Here we go!' With that, they were both inside the camp. Straightening themselves up, they looked around.

They stood on the edge of a broad space, criss-crossed with concrete roads, cracked and covered with weeds. Beyond were ranged line after line of low-lying buildings, grim, flat-roofed barracks with broken windows and sprouting greenery. Birds flitted off in panic, disturbed by their presence, diving into their hideaways amongst the undergrowth, squawking and chirping their alarm into the still, warm air.

Nothing else moved. Hand in hand, the pair moved steadily but warily across the roadway into the heart of the base. The place was eerie in its strange desolation. They passed pylons and stepped over fallen cables. All around them were the ghosts of long-gone comings and goings. The place had evidently been abandoned for years. Not far from the main entrance there stood the burnt-out remains of a couple of blocks, which were presumably the buildings the fire engines had been rushing out to.

'What was that?' Keith stopped dead still in his tracks.

'What was what?' asked Karen, clearly also on edge.

'I saw something move over there.'

'Are you fucking me about?' demanded Karen. 'That's not funny.'

'No. Look! In that window. I saw a face.'

'No you didn't.'

'I did! I promise,' Keith insisted. He made towards where he was looking.

Karen held him back, and hissed: 'Just what the hell do you think you are doing? If you did see someone watching us, then we get our shit out of here! Now. Let's go.'

Keith gave in, but not without looking back at the broken window. Nothing stirred there now. They almost ran back to the road they had arrived on; for a moment or two they couldn't recognise where they had broken through the gap in the fence. Then Karen spotted it, and they dived back through the hole, hurried along the track, where houses and hedges welcomed them back to safety.

'Come on.' Karen smiled at him: 'Were you having me on, or did you really see something in that window?'

Keith's heart was pounding. 'Yes, I definitely saw a face, looking out at us. It lasted a good ten seconds or so, and I just couldn't find the words to tell you at first.'

'Oh my god, really? That's so creepy!'

'But I'll tell you something else if you want to know why I ended up running as fast as you were by the end…'

'Go on!'

'Somebody followed us out. I saw him staring at us from that hillock over there, as we came along the track back to this road.'

Keith saw her face turn pale and serious. He wished he hadn't told her. She was terrified now, as she turned to look where he had indicated. Just above them, opposite the smart houses was a knoll, dark with dense thickets and brambles and undergrowth; tall trees towered above them. But somehow in the midst of all that shadowy foliage, a figure had been silently looking out at them as they fled. It was a man, though Keith hadn't been able to see the face clearly; instead, he had been more intent on getting back to the road.

'Enough!' cried Karen, and stamped her foot. 'You're scaring me now, and I still think you're doing it on purpose. We're going. Let's leave now!' With that, she turned, laughing, and headed back towards home, and Keith followed. Best let it all settle for now. No point in worrying her, no point in adding to the weirdness of it all.

They arrived home in good spirits. Shoes taken off, kettle put on, paper picked up, tea sipped… Suddenly it all felt like a strange vision, a dream even. Keith, though, couldn't quite put it to rest for now, and disappeared back into his study to look one more time at where they had been.

There had to be some explanation for all this, he mused. Perhaps he had missed something before. He decided to examine the satellite images again. Let's get a better look at what was actually seen on the ground, now that he knew what the place was really like.

Keith zoomed in on the base. There it all was: the little lane leading up to the entrance they had found, the wood beside it, through which the track had been made to get to the hole in the fence. Now he could see the roofs of the barracks where they had first emerged. There was the track they had followed to the centre of the base. And there the building where he was sure he'd seen the face. Surely not, though… surely he'd been mistaken? There was enough wildlife bustling around there to suggest no-one had entered for quite a while. The place was dead. His eyes and his imagination had played a trick on him. No other explanation for it. Keith didn't believe in ghosts.

Keith pulled the little figure over from the side of the screen, just to go and look again at the streetside image that had so confused him before. Maybe it was a simple glitch? Maybe the maps hadn't been properly lined up earlier…

The view on the screen slipped down into the landscape, a blurred patch of colours filled his vision, and there he was again, standing in the same strange village full of normal, but unrelated, life. He scanned about again, but this time, as his view spun round to take in what was standing behind him, Keith recoiled at the sight of something that had not been there before. The camera turned. Keith watched the other side of the road swinging into view. Suddenly he found himself face-to-face with a tall figure, standing right up against the vehicle-mounted camera, uncomfortably close, his face looking directly into the lens; pixellated still, this face nonetheless seemed to be staring right through the screen at him.

Above this pixellated head was what made Keith almost fall backwards off his chair. A sickness rose deep within him. He stood up, and stepped back away from the desk, his gaze fixed in horror on the screen.

There on a placard being held up high in both hands by this eerie, faceless figure were the words which now rang around Keith's head:

DON'T EVER TRY TO COME BACK. STAY AWAY FROM HENFORD.

Keith did not know what to do at first. Things were now suddenly moving far too fast for him, and he did not feel at all easy in himself about dealing with events such as these. Gripping tightly onto the side of his chair, he approached the computer with a fixed stare, as if face-to-face with a venomous snake. He sat down and looked hard at the image there on his screen. It was addressing him, and this was no mere, imagined paranoia. This was something meant for him to see, and a warning, too, a pretty obvious warning to stay clear.

Karen did not need to see this. Not now. He would show her later, when the time was right. For the moment, she was scared enough, and so: let it wait.

Now calmer, he moved the image around a little, to get a better view of the figure, and to see if there were any clues at all about who was behind this, and why. The first thing he noticed was that the figure cast no shadow. That was interesting… Not that this had any supernatural implications for Keith; it simply showed that the figure had been added or superimposed onto the *street view* image – someone had been able to access the image of the village and place this warning onto it. Likewise, Keith noticed that the pixellation had a slightly different appearance from that which covered other faces in the scene.

Well, he thought, sitting back and contemplating the figure, so creepy in its facelessness and its static presence, intended to make him jump; it certainly did just that! But do I mention it to anyone at work? Should Carter know? Maybe Samantha could advise…

Maybe she could. Or was this beyond her league now? After all, whoever did this had evidently just observed them both going to Henford base, and had somehow manipulated the satellite imagery in the meantime; this figure staring facelessly out at Keith was definitely not there earlier this morning.

Keith closed down the program, put the computer to sleep, and went out to join Karen in the sitting room, where he found her reading in the sunlit-filled window seat.

'Hello darling!' she smiled. Then, 'God, it looks like you've just seen a ghost!'

'I need a beer.'

'I'll get you one.'

Chapter Nine

That evening was one of the Saturdays when Karen would go out with some friends, two colleagues from work and an old girlfriend from years ago. While Karen was getting ready upstairs, Keith sat in front of the TV with his mobile in his hand. He finished the text and sent it off: *Hi! Hope you are having a great conference! Went to chicken crossing. Lots to tell. But still failed to catch the 1241. Hope to see you soon xxx*

She came downstairs all tights and straps, and he wished he was going with her. He missed their regular Saturday evenings out together, but maybe it was better for her to be out with others instead. She seemed happier without him these days, he wondered if that was the way things were drifting.

She smiled wistfully at him. 'You take your time, now.'

'You take yours! Where are you off to then, tonight?'

'I think the girls said we were heading off to Newbie's. Or maybe Jack's.'

'Great. Have a lovely time. I shall miss every minute you're away!'

'You're a cutie!' she said. 'I've begun pouring you a lonesome beer out in the kitchen, to complement your lonesome evening. Let me go and get the rest of it.'

She disappeared, then returned with the cool, refreshing beer and its bottle. Then she was out of the door and off down the street by the time he'd started missing her. Out of his life and gone. Keith sighed and returned to his computer. He did not want to freak himself out now he was alone in the house, but he had to look at it again, this uncanny figure who had intruded on his peace of mind. He had to confront him and face his fears, and work out what to do next.

Flicking the monitor on again, Keith dived back into the image that was haunting him so, and looked again for clues as to where the place was, who the figure might be, whether he could recognise the handwriting…

Ping! A message had come through from Samantha. He opened it.

Is this a safe line to text on? If not, wait till we meet.

Is that it? Brilliant. More mystery. He had a good mind to phone her now. *Ping!* Another message.

Am driving. Don't phone now. We'll meet. Wait till you hear from me.

OK, thought Keith, I'll wait. Fair enough. Cat and mouse, cat and mouse!

But she didn't get back to him. He turned off his computer and returned to the TV. But still no word at all from Samantha, as the hours drifted by. She was driving, after all, and it was getting late, too.

Something in the back of his mind, though, told Keith to delete these texts from her. It would not do for Karen to find them. What would she make of *xxx* or arrangements to meet up? Best get rid of them. *Delete…*

It was starting to become dark outside, and in the gloom Keith felt his head drop once or twice in front of some particularly unfulfilling TV, beer glass in hand, forgetting what had just been happening on the screen. He was beginning to doze off, exhausted by the day's riddles.

Riddles and riddles, endless riddles. A sequence of crackpot thoughts worthy of a fantasist. A spiralling of misinterpreted signs and signals…

Signs and signals, symbols and ciphers.

Keith, Keith… You must see it all, it all makes sense, it makes certain sense to see it as a whole! Linked up, tied together, all sewn up into a single plot.

Patterns, there are patterns here, Keith. If only you open your eyes to them… Patterns weaving their filigree way around your head and around the room and out into the street and over the houses across the woods right the way to the army base… A pattern which can't be understood by everyone, not even you at the moment… A pattern of signs. You can't deny it. They'll say you're mad, they'll say you've lost it… They will! They'll say you're mad… A pattern of ciphers and hints, a pattern so complex you will burn your poor brain working it out. But you're the only one, Keith, you're the only one who can do it.

The pattern is there. Just out of reach. Reach out for it. Reach out…

Keith… Keith…

He turned off the TV and put down his half-empty glass. Heaving himself upstairs, he eventually climbed into bed, and immediately fell back to sleep, later disturbed only by Karen returning loudly in spite of herself, and climbing into bed beside him.

'A good night?' murmured Keith.

'A good night!' she answered, and dropped off to sleep.

Out he gets, middle of the night again, dammit. Darkness entombs the bedroom this early in the morning, as it always does, but by the time he gets to the bathroom, the bright moonlight reflecting into the window from the back garden casts a silvery glow to everything. Come on, come on – let's hope that sleep will come back easily…

Into the darkness of the toilet bowl, Keith relieves himself gratefully. Done, he inevitably looks out of the window onto the little patch of lawn and across to the shadows of the hedge.

Christ!

Who the *hell* is that standing in our garden?

He blinks in disbelief, but the figure remains. There, in the middle of their lawn, bolt upright, arms down by his side, is a man. Is he staring up at this window? He is; oh shit!

'Christ! Christ! Karen!' he shouts, as he hurries back to the bedroom, where his girlfriend is already sitting bolt upright and blinking in dopey panic. 'Come and help me here. We've got an intruder in the garden, god knows how he's got in, but he is just standing there in the middle of the lawn! Get your phone, get ready to phone the police; we'll take a photo! I'm going to grab something heavy just in case!'

Pulling on her dressing gown, Karen followed him along to the bathroom, making sure not to turn any lights on. Creeping up to the window, they arch over each other to look out.

Nothing.

'Oh for fuck's sake, Keith. This is becoming ridiculous. Why are you suddenly seeing all these weird people wherever we go?'

'I tell you, there was someone standing there!'

'Are you doing this to piss me off? Do you know what time it is?'

'He's gone now. I swear he was standing right there, bang in the middle of the garden. I mean, Christ; he was in full moonlight, too!'

'What did he look like?' asked Karen.

'Long coat; really long. And, oh no… I thought he was looking up at the window, but… yes, that was because his eyes were so clear on his face – it was like a mask or something. Yes, a mask!'

Karen seemed to be persuaded by this detail. 'Really? Shit, that's horrible, oh god! But are you sure you saw something out there? Let's see again… I can't see anything at all.' Holding his hand tightly, she peered intently into the shadows of the hedge and the wall, where the moonlight did not reach; was someone standing out there in the darkness? Was he still looking up at them through his mask?

'I should go down and see,' suggested Keith.

'No, really?'

'Just to check the doors and windows are locked.'

'OK, but be careful. Here, take this vase!' She passed him a heavy piece of pottery that stood beside the bath.

Keith crept downstairs, knowing that every creak and groan from the old house would be announcing his imminent arrival if there was indeed somebody waiting for him downstairs. He turned into the hallway with the pot raised high above his head.

But nothing. Then on into the kitchen, and out to the back door.

Still nothing.

Locks checked. Handles tried. From the back room window Keith looked nervously out into the darkness, but all was still and utterly silent. His own heartbeat was deafening within his head, but nothing outside stirred in the shadows or on the lawn.

He came back upstairs, fell into bed and into his nervous girlfriend's embrace.

'Darling, maybe you were still dreaming? Your dreams are always so vivid, aren't they…'

'I wasn't, I'm sure.'

'Let's get back to sleep.'

'Let's.'

CHAPTER TEN

There had been no word from Samantha since the texts, which annoyed him; surely she must have known he was interested now… Well, if she could play hard-to-get, so could he. Cat and mouse, cat and mouse. So his Sunday had passed care-free; breakfast, newspaper and a walk over the fields with Karen.

When they returned after a pub lunch, Karen went into the kitchen to make them both a tea. She brought Keith's into the lounge where he was sitting, while she went back to hers and took it into the study upstairs to order something on the computer. She was always ordering something on the computer. Keith sipped at his tea and checked his mobile for any news from Samantha. Still nothing. He texted her a perfunctory message.

Hi there. Hope you had a good time in Manchester. Get in touch when you can.

It was then that Keith suddenly became aware of the flickering in the corner of his vision. It was a feeling, rather than something he could actually see, and he recognised it for exactly what it was. A migraine was on its way, and as he looked at his right hand now held up in front of his face, a hand strangely detached in his mind from the hand he knew he had at the end of his arm, only half could be properly focused on. Keith realised that the unavoidable was upon him, and that he would have to retreat to his bed, take some pills, drink lots of water, and write off the rest of the day.

Damn. He hated this, and they seemed to be getting ever more frequent. Upstairs, he pulled the curtains, said goodbye to Karen as she quietly closed the door on him, and drifted on into an uneasy semi-consciousness.

This kind of sleep was always punctuated by odd episodes that troubled his mind and didn't let him rest. Patterns swept frenetically over his mind, never settling, never resolving, always seething silently and menacingly through fields of blazing colours and bright splashes of light. An awareness of the light at the edges of the curtains permeated his visions.

Rick Astley… Rick Astley… Rick Astley… Rick Astley…

On and on they went, the pigeons outside his window, with their pointless, repeated refrain. Now that it was in Keith's head it wouldn't stop. Why *Rick Astley*, he heard himself wonder? No idea; but that's all he heard as he surfaced from his troubled dreams. Light still filtered around the edges of the heavy curtains.

What time is it, anyway?

From under the covers Keith now noticed the gathering darkness, and understood the evening to have already set in. That made a certain sense, thank god.

Not much else did. The scroungers outside, clambering over the hedge into his front garden, clawing at his front door. The bastard from number forty-four looking through the front window into their lounge. A slow sunset was congealing around the edges of the curtains, and all the worrisome ants and vermin that resided under the floorboards needed to be taken out, exterminated. Not a single finger of blame pointed anywhere, but overhead there was nothing more than a dark, frayed cloth fluttering in the breeze; it wasn't on their normal washing line, it was too high – after all, you could see the roof from here, reflecting the red sky. And the breeze wasn't a wind – if only it were, there'd be something more satisfying in that, something more tangible, more definite… This wretched breeze, dammit, an all-too-gentle, oh-so-gentle wafting without any form, without any substance… The day has already gone, hasn't it.

Fanfares. You don't often get those round here.

Without a pylon to support it, there wouldn't have been a room like this, high and shadow-filled, its hollow shape disappearing into the darkness of its vaults. Not many can boast of a bedroom like this. But the pylon, bang in the middle, almost swelling with its bulk, right here, right in the centre of the room, filling it with its vast presence, rearing high into the darkness – all very well, but down here in its shadow, faced with all its weird carving and scrawled messages, none of which seem clear, but, all the same, wheel out towards the eyes, fill the vision, float and lurch towards the beholder... Who else has a pylon in their bedroom? Where did it come from? Sure, it's needed for the roof, but what about those stuck here at its base, clinging on to reason, making sense of its bulging, swelling, throbbing form, as it nudges his bed to the edge of the room, pushing it outwards, ever further, ever more to the edge, where it has always been.

This room has no edge any more. The darkness goes off into the sides too, and into depths where the rats and ants and neighbours and lowlife and ex-lovers all grin, invisible, hidden by the shade. Why are you all here? Go away and shit in the forest! Don't mind me. I'm fine here. I don't need your judgment. I am all right. I am king down here in this cavern.

The rag is fluttering again. This time in the darkness, but Keith knows it is moving, he can see the wind, he can see the air.

The remains of Keith's consciousness are fluttering in his head.

He turns over onto his other side, seeking relief in a different position. But his head still buzzes with lights and colours and the weaving patterns of a frenzied delirium.

What the hell has happened? What has happened to you, Keith?

He was floating like a blimp. A colourful blimp, or a balloon. Full of air.

Keith, Keith, Keith... What do you reckon you should be doing right now? You should be sorting out some of those things we both know need sorting.

Both of us?

Both of us, Keith.

Who are you?

Who are you, Keith? If you don't mind my asking.

I'm Keith.

I'm Malcolm.

Malcolm?

Hello!

A figure stands in the corner of the room.

Keith is too tired and full of fog to realise that it's not normal for someone to be standing in the corner of his bedroom. Deep down he knows he's dreaming.

I can't see your face, Malcolm.

I can see yours.

What do you want?

I want you to relax, Keith. I want you to let go.

Oh my god, so do I, so do I… so much!

You've got to let go, Keith. You shouldn't worry so much, should you?

No. It puts years on my life, I'm sure.

Old before your time, Keith?

Feels like it sometimes.

Then you've got to start taking some risks!

I don't want to take risks.

You must. It gives life some edge. Makes you feel alive, Keith!

What risks?

Risks! Risks!

Risks? What risks?

Rick Astley.

What?

Rick. Malcolm.

Malcolm?

'Malcolm? Who's Malcolm? Are you OK, darling?' Karen was stooping over him. She had brought him some fresh water and placed it on his bedside table.

'Huh? Oh sorry.'

'You OK, honey? You were talking and shaking. You were calling out a name. You were calling out *Malcolm.*'

'I'm fine. And feeling better.'

'Good, I'm glad. You get back to sleep.'

'I shall be fine for tomorrow.'

'We'll see.'

'Come to bed soon. I'm going to sleep well now.'

And with that Keith turned over and fell straight back into a deep sleep, less troubled now, and so soothing that he didn't even notice Karen climbing in beside him twenty minutes later, snuggling in close for a while then dropping off as she rolled her head onto her own pillow.

Chapter Eleven

Sitting on the train, Keith looked through the grime-smeared window over the roofs of West London, and as he stared out waiting for his workplace to approach, he was waiting too for one of the few ways he had of distracting himself from the enveloping boredom.

Not far from central London, as the train pulled into Barons Court, a nondescript stop just past Hammersmith, there was a delicious moment to look forward to every day, when a vision of homely bliss, combined with forbidden lust, wheeled into view. Each morning at about quarter-past eight the train would ease itself past a second-floor flat boasting broad, featureless windows, one of which gave directly onto a modern kitchen brightly lit and filled with the routine of getting kids' coats on and pushing them out of the door. Keith had noticed this domestic scene a good year before, but after a few months had begun to realise how attractive the young mother was who presided over the daily drama. She was tall with long, dark hair flowing voluptuously over the collar of her pale beige trench coat. Sometimes she was looking out in the direction of the train, and it was clear she was pretty, even from this distance. But most of the time she was faffing around at the further end of the kitchen, bending over the children, kneeling to do their coats up or putting their lunches into satchels.

This was how Keith had come to know her, a distant, half-visible figure out of reach, trussed up in his imagination in boots and stockings; but for these few fleeting seconds she was all his, possessed by his gaze alone and fittingly unaware of his attention. Who was she? What might she be for him?

Then she was gone. If she had been there at all; some mornings she had already left, or was not in the room. Sometimes the light was not even on. But each day's anticipation of a glimpse, perhaps this time a closer, more intimate glimpse, gave a focus to this part of the journey, added a frisson of expectation for Keith to pin his mind to; or just as often, if she failed to materialise, left his spirits dampened, unfulfilled. Her routine, like his, was no doubt mind-numbing in its packed-in meaninglessness, and this shared, albeit unknowing, thread of experience appealed to him, as they participated in this same, timetabled moment in both their lives.

Today, though, there was not any sign of her at all. As they slowly pulled past the group of workers in hi-vis jackets who were seemingly always gathered around this part of the line, an empty kitchen made its way impassively past the train window, then they drew up hissing up to the dreary platform's edge. Plenty of other women here to look at and admire, but none of them so tantalisingly beyond his reach.

Keith winced as he realised how ridiculous the logic was that he was now following. As if any of these lithe beauties were within his reach anyway!

As the train started off again, Keith realised with a jolt that the station's name on the platform sign was where one of the witnesses to the M4 bridge crash lived. Leslie Trent had an apartment somewhere near Barons Court on one of the streets of terraced houses just beyond the station.

Two thoughts came together in his mind. He should visit this witness. He might also bump into the Kitchen Woman. The second idea was, Keith accepted, both highly unlikely and anyway completely tangential to his first.

But as Keith neared his stop, the thought of seeking out this witness and interrogating him seemed more and more like a good idea. Why shouldn't he pursue this himself? After all, he had opened this particular can of worms. And with access to the address, it would be as if it were official business.

Actually, given what had happened at the weekend, the whole disturbing saga with the army base, maybe it would be better if he didn't go in any official capacity. Just tell Carter, that's all. Keep it all in-house, as it were. Carter was on-side, in any case. But he need take it Upstairs only if something cropped up after speaking with this chap Leslie Trent.

What was normally a post-kitchen-woman slump on the journey into the centre of London had become a moment of sudden potential. Keith resolved to get out at her stop, on his way back home this evening, and to seek out this Trent fellow; what was there to lose?

He entered his office just as Carter was sitting down and turning on his own computer and printer. 'Hello, you all right?'

'Half left.' replied Carter with predictable inevitability. 'What about you? Good weekend?'

'Fine, thanks,' answered Keith with a sighed, unconscious expression of frustration at this empty banter. He waited till Carter had settled down, before continuing. 'Carter, what would you say to me going to meet up with that witness from the M4 crash later today? The Leslie Trent fellow who said–'

'Yes. I know. The one who saw a white man fall, not a Nigerian. Well, have fun. I wouldn't.'

'Why not? Don't you think I should do my job?'

'It's not your job to go round questioning police investigations,' Carter said curtly. 'The files said it was sensitive, too, and not to contact the witness.'

That was strange, thought Keith. He hadn't expected this from Carter.

'Fine,' Keith muttered back. 'If you reckon I should leave it, I'll leave it. Let's hope we don't miss something, though.' Odd, thought Keith – only last week Carter had been fired-up enough to do all that research. Well, tough… We'll do it on our own. Screw you, Carter, with your mood-swings, your I-know-best attitude. I'll keep you out of the loop for the moment, and see what I can dig up without you.

And so the day began, another Monday, another start to a week of sifting, processing, making piles of paper from other piles of paper. Behind him the serried ranks of filing cabinets released and later swallowed back the coloured files that passed across his desk. The whirr of a second-rate, yellowing shredder in the corner of the room occasionally interrupted his thoughts, and a photocopier which churned out only twenty sheets a minute hummed away almost imperceptible to his hearing.

First of all, he had to find out where this Leslie Trent lived and worked, then see if he could catch him for a chat. Keith quietly sorted out all the documents he'd need, the various warrants to make it easier to get a foot in the door. The exact address, the police records, if there were any. Then he'd have to try to cover his tracks, too; surely best to get hold of the warrants through the personnel office at lunchtime, and then to do them through Harvey, rather than Carter. Anyway, that Carter would be interested in something like this was highly unlikely; if he did end up checking up on Keith on this matter, then something most definitely was going on.

While his mind was buzzing with so many different activities, Keith suddenly found he'd brought up *Google Earth* on his screen and had zoomed into Henford, found the base, and tried to enter the *street view* image he'd seen at home.

Nothing. It was all gone. The whole village scene had disappeared, there were not even blue road lines anymore leading into the base. So it had all been done through his own home computer, somehow, god knows how…

Remotely at least, he hoped.

He entered the *street view* just outside the entrance to the base, and sure enough there were the normal images he'd seen before, the large houses, the hedgerows, the garden walls, the copse looming up on the right, and ahead, the military ambulance waiting to get into an evidently disused base. Come to think of it, looking at these images now, the base certainly wasn't looking very active even then, whenever it was these pictures had been taken; Keith noted the ivy climbing the fencing and the closed gates, and beyond these he glimpsed barrack buildings with broken windows and grass seeming to sprout from their flat roofs.

So even a few years ago the base was abandoned but still being used for something. What *was* going on here? Too many questions…

'What you mentioned a few days ago, Carter, about satellite images that are doctored and patched over… Who can we get to do that sort of stuff now? Is it just military, still, who can bypass the big corporations?'

'No, if the authorities don't want you sniffing, they won't want you sniffing, will they! Even we can easily paste all manner of stuff over what you're looking at – Brian on the third floor reckons he can do it from home!'

'Really?'

'Come on, you knew that, surely? You don't believe it's only in the hands of the satellite companies, do you?'

'No, of course not,' answered Keith with mock innocence. 'I just didn't realise it was so easy, that's all.'

'You can imagine what MI5 get up to, can't you? Someone prodding around a bit too close for comfort… Gets them off the track straightaway.'

Keith could indeed well imagine what the full weight of MI5 might be able to do. He knew what they were like, he'd seen them at work on the Gordon Alfonso case a few years before, when they'd had to infiltrate a gang of East European protectionists operating in Limehouse. And he had heard about some of their methods when they finally cracked into the jihadi cell whose case Keith had brought to their attention; the lengths they must have gone to get their mobiles and laptops bugged, and then to make them believe the various bits of false information they fed to them before the ambush…

Carter paused, and looked directly at Keith. 'Why? What have you found? Something to do with this dead Nigerian, still?'

'Oh nothing, forget it. Really nothing at all,' said Keith. 'Just wondering out loud, to be honest with you. How are you getting on with your case?'

'The Mahanu Brothers? Dead ends all the way. No line of enquiry to be had within a sniff of them.'

'That must be infuriating.'

'You're telling me. Even for an old pro like myself, I can't understand it. Anyway, that's the way the cookie crumbles sometimes.'

With that Carter's voice disappeared back behind his partition, and Keith resumed his own work. The morning bled into lunchtime. Keith passed his requests over to Harvey, across the other side of the courtyard. At last the time came to leave.

Carter packed up first and, saying goodbye cheerily, he left the office and headed off. On his own now, Keith printed out all his UK Visas and Immigration Services documents, his pass, his warrant – a low-level, straight-talking piece of ID which counted for hardly anything if push came to shove – and headed out into the warm evening air. There was the whiff of adventure on the breeze.

'Darling, hi!' he spoke into Karen's voicemail, as he made his way across the parks to his Underground station. 'Just to let you know I'm going to be late this evening. Something has come up here at the office, not sure when I'll be home, but I shouldn't be too long. Just didn't want you worrying or getting anything ready for me. I'll grab something to eat later, or on the way back. Love you!'

There were shouts from a small group of Brexit supporters brandishing signs and handing out pamphlets just outside the entrance to the station and milling around the Diana statue. Keith took one of them as it was foisted into his hand, and walked on. Their cries rang down the long entrance into the depths: *Give us our rights! Make Europe pay! Give us back our country! Break the stalemate! Who's paying now?* Before throwing the pamphlet away, Keith spotted many of the same, brash slogans plastered over its cover.

His train pulled out of its station, and within eight minutes was emerging from below ground and coming close to Barons Court.

What would he say, once he met Trent? How should he broach the whole subject? Especially if a loved one had been lost in the accident… Keith began rehearsing his opening lines.

Hello there, I'm sorry to disturb you at home, but…

Mr Trent? Pleased to meet you at last…

Good evening. Keith Hartman. Office of Homeland Security! That one would make them think! Maybe he should've printed off something fake. It would have been easy enough to mock up something from the US.

Hartman, Keith. FBI… Keith could do a pretty decent American accent, though it was more Alabama than Washington-DC-sophisticate. Quite how anyone would react to Deputy Dawg turning up on their doorstep, asking to conduct an interrogation on behalf of the US government he could not imagine.

And what if he bumped into Kitchen Woman? What would he say to her? The momentary realism of the scenario disappeared swiftly with an embarrassed gulp.

The train stopped. Keith stepped out, and strode purposefully through the crowds around the ticket office and on the pavement outside, past the paper-stall, the beggar, the children coming home late from school clubs and music lessons. Then he headed off in the direction of Leslie Trent's flat, a small terrace three or four blocks off the main street. Keith rehearsed his opening words more seriously now.

Mr. Trent? First of all let me say how sorry I am at your loss…

Leslie Trent? You weren't expecting me, I know, but…

Keith turned into the street and made his way past the plane trees lining the kerbs, until he found number 46. He opened the wrought-iron gate, stepped up to the front door, found a bell on the side with sun-bleached name inserted: TRENT.

Here we go. Deep breath. Shouldn't even be here, you fool…

Nothing. Keith rang a second time; finally, footsteps echoed within, and after a noisy fumbling on the other side the door opened. Out peered a plump woman in late middle-age, thick plastic-rimmed glasses perched awkwardly on a bulbous nose, greying hair pulled back in a scruffy bun. She eyed Keith with a friendly but questioning expression.

'Yes? Can I help you, my love?'

'Hello. I am Keith Hartman from Visas and Immigration Agency.' Keith held out his warrant and a small ID card. She glanced at them. 'I was hoping to speak to Mr. Trent.'

She raised her eyes to his. 'Mr. Trent, now? What are you after him for?'

Keith was beginning to feel uncomfortable. 'Well, I'm afraid that's something I'll need to talk to him about in private. Is he in?'

'No, he's not,' came the answer, brief and quite sharp, thought Keith.

'Do you mind me asking where he is?' he persisted.

'Who are you again, sonny?'

'I'm from the UK Visas and Immigration Services, the Home Office.' He paused, sensing a certain resistance. 'I can come back if you like, when it's more convenient. Is Mr. Trent not at home at the moment?'

She looked at him quizzically. 'Well, you could say that,' came the answer at last. 'He hasn't been back since 1988.'

'I'm sorry?'

'So am I. I think you're probably barking up the wrong tree, my friend. My brother died in a rail accident years ago.'

'Leslie Trent is dead?' asked Keith, astonished at the sudden turn of events.

'No,' came the reply. 'Certainly not! Not dead at all.'

Keith was beginning to sound exasperated: 'Does Leslie Trent live here or not?'

'Yes, she does. I am Leslie Trent.'

Keith sighed, realising his mistake. *Leslie* Trent. The flipping-over of his built-up reality shocked him for a few seconds. Then he regained his composure. 'I am so sorry, Mrs. Trent, Ms. Trent… Complete misunderstanding on my part. Do forgive me. But I wonder if you'd mind me asking you a few questions?'

'Fine,' she said. 'Come in.' Keith followed her into a dingy, ground-floor apartment that looked as if it hadn't changed in decades. Occasional, grainy family photos hinted at a lost past with her favourite brother. She led him into a fusty room with a couple of high-backed armchairs facing the small TV and a four-bar electric fire set inside a glaze-tiled mantlepiece. He sat down and took out a notebook and pen, though with little intention of writing anything; he simply wanted to look more official.

'You see, Mr. Hartman, my brother Anthony was killed on a level-crossing, when he was coming back from a football match over the other side of town.'

'I see,' said Keith. 'No, I do understand now. I had been misinformed, you see, and… Well, anyway, it's not about your brother; it's about you, and something you told the police back in May when you were involved in that awful accident on the M4.'

'Oh, I see. Yes, well I told the police everything then. Of course, if…'

Gradually, as he was talking to her, Keith realised that his silly error of presuming the name *Leslie* to be a man's had now opened up a gaping hole in the whole witness statement. Aghast at the extraordinary implications, he said:

'So you didn't lose *anybody* at all in the pile-up, then?'

'Well no, of course not.'

'You were on your own in the car?'

'Totally.'

'But you gave a full witness statement to the police… And in that statement you did not say that you lost your husband in the crash? Sorry to be so blunt about this, but you did not lose your husband?' Keith was feeling uncomfortably intrusive.

'I don't have no husband to lose, my love!' she smiled back.

'Right. No. No, of course not…' Keith closed his notebook, and made to stand up. 'Well, thank-you so very much, Mrs. Trent. That was very useful indeed.'

She stood up to show him back to the front door. 'Sounds like your boys have got their stories all muddled up, now, don't it!'

'It certainly does,' answered Keith. 'Just to confirm one fact, though, if you don't mind. The man you saw fall off the bridge – could you describe him?'

'Of course. About my age. Big fellah. Never forget that sight, not when it happens right in front of your eyes.'

'Was he black?'

She seemed shocked by the question: 'Black? You mean a coloured? No, definitely not. As white as I am!'

'Brilliant, that's really useful,' said Keith, and stepped outside. 'Well, thank-you again. If there's any more inconsistencies or problems, I hope you'll understand if we have to get in touch again.'

'You get in touch, love, if you need to!' With that, almost cheerfully, as if buoyed up by the authorities' ineptitude at dealing with her straightforward case, Leslie Trent closed the door on a now perplexed Keith.

What the hell was going on here? Why had someone doctored her statement? Why would they say she'd lost her spouse? To keep Keith or anyone else away from her, no doubt… And that's why they'd written that she was not to be contacted. Of course, it was all beginning to fall into place now.

But *what* exactly was beginning to fall into place? As he wandered back towards the station, Keith went over the events again and again in his mind. Nothing here was making any sense at all, unless one could bring all the various strands together into some vast, unfeasible conspiracy plot. That was unlikely, he thought; who was *he* to take on the responsibility of all that? Getting on the train, he realised as he drew out of the station that he had completely forgotten about chancing upon Kitchen Woman while out on the streets around her flat. His attention had certainly been diverted onto other things over the previous few hours.

And still something was not at all right.

As he finally turned into his front garden and entered his own house, Keith also sensed there was something not quite right here, either. No warm *hello!* from the kitchen or back room. In fact, strangely, Karen emerged from the hall with a serious look on her face.

Oh shit, was she really that angry that he was late? He wasn't *that* late, though, surely. Had she not got his message? Maybe she'd been preparing something for them? Or he'd forgotten that something was happening this evening; not *another* dinner guest? Keith searched his memory frantically.

Karen approached him, took his hand, and led him into the lounge.

'Darling, sit down.' she said. 'Something's happened.'

'What is it? Something serious?'

'Yes. Bad news. Awful…'

'For god's sake! What is it?'

Karen's eyes began to well with tears, and with her voice cracking, she sat down next to Keith and took his hands.

'Darling. You won't believe it. Sam Taylor. She's dead.'

Chapter Twelve

The empty silence which followed was something Keith had never known before. It lasted only a few seconds, but in that time Karen's face, the room, the whole world outside all folded themselves in on his vision and his consciousness, crashing down headlong into the centre of his head.

He had known sadness and bereavement before, but this felt different. Was it because he had loved Sam once? In the instants following Karen's bombshell he could not stop himself from entertaining vivid, bright, sensuous memories of her in his arms, in her bed, her thighs, her warm, fleshy embrace of his own body. He tempered these thoughts into an agony-seared sadness at all that life and warmth now fled, and at the potential closeness she still, in his imagination, might have offered him – offered anyone, in fact – which had now all vanished for good.

Vanished? Gone? It's unbelievable...

Keith's thoughts were struck too with the awfulness of her timing. Just as something big was looming into view… And that was what most scared him; just what might be happening to his ordered, rule-bound world, if the one person he had cajoled into helping him had suddenly died?

'How did she…?'

Karen was crying now: 'Car accident.'

'Where?'

'On her way back from some meeting, Saturday night. Motorway.'

'Coming back from Manchester? Christ! That was when she last texted me...'

'That's what the police said. They'd traced her last texts.'

Keith sat back, and felt something choking in the back of his throat. Tears clogged his eyes: 'The police? Here?'

'They came round earlier this evening, and I told them you hadn't come back yet. Carter had phoned, and–'

'Carter phoned here? When?' Keith's evening was becoming ever more surreal.

'Earlier on. He wanted to ask you something about work, and I told him you weren't back yet.'

'Was that after you'd got my message?'

'Keith! What's all this about?'

'You told Carter I was coming back late? That I had some work to see to at the office?'

'Yes, of course I did.'

Keith sighed. So Carter was checking up on him. He must have been. Why else phone to see if he'd got home yet? Carter never phones here, never!

'Then the police came to the door,' continued Karen, 'to see you, and to ask you about her last movements. And did I know Sam Taylor, were we friends, how well you knew her... Oh god, Keith. This is all absolutely awful.'

'I know, I know.' Keith finally put a strong arm around her, and held her close, as she sobbed onto his chest. Then she lifted her tear-laden eyes, and asked him:

'She'd texted you the night before?'

'Yes, about this bloody business...'

'Oh Keith. What is all this? What's going on?'

'Nothing. Nothing at all. I don't know.' He looked down at her. 'I don't know, I tell you... Just that something is definitely going on here. And I'm getting caught up in it.'

'The police are coming round tomorrow morning, first thing. They said they'll be needing a few answers, and that you need to be in.'

'OK.'

'You're not in trouble?'

'Hope not.'

Suddenly, the full implication of Samantha's death kicked in, and Keith felt a heavy sob burst from his lungs, followed by Karen's arms holding him tighter now, as he shook for a good half-minute with emotions as pure and raw as he'd ever known.

There on his sofa sat a stocky police officer, cap in hand, accompanied by a young WPC, whose eyes seemed red from crying. Did they know Samantha? Presumably. Keith didn't want to ask; it seemed topsy-turvy for him to be prying. It was early the next morning, and the inevitable ring on the doorbell presaged a difficult interview.

'You knew the deceased from a long time ago?'

'I did. We met on a course a good few years back.'

'And you and her had been… as it were, an item, sir? If you don't mind my asking?'

Karen wasn't around. She'd left for work at her normal time, but Keith still felt uncomfortable dealing with this side of things in the house he shared with her.

'Yes. But a long time ago, really, and not for very long.'

'But you'd begun seeing her again recently?'

'Yes, well, but not in that sort of way. I mean…'

'But she was in close contact with you, was she?'

'With both of us, yes. That's right. It was Karen, my current girlfriend – well, my girlfriend, full-stop actually, who… that is, it was Karen who got back in touch with Samantha.'

'Your ladyfriend stated last night, sir, that it was Ms. Taylor who had contacted *her*?'

'Well, yes. Actually, that's right. She was working in the area a bit more frequently, and wanted to get back in touch again.'

'With you?'

'Yes. Well, with both of us, that is.'

'And you were happy to see her again?'

'Of course. We'd been good friends. And she'd always been friends with Karen.'

'You'd had her round for a dinner party?'

'Just before my speed awareness course. Not that that's of any importance, though,' added Keith. 'That's a completely different criminal offence.' As soon as he heard the words blurted out of his mouth, Keith winced.

'Different criminal offence? What do you mean by that?'

'Different, as in whatever might…' Keith wanted to utter the word *murder*, but he knew this was not the right moment to do so, and instead continued: 'Adultery. Not that adultery is actually a crime these days, anyway… And I wasn't. I mean, we weren't. Oh god…'

'Shall we start again, sir?'

'Yes please.' Keith managed a weak smile.

The young policewoman now leaned forward: 'You appear to have been the last person to have received word from the deceased. Do you have those texts on your phone?'

Keith shifted awkwardly in the sofa. 'Well, no. I don't have them any more.'

'Why not?'

'Deleted.'

'Because…?'

Keith winced again. 'In case my current girlfriend found them. My girlfriend, that is. Karen…'

'You deleted texts because you were worried your current girlfriend might suspect something was going on with someone she had invited on several occasions to dinner, and with whom you say you were not having an affair?'

'Yes.'

Her colleague picked up the thread once more: 'And what was in those texts? Anything we should know about?'

'No, not really. But you have them yourselves, don't you? Aren't they on her phone? Do they contain anything of interest to you?'

The officer leaned forwards with a menacing smile. 'Should there have been something interesting in them, sir?'

'No. Not at all. Nothing I remember really.' Keith gathered himself up for a moment. 'Look, are you treating her death as suspicious?'

'To be honest with you, no,' answered the WPC. 'It was a shocking and tragic accident, that's all. But we did want to know who it was she had been texting, not long before her death, just to follow up a loose end or two.'

'Well,' said her colleague, beginning to stand up. 'Thank-you very much for your time, Mr. Hartman. We shouldn't be troubling you any more, but do get in touch if there's anything you think we should know, won't you?'

'Will do,' confirmed Keith. As he saw them out of the house, the woman turned one last time, and said with a serious tone:

'There may be an inquest, certainly before any funeral takes place. I hope you understand that you might be called upon to give evidence, Mr. Hartman? After all, if we need clarification about your *actual* relationship with Ms. Taylor, it may be that this will have to be discussed publicly. I hope you are prepared for that. And I hope your *current* girlfriend is, too.'

'No problem,' Keith smiled through gritted teeth, and as he saw them making their way down the front steps to disappear off along the street, he closed the door behind him, leaned against it exhausted, sighing heavily.

Marvellous. Now they too were convinced he had been having an affair with Samantha. Just like Karen. Anyway, they were definitely suspicious of him. Now he felt as if he actually *had* been unfaithful, and was furious with himself for speaking to them in a way that made his story sound so unbelievable.

Even Keith couldn't imagine believing himself after all that…

Still, on the positive side, he had managed not to let on that there was indeed something odd about their recent dealings. The timing of her death seemed too much of a dreadful coincidence.

What's more, the police's responses led him to conclude that they had no idea what Samantha had sent him. She must have deleted her texts to him, too. All that was left was obviously a trail of deleted texts that had led them to Keith. So he did know more than they did, after all.

His breathing had returned to normal, and he was feeling better about the whole traumatic event this morning. All he needed to do was make sure Karen didn't put two and two together about Samantha, and come up with five… Leaving the hallway, Keith went to find his jacket and keys, picked up his briefcase from the docking port, and set off to work.

Work for the rest of this week was going to be difficult. Keith was not in the mood to talk about events to Carter, nor to anyone else for that matter. With his head down, he ploughed his way through the work he had on his desk, and asked Carter things only when he needed to.

Early on at one point, however, he did put his head over the partition to ask the one question he had to know the answer to:

'Carter, I understand you phoned last night. Anything serious?'

'Oh, nothing really. Just wondered if you'd picked up the files I'd left on the Symonds and Grove case, that's all.'

'Ah.'

'No, it's all right, they were here under a load of stuff when I got in this morning. Just couldn't remember where I'd left them.'

Keith returned to his work. Something in Keith's own tone had changed; he sensed it, even if Carter hadn't. He felt more detached, almost dislocated. He was not smiling when he spoke, and he was sure Carter must have noticed. But then Carter was lying anyway, wasn't he… He had never before presumed Keith had picked something up from his desk – what a load of nonsense! He had been checking up on whether Keith had carried out his idea of visiting Leslie Trent. But why?

Keith now settled into the routine over the next few days of looking up information he needed about the two doctors, Daniel Smythe and Simon Hawes, who had been at the scene of the accident; but he did it incrementally, five minutes at a time, never leaving any windows up on his screen, and always with plenty of other paperwork and data in front of him, as a cover.

Still he seemed to get no further. One was listed as working in a North London hospital, the other in a private practice in Guildford. Two doctors who once knew each other were there at the scene. Hints of slight inconsistencies within their reports, but not much else… Perhaps after so many years and in the heat and chaos of the moment they simply had not recognised one another. Enquiries about their whereabouts on the day itself had brought up the link with a meeting of specialists in their field at a hospital in Bristol.

Was he barking up the wrong tree after all? Perhaps it was all just some awful set of coincidences, culminating in Samantha's untimely death. Perhaps his imagination, this bloody head that wouldn't stop buzzing and humming with thoughts and convoluted conversations, was playing him up, fucking with his mind. This was turning out to be a nightmare, and maybe it was all happening in a feverish vision, like a waking dream.

Why can't I just let go, sometimes? wondered Keith, as he headed home on the Friday evening, after an uneventful journey back through suburbia. A dull day, doing dull work, unalleviated even by a glimpse of Kitchen Woman, who seemed to have gone AWOL.

'Hi, darling!'

'Hello!' came the response from the back room, where Karen had not long arrived, taken off her shoes and put her feet up in front of the telly.

Keith put his briefcase in the docking port, slipped his own shoes off, and poked his head around the door. 'Won't be a second! Just popping upstairs first. Absolutely desperate!..'

Running up to the loo, which was inconveniently on the top floor, Keith hardly noticed at first a dark shape in a place where there was normally only white. It was an angular, irregular gash of black, a shard in the upper periphery of his vision. He looked up. How strange.

Returning to Karen, Keith said: 'You been up into the attic?'

'No.'

'You must have been.'

'No. Definitely not.'

'But the attic cover is half open.'

'Well, it's not me. Did you?'

'No.'

'Then it's been blown out slightly by a draught. Today's been windy.'

'Can the wind do that?' asked Keith, innocently.

'Yes, I think so.'

And that was that.

Chapter Thirteen

'There you are, Keith. Welcome back.'

'What do you want?' asked Keith.

'No, what do *you* want?'

'I don't understand. I don't understand anything…'

'It's all up to you now. You are a free agent, my friend.'

'That's what you said before, I remember. What do you mean by that? I don't really…'

'How do you sleep at night, Keith? Soundly? Deeply?'

'Yes, I suppose so. It depends.'

'It depends. Oh yes, it does depend, doesn't it.'

'On what?'

'You tell me.'

'I don't even understand your question.'

'You're surprised I know about you. Even in your sleep we've been watching you.'

'Somebody's been following me a lot, recently. Is it you?'

'It is.'

'Are you Malcolm?'

'If you like. I'm whoever you want me to be. Let's make a pact, you and I.'

'Oh, come on, for god's sake …'

Malcolm leaned forward, and whispered: 'Let's say I show you the way forward, first. Then we can talk about a contract.'

'Let's do that... Oh god, I am drunk,' muttered Keith. 'I had a few drinks this evening, I have fallen asleep and I'm dreaming this nightmare. You are not real.'

'Oh, but I am, old fellow,' came the reply. 'More real than you can imagine. You've been on quite a roller-coaster, without realising it; you probably don't know now just how much is real and how much is not.'

Coming to his senses a little, Keith tried again.

'I am dreaming, I have been drinking...'

'Oh, you've been drinking all right! It's been a while now, Keith.'

'What does that mean?' asked Keith. 'What does that even mean? How do you know my name? Who the hell are you, for Christ's sake?'

'Oh, you know me.'

'I do?'

'Yes, Keith. I am your guardian angel!'

'Are you really?'

'Oh, you've been through it, haven't you, Keith, just like we've all been through it; loss and bereavement, shock and anguish, renewal and rebirth, renewal and rebirth... But that's what our Society is for. Come and be a part of it, come and join us; there's no other way out now. We share your secret, after all, we know who you are, we know where you live...'

Malcolm's voice, almost chanting, almost ethereal and sing-song, infiltrated every corner of Keith's dream: 'Take the chance, Keith, take on the change. Keith, you know we know; and you know what it is you want to do, how you want to be. You've spent your life in the darkness, but now's your chance. You've been hemmed in, so constrained, so cut off and cut out of things. Why not bring about the change you want in yourself? And in the world around you, too? Why not bring on that freedom you've striven for, hoped for all your life, dared not dream of? We are here to follow you, we shall help you, there's no need to worry. Nobody will find out. Why should they? You're cleverer than most, you won't get caught. You just need to let go a bit, don't you? Let go... Why are you so uptight, Keith? When do you ever relax? Look at you, look where it has got you... Poor old Keith, always so upright, always so serious, so reliable... Where's it ever got him? Why does he still hope to change things, to do things for the world, when he just languishes in his old self? Why doesn't he break free, make the leap to a new reality, take the hand of those here to help him, who can support him as he steps out into this new adventure?

'Silly Keith, with his habits, his failsafes, his worries; which way should he turn when he has everything already covered? Come on, wake up! Smell the fresh air of a new way of life; breathe, breathe in deeply and feel it in your lungs, feel it seeping, then clawing right inside your body and your mind! This is the breath of the new, the cool, vigorous, life-changing elixir that you need to take a gulp of! Why do you want to rely on the crutches you surround yourself with, especially as you're on your own now. You can please yourself, you can throw away the stifling constraints and restrictions you built around yourself and your stiff life, like scaffolding – scaffolding so dense you can hardly see out from behind it... You won't need it any more, you won't want it any more, never again... And if you find yourself in trouble from now on, it won't matter, because you're going to be able to cope without it, you'll find a different way around, use a different mindset, Keith!

'Look, here's your problem – why don't you admit it? You've never been able to let go, have you? Always worried about the risk, always afraid to stick your neck out. Good old Keith, he means well, but he'll never put his money where his mouth is...'

'What do you want me to do?'

'That will come later. For the moment you should do what you want to do – or have always wanted to do... Who have you always wanted to get their comeuppance? Who in your book deserves some mild revenge? Start close to home, Keith... Test your wings!'

Keith thought for a moment, and in the gloom, taunted by this strange saviour sitting across from him, one thought popped into his head.

'The man from number forty-four.'

'There you go, then. The man from number forty-four.'

'He's a smug bastard.'

'He is indeed. He's a smug bastard, Keith. He should be taught a lesson.'

Chapter Fourteen

Keith looked his girlfriend up and down as they set out for one of their weekend treks across the estates and out beyond the stiles that led to the nearest stretch of unbroken countryside.

For god's sake, Karen, what the hell are you wearing? I mean, dressed like that, just for a walk through the fields – we're only walking off last night's curry, after all…

In recent months she had become increasingly keen to be well equipped, *just in case*, she'd always say.

Just in case what? Just in case they happened to lose themselves amid the copses and brooks, and couldn't find their way back to the metropolis of West London? In case they were attacked by feral rambler-rustlers, out to stalk and shoot at them for sport? Or in case nuclear war was declared while they were out, and they had to seek shelter from the blast, live out in the country for days on end and claw out their existence in the wilds of Middlesex, till they made their way to the nearest colony of refugees?

Keith was a child of the late eighties, after all, and his mind often still wandered into the realms of nuclear holocaust scenarios…

Karen wore a double-lined pair of lycra leggings, a sporty crop-top emblazoned with some meaningless logo and lifestyle motto, *Live The Moment!...* and not only a rucksack too small to put anything worthwhile into, say a bacon bap or a couple of cans of chilled lager, but also a bum-bag, sported at a jaunty angle over her slim hip, and filled with a number of packets of headache tablets and mints. Also, snaking over her right shoulder, was a hydration unit, that most pointless of items for a walker beating the fields of the Home Counties, with its nozzle that constantly hung beside her lips in what looked like trembling, sycophantic attentiveness, dribbling and spurting unattractively. Finally there was the bandana, and it was this that made Keith bristle with unexpressed rage. *Why the need for a bandana, Karen? Really…* The look of the hip-hop bad-boy, the look-at-me accessory for anyone too uncool to realise they didn't look cool. *Oh Karen, what are you thinking of?*

'Ready, darling?' she asked. 'Do I look all right for you?'

'Ready, darling. You look great today…' Smiling, he reached for the front-door key from the kitchen, and while he was there stuffed a couple of paper towels into his trouser pockets, *just in case*, and followed his adventure-ready girlfriend out onto the street. Off they went, down their usual route, past the off-licence, the newsagent, across the main road and out away from the centre of town. After a few minutes, Karen grabbed Keith's hand.

'What do you make of the chap at number forty-four? Has he just gone even weirder than usual?'

'Why do you say that?'

'Silly behaviour, really. Just hanging about at the front door when I come and go, as if to make some sort of point.'

'What point?'

'I dunno. Territorial idiot…'

'We've got our fair share of them, haven't we? Noisy kids and Civil War enactments next door, spider man at forty-four.'

'Then there's the other side,' agreed Karen, 'with their studenty habits and darkened curtains drawn. I never see them at weekends before midday, do you?'

'Oh, to be a student again… Mind you, at least the end house is being done up. Whoever moves into number forty once it's all been refurbished, let's hope they're normal!'

'They've been working on it for ages, haven't they.'

'Months now. Though I rarely see any builders going in and out.'

'Have you spoken to your parents recently? I thought about it when you mentioned the man on the bridge. When was the last time you rang them?'

'A fair while ago.'

'You should ring them.'

'I know.'

'Do it. They're getting older.'

'I know. I'll get on to it.'

'I understand they're a bit, you know, but…'

'I know, I know…'

'Did you enjoy the film last night?' asked Karen, changing the subject at the sight of Keith's discomfort.

'I did, though I found the plot a little far-fetched, especially the ending.'

'God, I thought you liked a good conspiracy, darling?'

'I do, but not when it becomes so complex that… I don't know, it just seemed a wee bit silly. Curry was nice, though, wasn't it?'

'Mmm. Tasty. I preferred it to the new takeaway that's opened on Barnwell Road.'

'I'll tell you what, the one we used that first time when Sam came over was superb, wasn't it?'

'Absolutely…' Karen stopped herself momentarily. It had been a week now. 'Poor Sam. Still can't believe that, can you?'

'No. Still really odd,' Keith admitted.

Keith readjusted his thinking, and added: 'It's just that Nigerian fellow. I cannot get this whole saga out of my mind.'

'Are you still completely sure you saw a white man? Could you not have been mistaken?' Karen's tone was genuine, but her words still showed she was unconvinced.

'I did. It is definitely connected,' he affirmed.

'Honestly speaking,' said Karen, climbing over a stile and setting out across a field full of sheep, 'how can you truly say you believe there is a connection? Seriously?' she added, ahead slightly, and turning to look directly at him: 'Do you honestly think in your heart that she was killed… and killed, because of *you*?'

'Well,' he began.

'Because if you do, then you really must tell somebody. And soon.'

'What if I am worried about who to tell it to?'

'What do you mean? You're saying you think Carter's in on it as well? Oh my god, Keith! Is this a whole conspiracy theory taking shape in your head?'

'Well, if whoever is behind this can take out a policewoman just like that… I mean, who the hell can I turn to? Hardly the police…'

Karen laughed. 'You'd better go above Carter's head, then, hadn't you!'

'Maybe I will. It's no joking matter, you know.'

'I never said it was,' she answered, sucking at her hydration tube.

'Well, I just cannot see how to go ahead. If they decide to take me out as well, I wouldn't stand a chance. I know too much.'

Karen snorted.

'What? You really don't take this at all seriously, do you?'

'Well, it does seem a bit far-fetched…'

'And the deserted army base? The figure in the woods watching us? And the satellite image–' He broke off suddenly, realising he was in territory she had no idea about.

'And the what?' she asked. 'What satellite image?'

'Well…' Keith took a deep breath. 'I didn't want you to worry about this, and so I didn't tell you at the time, but… When I went back to look at the *street view* version of the base, someone had inserted a figure telling me to back off and stay away.'

'What! You serious? Is this really true?' Karen stopped in her tracks for a moment. 'You didn't tell me? But, oh my god, that's seriously creepy. You sure you didn't imagine it?'

It may have been a reasonable question, but Keith responded with quiet frustration. How typical. Just the same as when he had said he'd seen the chap falling off the bridge in the first place… Why did she always have to give the impression of not believing him?

They moved on through a line of trees bursting with spring blossom, and crossed a brook over a rickety, wooden footbridge.

Beyond lay a low rise with copses snaking up left and right. A farmhouse lurked silent and empty to their left at the end of a muddy lane.

'Yes.' he retorted eventually. 'It was there.'

'What do you mean *telling you* to back off?'

'He was holding a placard or something. The words were written on that. *Don't come back. Stay away from here.* Really fucking weird, I tell you.'

'And you didn't dream it? You must show me!'

'I can't. It's gone. And what do you mean, *dream it* ?'

'Oh well,' she continued, as if all her assumptions were suddenly proved right. 'There's no hope of telling anyone that, then. They'll think you're mad.'

'I know.'

'Or you imagined it…'

'For god's sake,' Keith erupted at last. 'I saw it, I tell you. Do you really not believe me?'

'Why didn't you take a screen-shot of it?'

'Damn,' Keith exclaimed. 'I don't know why I didn't. It's daft, I know, but I just was not thinking straight, I was in quite a bit of shock. It had been a tough day, if you remember, what with the visit to the army base, and all that.'

Karen took his arm in her hands: 'OK, OK, I do believe you.'

'Good.'

'I'm sorry, all right?'

'OK.'

'It's just a bit too weird and, I don't know. You're supposed to be a straightforward civil servant, not the object of an assassination plot.'

'I can't help it. It's *me* who's opened up the whole Pandora's box. Let's leave it, hey?'

They walked on again in silence for a while. Karen ventured the beginnings of a conversation: 'Did you see those latest photos from NASA? Almost too good to be real.'

'Could they be faked, do you reckon?'

'I wasn't saying that.'

'Do you believe in conspiracy theories when it comes to NASA?'

'Do you?'

'No.' Keith searched around for another thread: 'Only a couple of months till your birthday. Any ideas for presents?'

'Not really. What did you get me last year?'

'Forgotten?'

'No.'The words stumbled out of both of them like a slow growth, the stunted tendrils of a drawn-out relationship gone cold. Only with the clasping of hands did a hint of warmth return, though this was short-lived, as stiles and a high bank of nettles followed on from each other in quick succession.

'Any ideas, then?'

'Not immediately. Have you?'

'Surely no more hiking gear? You look kitted out like a trained assassin, a forest hunter.'

'Well, since you mention it, you can never have enough gear. Only this week I was looking at the catalogue for socks and insoles, and now there's a new type of–'

'Ssshh! Look!' Keith cut her off and stared into the middle of a dark, dank-looking hill above their path, covered with trees and brambles. 'Stay still. I saw someone.'

Karen froze as ordered, then slumped in a wave of tired recognition. 'Oh god, what have you seen this time, Keith?'

'I tell you, I am getting so freaked out by all this.'

'So am I. Who did you see this time?'

'I don't know. He was too far away, but there was definitely someone there.' He turned to look at Karen's face, and realised she was not buying it. 'Oh my god,' he hissed, 'you don't believe me, do you? Again! I mean, how much do I have to see till I can get you to believe what I am saying?'

'Well, look – what did you actually see there? Hey! Where are you going?'

Keith had started to climb over the retaining lane wall and up into the copse. Karen tugged at his coat and pulled him back onto the path. 'What the bloody hell do you think you're doing? If someone is up there watching you, you might get yourself killed. Just hold your horses!'

'So you *do* believe me, then?'

'The jury's still out.'

'Ouch…'

'Did you see his face?'

'I never see his face. Oh my god, I hope I'm not getting Alzheimer's. That's what happens, apparently. But it looked like the same figure I spotted when we left the army base. Just standing there watching us from a distance.'

'Right, let's keep moving.' Karen dragged him onwards, and he acquiesced.

They walked briskly, almost hurriedly away from the copse. Inevitably, Samantha's ghost now caught up with them, and stalked along beside them for a while.

'Do you still want to believe she didn't die accidentally?' asked Karen at last.

'Yes,' he answered earnestly, 'I do.'

'Did you really delete those texts because of that?'

'I did delete them, not because of any real, definite worries – I didn't know she'd die that night, after all. But I did feel it was going to be better for me not to have them on my phone. Does that make sense?'

She nodded, but Keith saw in her expression the look of someone unconvinced, uncertain of quite what to believe. He was beginning to despair of Karen's default to doubt, he might as well give up on believing in anything himself. Does there come a point, he wondered, when the whole edifice of what one thinks one knows is so undermined that it cracks; that the individual self just gives in, and surrenders to a different reality? Is that what it must feel like to live in a totalitarian state, a state that is asking you to join in with its own confection of reality? Keith shuddered.

'You shuddered!' observed Karen. 'Is it her you're thinking about? Are you desperately sad at her death?'

'Yes, of course I am. You know I am. It's awful.'

'And *was* there anything else?'

'What do you mean?'

'You know exactly what I mean.'

'Did I ever have another fling with her? Is that what you're saying?'

'You know that's what I'm saying.'

'Why does it matter to you? Haven't you made up your own mind already?'

'No.'

'Yes you have. You're convinced I was seeing her again.'

'Were you?'

'No.'

'Good.'

'There we are then. That's sorted that. I told you before I wasn't. I wouldn't do that to you, would I?'

'I'd be devastated. Oh my god, I tell you I couldn't bear it if I thought you were lying to me about her. She might be, well, gone, but you and me, we still have… Do you know what I'm saying? I mean, even if – '

'I said I didn't and I didn't.' Keith's answer was intended to sound curt and definitive.

'She had meant something to you in the past, I know.'

'Nothing more than a silly, flirty thing,' he said, with a shudder.

'There you go again. You shuddered! I saw you!'

'I know,' admitted Keith. He paused, then confessed: 'I'm suddenly desperate for a shit.'

'What? What *are* you like!' exclaimed Karen, half laughing, half appalled.

'I reckon it's last night's rogan josh.' he shivered again, and began to feel the beads of sweat on his forehead that meant there was going to be only one way out of this situation. A deep, audible rumbling emanated from his bowels in timely confirmation.

'My god, you mean it, don't you?' Karen's face had settled on an appalled look now. 'Well, god knows where you're going to go… Maybe over there?' She pointed at a hedge. Traffic flowed visibly beyond the further field, and a farmhouse overlooked the whole scene from a nearby hill.

'I'll hold out.' retorted Keith unconvincingly.

'You've gone pale.'

'I'll hold out.'

They crossed another couple of fields.

God, Karen must feel like the compassionate carer of a man suddenly afflicted with an unnatural, racing onset of old age.

Bent double and wincing in pain, Keith's legs were hardly able to open as he half-tumbled over stiles seemingly designed to increase his discomfort. An occasional groan was accompanied by the growing rumbles in Keith's lowermost regions.

They entered a wood.

'Here's your chance,' urged Karen. 'Mind you, better hope that your stalker isn't around to see you!' She seemed surprisingly keen on his relieving himself. *Why might this be?* Keith wondered. *And what about his trousers? His light beige trousers would be in the direct firing line once the curry was released. Oh god…* He stared through his weeping vision for a safe place away from the path, looked around for signs of other walkers, and then struck out through the bracken and brambles to a spot hidden down a small gulley.

'Go on ahead!' he rasped. 'Shout if…'

Keith had spent a lifetime not allowing the realities of the body to impinge on his normal routine, and taking the right precautions to make sure they did not. Now here he was outdoors, trousers right down, crouching vulnerably and letting go in a manner he found alien to everything he had ever striven for.

But it felt so good.

The sudden ejection of pent-up pressure immediately released an almost euphoric delight in him. He heard himself sigh. A beautiful sigh of inner release, something like childish joy. He didn't care any more. It was the lancing of a boil, it was the same as having to be sick in order to start feeling better again… More, it was relief combined with a transcendental ecstasy.

My god, it was almost as satisfying as sex.

On top of all this, Keith was able to congratulate himself on having grabbed some kitchen roll before leaving the house. There was now a rightness to this whole episode, and as he made his way back to the path, walking upright now, lighter both in body and mind, he wondered why he had not done this before, more often. Was it the *al fresco* element that had always put him off? Whipping one's trousers down, squatting amid stinging nettles, everything hanging out, with bowels straining behind the modesty of just a single tree and some bushes.

And the visceral, primitive result! A vast turd, animal-like and sitting half-curled up, half splattered on the ground instead of semi-dissolved in the dip of a U-bend, only to be flushed from view. Its presence was something quite shocking to Keith, the sound, the sight and the smell, which pervaded the air all about. This was nature, this was to be a source of curiosity for the wild beasts right across the neighbourhood, and to an animal instinct it would be something ripe for investigation, something to be analysed.

How very different from the sanitised, bleached lives we inhabit…

Keith caught up with Karen.

'Better?' she enquired.

'Much better!' he replied, more honestly than he realised. 'That's a weight off my mind.'

They marched on, in lighter spirit now, emerging from the dank wood and made their way over the lower valley towards a village pub they knew would be open. Keith felt he had learnt a great deal today.

CHAPTER FIFTEEN

It was night. Deep night. As he walked towards his house, Keith finally heard the first car to interrupt his impromptu walk. As he had pounded the pavements and ranged around the centre of town and beyond, through tree-lined suburbs, he had seen nobody else on the streets at all, not a single soul – it was late, after all. Karen had gone out, so why shouldn't he? Out for some fresh air, that's what he had needed. Out and about, out and about… A walk through town and along the canal, lungs filled with fresh air.

Then suddenly, around the corner behind him, spluttered the engine of a small *Peugeot*, profiting from the quiet of the streets in the small hours. A glimpse of the driver as he went past suggested someone around Keith's age, with a wife beside him and elderly parents in the back, coming home no doubt from some dull dinner party or family event.

As they raced along the empty road ahead, Keith saw the sudden, shocking flash of a camera, followed by the red glare of their brake-lights, a sign of the frustrated realisation within the car that they'd been caught. Then it moved sheepishly on, disappearing round a corner and finally out of earshot.

Keith could well imagine the conversation that was now taking place within that car, the recriminations, the apologies, the regret at speeding; and the silent justification, too, of an empty road, and of a risk having been taken.

CHAPTER SIXTEEN

Malcolm flicked a glance over his shoulder. 'All our attic spaces are linked. He went out hours ago, to visit his daughter as he always does. Won't be back for ages.'

'What should I do?'

'Well, that's up to you, isn't it. I wouldn't burn his house down, though, that might be going a bit far, given that your own house is only two doors away from his…'

'I could really worry him, though…'

'You could. Why don't you climb in through his attic door and have a look at the layout of his place, and see what devilry you can get up to. If I hear him coming back, I'll whistle down to warn you.'

Keith got out of bed, walked as if in a trance away from the figure standing motionless in the shadows in the far corner of their room, and went up to the top floor, where he pulled down the ladder and began pulling himself up into the loft. In the darkness, he clambered over the low partition separating his loft space from that of his nearer neighbour's. Keeping carefully to the wooden planks placed on top of the thick rafters, he found himself amongst piles of cardboard boxes, toys and an old pushchair, through which he negotiated his way, until he reached the next partitioning wall. He climbed over this, waited for a moment until his eyes accustomed themselves to the now complete darkness, then felt his way half-crouching towards the hatch that led down into number forty-four.

He lifted it easily enough, released the ladder down onto the landing, then lowered himself into the house below.

He was standing in surroundings almost identical to his own, but with heavy, claustrophobic wallpaper, endless pictures and family portraits, and a paisley carpet that snaked its way from the bathroom down the stairs and to the floor below.

Keith tiptoed down step by cautious step, still unsure whether the owner might be at home. First he glanced into the master bedroom, the bed made and covered with carefully laid cushions; then into the spare one opposite, where he turned on the light. Here, heavy drapery and an old sewing machine filled the space, as well as a table with piles of old family photos and a genealogical chart, half-completed.

He crept downstairs to the ground floor. Opening the lounge, he surveyed the dreary, 1990s style sofas, the ornate but modern mantlepiece clocks, the silver-framed photos of grandchildren and nieces. Paisley carpet had now given way to beige patterned thick-pile.

The hallway was lined claustrophobically with a mish-mash of cabinets and trestle-tables, on which he found a number of unopened letters, some driving documents, various pens, more photos and reassuringly, thought Keith, a set of spare car-keys.

So we all do it, then…

The kitchen was thick with clothes drying and washing-up ready to be put away. In front of the back door was the blanket where his little dog evidently slept. Keith sifted through some of the notices pinned up on a cork notice-board, and glanced across the memos and grandchildren's paintings clinging to the fridge. He left, uninspired, beginning to lose interest in revenge.

Then he opened the door to the back room. Here was the collection Keith had been dreading to find. He had to switch this room's light on, and he immediately saw its reflection catching the array of glass cabinets and tanks lining the walls. A musty, damp smell filled the air, and he felt himself itching involuntarily. Maybe he could let them all out. Well, he might, if he could bring himself to get close enough, but that wasn't going to happen. Keith couldn't even enter the room. And, for god's sake, what would be the point of letting things out which might eventually make their way over to his house? That was what Keith himself was doing, after all. Slipping and sliding, creeping and crawling around the hidden corners of the building. No, better to keep it subtle, at first.

At first?

Yes, there'd be another chance, there'd have to be.

So he left the lights on, here in the back room and upstairs in the spare bedroom. As he went back upstairs, he passed the thermostat, and another idea struck him. He went along to the bathroom, opened the cupboard where the boiler hung, and turned it off. The whole system, everything.

Oh my god, what the hell have I just done?

Keith placed the trapdoor back into place, turned around in the pitch blackness, and aimed back for the faint glow of light coming up from his own house. He clambered over the partitions, in his neighbours' attics, and found himself back where he'd begun the evening.

Malcolm had obviously gone. The room was in darkness. Karen's sleeping form was breathing beneath the duvet.

Keith crept into the bed, and drifted back to sleep with disturbing swiftness.

CHAPTER SEVENTEEN

The days passed, then the weeks. The trail around the Nigerian had gone cold. Keith slipped back into his routines, the cycles of work and sleep, the tedium of a life aching to know more, to understand what lay beneath the surface. And all the time a biting frustration was gnawing away at him, drilling into his neck and ears, behind his tired eyes, and driving him mad, buzzing with questions and an unsettling fear.

What had been happening to him? Keith wondered how he had ended up so involved in something he didn't even understand, something he didn't even quite believe was true… Again and again he pored over the details: Samantha's death; the impending inquest he had been informed would soon take place; the strange, eerie figure watching him; the Nigerian; the man on the bridge; the abandoned base at Henford; the doctored satellite images…

All these disturbing details seemed to be conspiring to send him over the edge. In the meantime, Carter had stopped talking about the issue, and as for Karen, well…

Karen's indifference seemed to be that of the kindly nurse, tending to the raving patient. Keith was the one who was mad after all, it seemed. She had tried to talk to him about things on a couple of occasions, they had stumbled into a convoluted conversation about his mental health, but then Keith had closed up on her. He hated all that sort of stuff. She seemed more concerned about his well-being, which was fine, but utterly incapable of hearing about his fears and concerns.

Then there were the dreams, these recurring dreams with Malcolm, whoever the hell he was, always emerging from the shadows. The attic. The voices. Number forty-four.

Oh god, number forty-four! That was weird, thought Keith. It had felt so real, and the conversation afterwards with Malcolm, that too had lodged itself into his mind like a reliable version of reality.

Maybe it was reality? Keith's new reality.

Keith withdrew. He felt himself draw back from Karen, and from Carter too. His days at work he increasingly spent with his head down, fumbling alone with his daily tasks. At home, even in bed, he found himself being ever more distant, more rigid, dislocated, even, from the girlfriend he had once felt to be so close. He retreated into his own imaginings, his world filled with shadowy plots and blurry figures sneaking around at the periphery of his vision.

Now he helped himself to drink as soon as he got in from work. More than was healthy, he knew, but to hell with it. Nobody noticed, nobody cared. Least of all Karen. One beer, then another and yet another, then a wine or two, all to fill the gaps, to fill the areas of his life he had no answers for. But his nights became ever more disturbed, waking in the darkness, hearing the creaks above, wondering whether his stalker might be standing in the garden looking up at the house…

Oh god, I *am* going mad, thought Keith as he looked into the familiar, brightly lit kitchen on his way to work one day, convinced that the young woman, looking for once directly at the train, seemed to smile and wave at him as he passed. Was it at him that she was waving? Surely not…

It had been three weeks now since he had visited Leslie Trent and first heard about Samantha's death. Three weeks, in which his life had suddenly closed in on itself. Perhaps, he thought, this was grief? Grief for a lost love? Or was it grief at the passing of his present relationship with Karen?

Sex had more or less stopped. There was little affection at the moment between the two of them. Was that his fault, he wondered? Did she know how much he was suffering? Maybe she didn't care any more. She didn't seem to. Empty nights and long empty weeks passed now without a touch or fleeting smile.

There was, of course, the inevitable reconciliation and remorse, usually centred around Keith nuzzling up to her and apologising for how things were at the moment. But hardly any meeting of minds. And precious little sex…

The old fool at number forty-four was heading out with his dog. He'd be away for an hour, at least. This was Keith's chance.

He grabbed a screwdriver from his toolbox under the stairs, and climbed up into the attic. Carefully, quietly, he made his way above the two houses, knowing his way this time. Then he lowered himself down into the now familiar house and stood to get his bearings on the landing.

Lights were on all over the place this time. Keith crept along to the bathroom, and looked around. On the shelf above the sink were the usual items; stuffing the two tubes of toothpaste he found there into his own pockets, he opened the airing cupboard, and this time, instead of turning off the heating he switched the whole system on, and turned the nearby thermostat up to twenty. Then, finding an old toothbrush stuffed behind the sink, obviously used for cleaning around the rim of the toilet, he swapped this for the one he saw on the shelf.

As he made his way out of the bathroom, he heard the heating system clicking into life, the hot water pumping through the pipes, seeping through the whole house.

Then he went downstairs, to the spare room. On the table were still laid out various old photos and labels meticulously placed over a complicated family tree. Keith picked up one, then another, then moved around a good six or seven photos, and swapped over some of their labels too.

Downstairs now to the kitchen. Hunting around the cupboards, Keith was toying with what to change, which part of someone's everyday life he could shift into the strangely unfamiliar. Suddenly, opening a door low down beneath the sink, he chanced upon the stopcock to the water mains. He turned it three-quarters, reducing any flow to a trickle.

Then he returned to the first floor, and taking his screwdriver out, he loosened all the screws on the handle to the master bedroom. The delicious thought of this dreadful man trapped in his bedroom until his daughter came round was almost enough to send Keith into a reverie, when suddenly he heard a key in the latch, the front door opening, and the sniffing and yapping of a dog.

He was back. Sooner than expected.

Christ! Shit! What will he say?

Keith placed the screwdriver back in his pocket, raced as quickly as his tip-toes would allow him up the next flight of steps, avoiding the creaky step he'd noticed on the way down, straight up the ladder, hearing the dog sniffing its way upstairs and now barking at the scent of an intruder. He breathlessly dived into the attic, turning round to pull the ladder up through the hatch, and disappeared into the all-enveloping darkness as he dropped the cover back into place.

That was close…

'I thought you were supposed to be keeping a lookout?' said Keith, turning breathlessly on Malcolm, who was somewhere in his house, but not visible today.

'I *was* looking out for you,' answered Malcolm. 'And you survived. And you are back. Safe and sound. How does it feel?'

Keith sat down. He drew breath.

'Weird.'

'Weird?'

'Yes, weird. Being in someone else's house, going through their stuff, looking into their rooms, being able to just fuck with their minds. Oh god, he'll really think he's going mad, or something.'

'You're good at it, that's your trouble. Very good, in fact. It's why we want you.'

*

Their holiday, booked months before, now loomed. At first they had thought about going to France, a car-bound exploration of the northern coast, maybe even Paris. The city of love and romance beckoned, like an old aunt with sloppy kisses.

But instead they had decided on a short city break in Brighton, which Keith hardly knew. Well, this could be a way to get back on track with each other, mused Keith equivocally; or maybe a way out.

A way out? Oh god, was he really thinking like that?

Whatever the case, it would get him out of the house, away from work, away from Carter and the whole sorry mess with Samantha.

'Looking forward to getting to know Brighton,' mused Keith, as they packed the car high with bags and boxes, the sun barely up, a cold chill in the late August air.

'Oh, I know it quite well,' replied Karen. 'I lived there for a year or so after uni.'

'Really?' Keith was taken aback. 'I never heard you mention that before? When were you there?'

'Like I said, just after uni. I'm sure I've told you about it.'

'No.'

'Yeah, hung about with a load of us in a squat for a while.'

'A squat? I had no idea!'

'Only for a while. Well, it was the early 2000s.'

'Gosh. You learn something new every day...'

'Darling,' ventured Karen, as she put her bags of toiletries on the back seat, 'This will do you good. You need the break.'

'I do?'

'Yes. You know what I've been saying about your stress levels recently, your state of mind.'

'My state of mind? My state of mind? Just what is it that going to Brighton will help me with?'

'Getting away from work, and out of this house.'

'Out of this house? I'm fine in this house.'

'I'm sure you are. But…'

'You think it's this house that's making me like I am?'

'I don't think it helps.'

'And it's making me mad, is it? Is that what you're saying?'

'No. I just…'

'Just what? Why don't you come out and say it? You think I am going mad. I'm having a mental breakdown. Don't you!'

She walked away to pick up the final bags from inside the house.

It's just as Malcolm had been saying. She was no longer on his side. She was steering him this way and that. She was acting against him and his better judgment. Who *was* she really?

Malcolm had suggested she was spying on him. Maybe she was.

But who for? For the people out to get him? For MI5? For Carter?

Maybe for Malcolm? No, that didn't make any sense.

All the way along the motorway, as they swung beneath London on the M25, while Karen dozed beside him in the passenger seat, Keith's mind was playing things over and over again. Could anyone really be after him? He wondered whether it was a mistake to get out of London. The house was empty, maybe someone would be going over it while they were away.

Oh, come on, that's just paranoia, for god's sake! Why would anyone want to rummage around in your house? There's nobody after you, you idiot! You've let your imagination get the better of you, and you just can't switch it off…

He couldn't switch it off, it was true. One or two cars seemed to spend an uncomfortable amount of time behind him, even when he allowed his speed to go right down into the sixties. Why weren't they overtaking? Are they checking he was on his way, and not likely to be turning back? Were there already people in his house, now, even before giving him the decency to get himself away from the M25? In the rear mirror, the headlights and radiators on the fronts of various cars lingering within his vision grinned like the gaping-mouthed masks of a Greek tragedy; expressionless and horrid, they seemed to be hiding shadowy faces behind them. Keith tried to get a glimpse of exactly who was behind the steering wheels, but could not penetrate the reflection of the morning sun on their windscreen.

Sweeping onto the M23 and then heading south towards the coast, Keith looked up ahead at the cameras positioned atop the high poles and pylons beside the grass verges. The road this early was quite empty here, he had a free run, but pulled back from careering too fast across the tarmac. Suddenly, looking up again at the cameras, he could hardly believe his eyes; as his *Mégane* entered their range, he saw them turning around to focus on him. Coincidence? Maybe. Keith had never witnessed such cameras actually moving, he presumed they did it automatically, and so slowly that one never noticed them doing so. As he passed them, he peered up out of the window, and saw their pitiless gaze following him.

So the scene was set for an unsettling few days in Brighton. Keith's worried expression stayed with him like a raincloud as they traipsed around the Pavilion, the Marina, the Sea Life Centre and the shops, and his silent frustration continually brought out the worst in Karen.

Brighton should have been the perfect place to let things go, with its happy-go-lucky vibe, its shabby-chic cafés and pubs, the thousands of free-living beach-bums with barbeques on the promenade. But Keith found it unsettling, especially as Karen seemed to know so much of it already. She reminisced about this place and that, as if she were enjoying some kind of hippy homecoming, which felt to Keith like a constant sparking underneath his dry tinderbox of inner conflict.

'Who exactly was it you were here with, then?' asked Keith as they went into a grungy pub that stank in a way that would be pleasant only if you had the memories to accompany it.

'Oh, mates, some pals who I hung around with in my final year.'

'Anybody I know?' he ventured.

'Probably not.'

By the end of their stay, Keith was ready to return home. They had both booked another week off work, so there was still some space for spending their time together at home, if that was what was wanted…

They dined out for their last night in a small restaurant in the centre of town. The bread was stale, the meal itself hackneyed and predictable. Karen drank more white wine than she could take, became argumentative. As they strolled home between drab, concrete apartment blocks, Keith heard her say something about the way he'd spoken to the waiter, and how offended she'd felt on the man's behalf. Keith was as drunk as she was, and began to argue back about her flirtation with the barman earlier in the day.

Which, of course, was not *relevant*.

Karen blasted several volleys of fury at Keith and they must have spent the rest of the walk to their hotel arguing. As ever, the memory was faint and patchy on what happened next.

Keith was beginning to think things really might be better once they called the whole thing off.

Could he? And wouldn't she want to, anyway? After all, he knew she was still harbouring the idea he'd been seeing Samantha.

Chance would've been a fine thing.

Good god, Keith, that's a dead woman you're talking about. Give it a rest, for Christ's sake!

Will we make it back home as a couple still? Do I want us to?

I think so… thought Keith, as he looked at Karen sleeping beside him through some interminable but inexplicable queue on the M25. As their car inched forwards he turned to look again at her sleeping form. Head back, neck rigid and hair pulled right over her forehead and down behind her ears, she exuded a beauty Keith had always admired in her, an inner equilibrium of quiet confidence and wonder. Surely they could stick it out, couldn't they? Surely they'll both see this through now?

Keith began to feel at ease for the first time in ages. Was he over it all? he wondered. Perhaps he had been unnecessarily anxious about everything. Maybe he just needed to get back home now, and forget about recent events – they had clearly knocked him quite a bit. Poor Karen; as if a fog was lifting, he suddenly realised what difficult company he had been.

Karen slept on. And on and on, all the way home. For some reason, Keith felt extraordinarily relieved, but was not sure why.

Chapter Eighteen

First he checked whether there were any mini cameras on the back of the machine, spying on those climbing up to do damage.

There weren't.

He reached up and lifted the spray can into the eye of the lens, making sure he was not visible himself in the camera's field of vision. Pushing down hard on the top of the nozzle, Keith felt it release its load, and smelt the sweet, toxic fumes. He'd done his job, and climbed down from the post.

Now he raced away as fast as he could, into the night.

This was exhilarating.

What next? There was a whole list of things to do, he knew, but the more carefully he worked on them, and the more measured he was in his endeavour, the less chance he would have of being caught.

One or two cameras on roads nearby, especially on the busy road by the canal, those could be usefully tackled this evening. Then after that it would have to involve cycling out to others, to avoid any suspicions about where the culprit might actually live.

Good idea! You're clever enough to avoid capture, Keith!

God, it was like having Malcolm right behind, egging him on.

In the pitch blackness of the early hours, Keith made his way stealthily across a park and a recreation field, through an estate and onto the main road, where he located his next all-seeing victim. It took only a second to shimmy up, lean across and spray it, then his work was done, and he was off. He decided not to do the other one on this road, for fear of attracting too much attention. He had another one in mind for this first evening, about twenty minutes away, but worth the walk. It was the very one that had caught him out earlier in the year, and for which he'd had to pay the ultimate price of attending that interminable driving course.

He found the task easy. Returning unseen to his smart, Victorian terrace, Keith let himself in, grabbed a pen and notepad and started to make a list.

A *to-do* list. Right up his street, he chuckled to himself.

Keith's life had become a routine he had always hoped for, a routine of mindless worthiness, success measured in the absence of thought. But this was offering something quite different. A full draught of adventure, laced with improvisation and danger. Could this be a new path entirely for him, he wondered? Is this what he'd been looking for all along?

Karen was out a lot that next week. She had engagements here, there and everywhere, apparently, work-meetings late at her office... Keith wasn't even sure what she did at work any more, there'd been all manner of shifting job descriptions just recently, and he couldn't keep up with it. Then there were meals out and even a house-sitting appointment over a couple of nights for her friend, Ruth.

Keith was on his own again. He had the nights to himself.

He ranged his speed camera activities across a wide area of West London, which could be covered at a surprising rate by night, routes planned, suburban, CCTV-free shortcuts adhered to, the same routes avoided on the way back.

It was an adventure, to be sure, and one which Keith suddenly found he was relishing, not least for the sheer logistic preparation involved. This was right up his street, and by the end of the week he had put at least two dozen cameras out of action with permanent black spray paint, industrial-strength, all bought at a number of different outlets in very small quantities.

Local councils were also on Keith's list for another reason. Clutching heavy-duty superglue and with his head covered by a thick, black balaclava, he walked slowly past a number of prominent parking meters on roads where drivers were always desperate to park, and where he too had been fined for overstaying his allotted time. It took a single, nonchalant squirt into each one's coin slot and all over the contactless card-reader as he made his way up the high street, then on to the next row of restriction-enforcers, all the way out of the town centre.

Then he was gone, back into the shadows.

Chapter Nineteen

'Why the fuck do you say those sorts of things?' yelled Karen.

'Say what sort of thing?'

'What you just said.'

'What did I say?'

'What you *just* said, for god's sake. Don't you remember what you just said?'

'Well I happened to mention the dynamo on the bike.'

'You know full well what I am talking about. I'm not talking about the bikes.'

'I was.'

'I wasn't. You deliberately... Oh, forget it. I've had enough.'

Three drinks in, and an evening argument had suddenly begun revolving around something Keith had not quite meant. Unfortunately, he had risen to it with evident gusto. Karen had folded her arms. Keith realised there was clearly no going back to the film they had started watching. Sometimes it reminded him of how wars begin – always the thing that triggers it comes out of nowhere, completely left-field and unexpected, despite all the preparations one has been making to dam up other sources of strife...

She turned away from him. 'I can't believe you told them at work. About how I felt.'

'I didn't. I swear there was nothing in it.'

'You think I'm a walkover? You reckon I couldn't hold my own in that sort of place?'

'No. Sorry if it sounded like that.'

'Well it did.'

'It wasn't meant.'

'How would you feel if I had said you couldn't do your job properly?'

Keith paused. 'To be honest, I'm not sure I *am* doing things properly at the moment.'

Karen rounded on him sharply. 'What do you mean? Why are you suddenly talking about *your* work?'

Undeterred, Keith went on: 'I have no confidence at the minute that what I am doing is of any use,' he ventured. 'What with all this business to do with Samantha and the man on the bridge …'

'I do not believe you!.. Why are we suddenly talking about *this*? God, you are obsessed, aren't you?'

'You don't seem that bothered by my concerns,' answered Keith, flatly.

'I'm not. You know what, I'm not really that bothered with your conspiracies and your cock-eyed theories about dead people in a motorway accident. Honestly, if you're that worried about all the people out to get you, or if you really believe that Carter is in on it all, why the hell don't you go and speak to someone above him? Surely there's somebody you can speak to?'

'I don't know. I really don't know. What if they're all involved?'

'For Christ's sake, are you serious? You honestly reckon you've unearthed some crackpot, all-consuming…'

'Yes, actually. That is how it feels.'

'You know how crazy that sounds? You want to know how crazy *you* sound? *There are all these people after me 'cos I've stumbled on a plot to cover up an accident! They're after me. I've got to hide!* And in the meantime, you're spouting all this bullshit to me, I don't give a toss quite frankly, because you're acting like a weirdo and you're turning into someone I don't really want to be around.'

'Well, thanks for all that,' muttered Keith.

Karen persisted: 'Don't you see what's happening to you? What's going on with you?'

'With *me*? What about you? You've turned your back on me completely. I come home and it feels like there's nobody here in the house. Sometimes it feels like you've already left me.'

'Perhaps I have.'

'Perhaps you have. Perhaps you have…'

Karen turned away, and then stood up. Walking out of the room, she cried back at Keith: 'Oh just…'

'Where are you going?'

'Somewhere.'

'Where?'

'I don't know. Somewhere.'

He followed her up the stairs. And into the bedroom. There he found her reaching into the wardrobe and fishing out a large rucksack. Then she started flinging clothes into it, pants, socks, two pairs of jeans, several skirts, a couple of jumpers, tights, shoes, trainers, jogging wear…

'You're joking, right? You're actually going to leave?'

'Looks like it, doesn't it.'

'Oh, come on, sweetheart. Oh come on, don't do this.'

'Why not?'

'Please…'

Karen rounded on him: 'Why *not?* I asked.' She carried on throwing things into the bag.

Keith sat dejectedly on the end of the bed watching her in disbelief. 'Why would you want to just get up and leave like this, though?'

Karen put the bag down onto the bed and sat beside him. Taking his hand in hers, she looked into his face, tears welling up in her own eyes. Keith saw this as a stepping-back from the brink, the beginnings of a temporary reconciliation.

It was not. Softly, Karen said: 'Darling, it's just not working at the moment, is it? You don't need me to tell you that. You said yourself that you're not coming home to a loving, engaging person, didn't you?'

Keith nodded.

'So let's just accept what is happening, shall we?' she continued. 'I don't feel I am wanted here, and I certainly don't feel I want to be a part of this as it is.'

'You'll be back?'

'I don't know. Not for a while. Maybe not…'

She stood up and continued with her packing.

'Where will you stay?'

'Not sure. I'll text Beth. She's got a spare room at the moment.'

Keith erupted. God, he could kill her sometimes. 'For god's sake, what is *wrong* with you? Why are you just so happy to throw all this away now? Just after a silly argument… For god's sake, Karen! Come on, baby, think about what you're doing…'

'I have thought. I have thought for quite a while.'

'You've been planning this?'

'Not planning it…'

'Look, you don't have to go now. Let's talk about it in the morning. We've got a whole Sunday to talk things over.'

'That sounds like fun.'

'You really are so unfair sometimes, you know.'

'And you have driven me out of this house with your *stupid* conspiracies, your bloody annoying habits…' She was now starting to find traction in her arguments: 'Your drinking, your drunken accusations, your blundering conversations with your colleagues at work, your insensitivity, your…'

'Insensitivity? When am I ever insensitive to you?'

'Every time you don't think about my health, every time you ignore my asthma, every time you don't believe me when I need my inhaler, every time you leave the door to the bedroom open after we've cooked, or when there's a draught…'

'And you're leaving me for that? Oh Christ, I don't believe it.'

'Exactly. You don't give a toss, really, do you?'

'Nor do you! We both forget things.'

'You're right. But I try to give a shit. You don't.'

'You don't pick up on when I think something's important.'

'Such as what?'

'The shed door.'

'Brilliant.'

'Where to leave the spare keys so no-one can catch hold of them through the letterbox.'

'Even more brilliant! Here's my health at risk, and you're thinking once again about complicated plans to steal our keys in the dead of night by fishing for them through the letterbox with an angler's rod. You really do surpass yourself sometimes, Keith.'

'Oh, sod off! You're not perfect.'

'At least I don't leave things open which can cause dangerous currents of air for an asthma suffer.'

'Come off it, you're not a high-risk patient. Stop hamming it up.'

Furious, Karen slung the bag over her shoulder and headed downstairs.

Keith persisted: 'Well, it's not as if you don't leave things open, is it?'

'Go on…'

'Again yesterday, the attic trapdoor.'

'What about it?'

'You must have gone up there, and then left it open again.'

'Keith, I never go up there. We hardly keep anything up there. I have not been into the attic. And, for the record, I did not leave the door open after not using it. OK? Anyway, it's you, isn't it? You're the one going up into the attic. I'm sure it is.'

'No! Definitely not.'

'Well, I'm not.'

'So it's the wind? The wind did it, then? Again.'

Karen stopped still and looked at him in disbelief. 'Why are you so bothered about that attic door? For fuck's sake, what does it matter to you? Here we are arguing about us and our future, and all you can do is wonder whether I've been up into our attic. What is your problem?'

'My problem is the fact that you sometimes leave things open.'

'But I haven't left that open, I keep telling you. I have not been up there.'

'Anyway,' ventured Keith, 'It's no less important than what you're going on about. Just a draught, that's all.'

'But to me that's important.'

'And to me, so is the attic door.'

Karen snapped. 'Right. That's it. Fuck it. I've had enough.'

'Sit down. Sit down at least for a moment.' Keith caught his breath and felt the need to deal with a situation swiftly getting out of control. 'Just wait for a while. Don't do anything we'd both regret.'

'I am not going to regret getting out of here, not now.' Karen strode towards the front door, opened it and walked out into the warm, late August night. It was still light, but the streetlamps had already flickered on. 'Goodbye. I shall be back to get more stuff at some point. Don't come after me.'

'Don't worry, I won't,' Keith heard himself answer, his voice filled with self-righteous anger. He closed the door with a slam, and went back into the lounge.

At first, numb with the shock of her departure, Keith sat and watched another five minutes of the film they had been enjoying up until the argument. But he could not concentrate. The characters on the screen came and went like marionettes in and out of rooms he could no longer put into context, like the way an old person must live their life when warped with dementia.

He poured another beer, flicked over to see what else was on, put his feet up on the sofa where Karen had been sitting. He drank fast, still furious that she had ruined his evening.

He flicked channels again, then rose to adjust the screen so it faced him more directly now, he turned too quickly back to the sofa, and fell bodily into it. A slop of beer from his glass landed on his leg and on the carpet beside the sofa.

Half an hour had passed, and she still hadn't come back. Should he be worried? Why should he be worried? Was *she* worried? Probably not.

Get another beer. Why the devil not? After all, he didn't need to care whether he was having too much now, anyway. He stood up, wandered over into the kitchen, grabbed the bottle-opener, missing the cap the first couple of times. His evident fuzziness amused him. Then he thought he caught himself crying, but wasn't sure. Another half-hour, and maybe he'd text her. At least to find out where she was. See if she was safe.

It's not good, this, though. It's dark. It's getting later and later and later…

OK. So it's not all right. But it's all right, too. Because we can both calm down. And have a bit of space. It's what we needed. I do. And if I do, then god knows Karen does. She is within her rights, too. But so am I. She left me, after all. She left me. Sit down. Relax. Take your time. There'll be no driving out to pick her up, not now – way too much booze in the blood.

Too much in the blood.

She'll be back, of course. She will.

He knew it. Why wouldn't she?

Oh, shit. She had left, though. And he didn't really care where she had gone. She's out there fending for herself. She'll have gone to Beth's. Or Tamsin's. Or the other one... Ruth. Who were all these girlfriends, anyway? He'd never met any of them. God, it doesn't matter who she was staying with. She'd be fine. She was the one who walked out on him, after all. Not his problem… Not his problem.

I'll do the washing-up, decided Keith, and headed off into the kitchen, catching the side of the doorframe as he went through with his shoulder. He had had a few by now, clearly, but so what?

Who cares, who really cares? Have another one. Have one while you do the washing-up! Who's here to stop you?

He poured himself a finely headed pint of lager he had found in the fridge, and he delighted in the fact that he could rinse a mug and follow this up with a slug of cool beer as a well-deserved reward. Actually, there was hardly any beer at all! Fancy a beer with that head, sir?

Ow! Shit!

Lots of blood, too. It was a sharp knife. Idiot!

He had caught his finger on the knife which he'd forgotten he'd put into the bottom of the washing-up bowl. Idiot…

He opened the cupboard with the plasters inside. He put one on over the wound, which was deep and had stained the washing-up water red.

Then he went back again into the lounge and sat down. Leave the rest till the morning. It would wait.

Could she wait? Yes. Let her wait. She didn't want him to follow her. Well, let's leave contact now for a decent time, shall we?

He poured the rest of the beer, now that its head had gone down, and decided that it would serve as an excellent anaesthetic for his injury, and resumed the film that had been interrupted. He was in the mood for it now. Picking at the remains of the pizza still to be finished, Keith dozed at one point, glass in hand, and woke with a start to find the film's credits rolling up the screen. Damn!

Toilet…

Keith climbed up the stairs towards the bathroom. This was bloody necessary now… He found it easier to slap his hands down on the steps in front of him as he went, but suddenly caught himself feeling quite gorilla-like as he passed the first floor, his simian gait accompanying him as he stumbled along the landing to the next flight upstairs.

Head down, reaching the top landing, Keith made his way to the toilet, where, to avoid any easy splashing while drunk, he stood legs splayed astride the bowl like a giraffe at a watering hole. The relief was palpable.

He left the bathroom, toilet seat up, and made his way back towards the top of the stairs. More booze awaited him below, he decided, if he was so minded, and a quiet, though lonely, evening in front of another film. Damn her; he was looking forward to it. There was no work the next day, anyway. They could sort out their differences either tomorrow; or next week. He was in no hurry.

He reached the top step. He remembered with a wry grin coming up only minutes before with his head almost touching each step in front. He looked up.

Oh no.

Keith froze. He stepped backwards, physically recoiling.

The whole trapdoor was open. Blackness returned his terrified gaze.

Keith stared up into the darkness. Was it his imagination, or was there the faint flicker of a light up there? Surely not.

Regardless of his ability to climb a ladder in this state, Keith resolved to go up and see once and for all what it was that had been haunting him. He reached behind the spare room door and picked up the hook that was needed to pull down the attic ladder. Standing on tip-toes, careful not to fall down the stairs just beside him, he hoiked the bottom rung of the ladder towards him, and pulled it down.

Oh god, really? Is this a sensible move? Keith heard the inside of his head resound with questions he didn't want to think about right now. Like the story he'd heard about someone who'd gone up into their attic for the first time, to discover that the previous owner had left some of his tarantulas up there, which had escaped and were waiting for him, as he felt around for a sōlid beam to pull himself onto… The size of a saucer, he remembered reading, striped all red and black!

Number forty-four keeps spiders. Stop thinking, Keith. Stop itching. There's nothing up here…

Mind you, on the occasions he had been up here, Keith remembered that the attic space did indeed stretch largely uninterrupted across all five houses in the row. If he did keep things up here, they might well have got out. Or had Keith been over already and released them, as he'd often thought he should have done? But that had only ever been in dreams, surely? None of those episodes had actually ever happened?

Up he climbed. Looking into the darkness, Keith was more convinced than ever that there was some kind of light up there. Was he dreaming it? No, there it was again. Perhaps someone else was in the attic at the same time as he had decided to come up.

Actually, he hadn't decided to come up. The attic had been left open, it had beckoned, summoned him even. Maybe it was a neighbour who had accidentally knocked this attic door off its place… Could be him at number forty-four spying on them. Or just causing trouble… God knows.

And god knows what I'll find up here, he thought. Let's get it over and done with.

He reached the top of the ladder and poked his head in.

As his eyes adjusted to the darkness, he turned to look at the space behind his head. There *was* a light after all. Keith blinked. It was a flickering torch. He climbed higher into the attic and squinted.

'My god, what the hell is this?' he asked.

Almost immediately, with an involuntary gasp, Keith backed down, away from the figures sitting up there. Then, when he saw they were not moving, he lifted himself up into the attic, and stood on the flooring placed there.

'Who are you?' His voice was weak. His heart was on fire.

Now he could see them all fully, and a sudden fear gripped him, a fear that was making his stomach lurch with a deep, sickening feeling. Staring back at him were four or five faces, and straight ahead sat a tall man, reclined in a worn and shabby high-backed chair, dressed perfectly normally except for the one thing that now struck terror into Keith's heart.

Around his head was wrapped some kind of cloth mask, tattered and stained, with just two holes crudely cut out for the eyes, and another for the mouth.

'Hello, Keith,' said the figure. 'I've been waiting a long time for you.'

Chapter Twenty

'What on earth is going on?' asked Keith. 'What the hell is happening here?'

'Oh, I see you've cut yourself,' came a thin voice from somewhere deep within the mask. A hint of movement behind the mouth-hole revealed teeth.

Keith was shaking now. Struggling to stand up, he watched as the whole space around him seemed to swim in and out of his vision. He felt his knees crumple. 'I… I need… need to,' he began to say, and yet the words were coming out blurred and broken.

'Sit down just there,' said a woman's voice, and gestured towards an empty armchair nearby, equally shabby, slightly lower than the one she was occupying. Catching the arm of it just in time to fall, Keith lurched bodily into its springy embrace, and lay his head back against the upholstery behind him. He may have slumped to one side. He might even have allowed one of his arms to dangle lifeless over the side of the chair. Is this what a stroke felt like? Was he even still conscious?

The voices and noises and creaks and scuffs seemed to invade his head like patterned light flickering over a trellis, casting shadows of interminable complexity. Whispered, hissed tones buzzed like gravel behind his eyes, as a spiral of redness at the top of his vision wheeled into the space in front of his slumped body – Keith felt his legs jolt, and his whole body suddenly arched, as he tried to sit up. The glowing spiral turned into a flickering torch, and then he realised that he was still in the attic, sitting amongst the nightmarish company. Across from him still sat the figure in a mask.

It was a nightmare. It must be a nightmare.

'Don't try to move too much. You need to conserve your energy. You have had quite a shock.'

Keith said nothing. He sat gazing through tired eyes at the creature that lounged opposite him in the half-darkness. Apart from the nod of the head, the movement inside the mouth-hole, no other part of the man stirred; motionless he sat facing Keith. His eye-holes were a deep and hollow black with not a glint of reflected light to show where the eyes might be. He wore a check jacket, a blue shirt open at the collar, and dark corduroys. His polished shoes looked new and expensive. This detail annoyed Keith.

He made to stand up. Pushing himself forward from the arms of the chair, Keith steadied himself to stand upright, and then took a step forwards, ready to lunge at this intruder. But half-way up he realised he was never going to make it; he lurched sideways, staggered backwards, and then, as he raised his eyes towards the faceless figure sitting still and calm on the other side of the attic space, he noticed why he would not have stood a chance.

Still holding the torch in his left hand, the man had now raised his other hand, pointing towards the large man sitting beside him, who held a pistol levelled directly at Keith; in silent, incapacitated fury he slumped back in his seat, and glowered back at his adversary.

'You see, Keith, you aren't awfully steady on your feet, are you?'

'I... I've been drinking.'

'And I'm telling you: you have no idea how much...'

'Did I lose consciousness when I came up here?'

'You'd lost consciousness long before.'

'My head is taking a flight somewhere.'

'You will take some time to recover, you have to understand that.'

'Recover? Christ, it feels like I've been doing drugs or something. What the hell's been going on?' Keith's hearing had suddenly become so pronounced that he thought he could hear... hear what? It was as if all the fibres in the roof timbers, all stretching and straining and pulling at each other, were no longer happy with their delicately jointed union and wanted to separate.

'Where's Karen? Has she come back?' he asked, reminded fleetingly of the evening's earlier agony.

Does Karen have any role to play in this? Has she set me up? What the hell is going on here?

'Well, Karen won't be coming back, will she? Not after what you have done.'

'Oh god, I didn't mean anything, not really… Surely she hasn't gone for good. How do you know about Karen? How long have you been watching us? Are you the one who's been spying on me all these weeks? Have you been living up here? Was it you in the garden?'

The man chuckled. 'Have I been living up here!.. Oh dear, Keith. You have got a shock coming to you, haven't you… Is it *me* who has been living up here in this attic? Really…'

'How long was I out for just now?'

'Well, what if I told you you've been out of the picture for quite a few days this time?'

'Days? That's rubbish, isn't it… For starters, I only just came up here.'

'Come on, Keith. You practically live up here now.'

Keith looked around. In the darkness to his left he could see a table, some scraps of half-finished meals, some silver takeaway packets, a couple of used knives and forks, several empty cans of his favourite beer, opened bottles of wine. Then he turned his gaze back towards the figure still nonchalantly pointing a gun in his direction. *Was all this mess his own? And how long had this creature been up here watching them?*

'How long have you been watching me?

'Oh, a long, long time.'

'Why?'

'I think you know why. I'm your guardian angel, Keith.'

'Why are you my guardian angel?'

'You need protecting from yourself. You know how dangerous you are.'

'What do you mean? And who are you? Come on, really; who are you all?'

'Who am I? Let's just say you don't need any other name for me at the moment, other than Malcolm. But as for the rest of us… Let's say, it's a welcoming committee, shall we?'

'A fine welcome this is. Why have you got a pistol aimed at me. Am I so dangerous?'

'You are, Keith, yes. You are very dangerous.'

'Do you belong to the same people that have been playing about with my computer?'

'You could say that. I am a representative of a very elite club, my friend. Very elite, very hush-hush…'

This was nonsense. This was theatre, pure and simple. Why were all these jokers going along with this? Why, indeed… How could a whole parish council of misfits sit up here in the darkness, thought Keith, in the attic of my own house, hold me against my will, tell me all this baloney… It's not happening, this is a hallucination. The gun is not real. I need to get hold of the gun. The gun is a fake. This is all just fakery.

He stood up again. Behind him a woman hissed: 'Sit down you fool. Do as we say.'

Keith did as he was told. His vision began to swim again momentarily, and when he looked up, Malcolm was still looking at him with eyes now glinting intently through their holes.

'I need you to understand,' said the disembodied voice, 'that you are now in a great deal of trouble. But with trouble, with your own, particular situation, come phenomenal possibilities. A great liberation, you might say.'

'What club is it?'

'A club you're now being invited to join.'

'Go on.' Keith almost sighed this, as he slumped deeper into the armchair. He felt ready to give in at last, and to accept whatever was about to happen to him. All too quickly he realised he was letting go of the ropes that had moored him to a reality he'd perhaps too long taken for granted. He was slipping into the mists. Loud murmurings echoed around inside his head. A quiet insistence knocked repeatedly on his skull.

'Oh Keith,' replied the smiling teeth within the mask. 'You must know. After all you've done.'

'What have I done?'

'You have freed yourself. You are ready to embark properly on the second half of your reign, just like Caligula, the Roman emperor.'

'Fascinating. And what does this have to do with me?'

'Oh, everything. You're alone now. You're free. You can do what you like.'

'Karen will come back. I know what she's like.'

'We shall see.'

'Who's in this club, anyway?'

'Oh, people who count, Keith, people who count, believe me. But what is important is how you fit in, and why we want you to be a part of our group. After all, it's not often that one gets an opportunity like this.'

'An opportunity?'

The figure sat back again. There was a long pause. Then:

'Do you know what has happened to Karen? Do you remember anything at all?'

'No. Why? Is she all right?'

'Not really. Oh dear, dear… I think you should sit back and prepare yourself for some bad news, Keith.'

'Go on. I need to know.'

'Why, Karen is dead.'

'What?' Keith began to drift back into a redness that was surrounding his vision, and the voice from this nightmare sounded as if it were echoing from the far end of a long, dark tunnel. 'She can't be. What has happened to her? She only just left this evening.'

'Keith, she's been dead for about a week now.'

A faint, whispered question flickered from the edges of Keith's lips, and hovered butterfly-like in the red mist around him. It flapped queasily around the air:

'How?'

'You killed her.'

'I did?'

'Yes, Keith. You killed her while you were in Brighton. You finally lost it, punched her awkwardly during a drunken row, and when she didn't wake up next morning…'

'What? Impossible!'

'Oh, but you did, Keith. Somehow you managed to bundle her down to the car and back home without anybody spotting. We were impressed, we really were.

'No,' said Keith, suddenly sitting bolt upright. 'No, I did not kill anybody, least of all Karen. This is bullshit. No! I have to go.' He made to get up again, and as he did so, headed towards the bright light coming up from the trapdoor.

'Stop! You must listen… Keith, sit down, sit down please.' Again, Keith caught a glimpse of a gun. There was a hint of urgency in the other's voice now, though not the urgency which comes with losing any control; this was more like an expression of the need to move things on, sort things out. Feeling as if he'd been broken at last, Keith returned to the armchair.

Looking intently through his eye-holes directly at Keith the intruder leaned forward and continued: 'Now, let's get things straight, shall we? Let me explain one or two things.'

A sudden and fierce headache started to kick in, a migraine-like thumper Keith was hardly used to. He'd always had to lie down in a darkened room, but here Keith was in an already dark space, and there was going to be no opportunity to lie down, let alone sleep. He let the headache have full rein of his mind, rested his head on the back of the chair and allowed the words spoken in his direction to swim into his consciousness, like fish in a shoal.

'Keith, the truth is you've been out of the loop for a good while now. After bringing Karen's body back home and disposing of it, you have retreated up here and been pretty well out of it. I'm sorry for your loss. And I am sorry for what has happened to you. But you do now need to get a grip on yourself. We should talk about your future, really, and how you're going to cope. We need to chat about what you're going to do, and how you might be able to help us. But first of all you need to rest, to get back on top of things, to make yourself well again.'

'How did I dispose of her body?'

'That can come later. Don't worry for the moment.'

'I wouldn't know where to start. I've never done anything like…' Keith's voice tailed off imperceptibly. 'I remember nothing. Have I been back to work?'

'No, but you're still on holiday leave, so no-one has missed you.'

'I'm still on holiday. What a lovely time I'm having.'

'Quite. Now, we do need to sort some things out. Let's see. How about you come back downstairs into the house? We need to get you sleeping back in your bed, don't we.'

'I've been sleeping up here?'

'Yes, but I've been keeping an eye on you.'

'You've been in the shadows? While I've been sleeping?'

'Yes.'

'What did you do to your face?'

'Burnt it badly. Not nice. Sorry if my appearance like this gave you a shock, but I can promise you it's a lot nastier underneath.'

'What should I call you?' ventured Keith again. 'Who is Malcolm?'

'Come on, let's get you up,' replied Malcolm, standing up and reaching down to Keith's hands to pull him up from the chair. 'Steady now, we need to be very careful getting you down this ladder.

'Do you have a real name?' persisted Keith.

'I do. But that's not important now. Hold on to me. That's right, well done. And down you go…'

Keith found himself standing back on the landing. Above him, the masked figure was peering out from the darkness, a half-visible totem of a receding nightmare. He evidently wasn't coming down himself, but was going to remain in the safety of the attic gloom.

Keith looked around. Things looked different. He made his way tentatively down the stairs to the first floor and into the bedroom, where his eyes immediately alighted on the carpet; it was no longer covering the wooden floors, but had been rolled up against the far end of the room. The bed was unmade and unslept in. The wardrobe, where he thought he had watched Karen pack her bags earlier that same evening, was open and empty.

Finding a sudden source of strength, Keith went into his study opposite; a half-eaten pizza lay in its open box on top of his keyboard. He didn't remember eating that, not there. Whose was this? He picked up an empty bottle of gin lying next to it.

'Oh god, oh god…' Finally he was starting to see it all. He had had a breakdown. A complete mental breakdown. He put a hand to his face and peered out between the fingers.

Then he wept, sobbing big, heartbroken bellows of air out of his lungs. A voice from above reminded him he was not alone. He'd never been alone.

'Get yourself some proper rest,' said the dislocated voice. 'Come and find me tomorrow.' Step by step, burdened by the knowledge that his world had changed beyond hope, beyond redemption, Keith steered himself back into the bedroom he had shared with Karen, and walked towards the bed.

'Thank-you,' he murmured, half-dead himself, and slowly pulled off his shirt and trousers, his pants, his socks. Then he clambered under the duvet and fell into a deep and troubled slumber.

The first night of Keith's new life had begun.

Chapter Twenty-One

He didn't remember having drawn the curtains closed the night before. In fact, he was sure he hadn't, hoping that the light of the morning would make sure he'd wake up.

Did he, though? Did he really? Come on, Keith… You were capable of very little independent thought last night.

He pulled his stiff limbs out of the side of the bed into the cold air, and sat up. His head physically throbbed with a thick pain.

What the hell has happened?

Standing up, he took his first steps around the room. A chair in the corner piled high with the clothes dispensed with each night provided a sudden, much-needed support for him as he had to sit down again.

The carpet. Rolled up against the wall. The empty wardrobe. The half-eaten food. The half-drunk bottles. The air of musty neglect. Now it all came back to him in a wave of shocked horror. He clearly had lost it. Truly lost it…

And Karen? Really? Had he really?

He stood up again. Pulling back the curtain a little to look outside, his gaze fell on the busy evening street below. Cars, lone pedestrians, delivery cyclists – all racing past to their various timetables, heading off to known destinations…

Befuddled, that's a good word. Hardly enough to describe this, though. Addled… Screwed up… Stranded. Aground. Marooned. Becalmed.

Not becalmed. That's too…

Groping for the handle, Keith is able to pass through to the next room, then across to his study. *Which is too depressing to stay in for long. The lounge. Downstairs.*

But the steps are too much.

Back to bed.

He lies down again, exhausted, and slips off into sleep, troubled by his parents, and their insistence on a cake for Christmas. Keith has never baked a cake in his life.

Despite gateaux not being his forte, Keith reluctantly summons up the energy or imagination to go downstairs to the kitchen, in order to put together the ingredients for a chocolate sponge. Or a Black Forest. Or Death By Chocolate.

On waking again, he is back in his bed. The salty taste of his breath forces him to make his way to the bathroom. It is up one flight, and he will have to pass beneath the open attic.

Still in bed, he raises his naked body up on one elbow.

It is completely dark. And not just because the curtains are pulled. It is night outside.

Toilet can wait.

No, it can't. He swings his legs out onto the floor. And standing up, he moves painfully to the door, reaches the landing, clings heavily to the bannister, pulls his weight up the first couple of steps, clambering one foot after another, then half-way up, he bends back his neck, raises his head, lifts his eyes, looks up at the ceiling above the stairwell; and he winces to see the ladder still down, the trapdoor still wide open.

Squeezing past the bottom of the ladder, Keith makes it to the bathroom, trying to be as quiet as possible. But as he flushes the loo, and as he fills his glass with cool, refreshing water, he realises his cover has been blown.

'Keith!' At last, the disembodied voice wafted thinly down the corridor from above the ladder. 'Keith… Can you hear me?'

Keith could hear him all right. He approached the ladder. He walked past it, ignoring the light he could see up there, flickering.

'Keith? Come and speak to me.'

Keith went down to the bedroom. He would have to get dressed, before he started clearing up the mess left all around the house. After switching on the light, he pulled on his jeans, a shirt and sweatshirt. Socks were to be found not in the usual drawer, but slung under the chair. He pulled open the curtains to see better. The streetlight shone intrusively in, as always. It was late night.

Standing limp and exhausted in the middle of the room, Keith surveyed the mess. Perhaps he should go straight downstairs, start on the clearing up. Get on with the washing-up, the dirty laundry…

But at the foot of the stairs, he turned, and as if still in a dream he started the climb up towards the ladder. Then, wearily, he hoisted himself up the first rung, then the second, then the third, on and on until he felt himself embraced by the semi-darkness. One final pull and here he was again inside the loft.

He knelt to raise himself fully inside and then hauled himself up into the armchair opposite the trapdoor. It was not until he was seated, slumped with the effort, that he raised his eyes and looked across at the same, bandaged face and seated figure on the far side of the attic.

It was just Malcolm and the woman this time. Other chairs were still up here, but empty.

Keith heard Malcolm's voice first, wafting across the semi-darkness.

'Now you know.'

Keith said nothing. The silence hung painfully between them.

The woman now stepped forward. She had downy jawlines and a sinewy, slender neck. 'Come off it, Keith. You know as well as we do; you'd fallen out of love with Karen long ago. You were finding life with her tedious and dull, she had become a bore, she didn't light up the room for you any more, did she? You were having precious little sex. And what sex you were having was uncomfortable, boring, unsuccessful… She was a stone around your neck. And so was your job, and your circle of friends. A petty, boring, bourgeois existence, lived out day after day, leading nowhere for you, and achieving nothing.'

'Exactly,' continued Malcolm. 'Your whole existence had telescoped into such a small, restricting space, that you were simply crying out for change. Your whole being was screaming for something to crack, for something finally to happen. And you made that change happen, Keith! You took that big, shocking step that most of us don't.'

'I did?' muttered Keith finally. 'I thought that was called murder?'

'It is.'

'Which is illegal…'

'Well,' smiled the woman, 'that's where we come in, isn't it… We won't tell, if you don't.'

'Why should you cover for me?'

'Because we want something from you.'

'What?'

'We want you to join us, darling. We know what you're capable of – now we want you to fulfil your potential.'

'After all,' added Malcolm, 'we've all been through loss of this kind, we've all seen how a disruptive change can shake us out of our lethargy, even if it is painful… Very painful.' Behind his mask, Keith thought he glimpsed the reflection of moisture in the depths of the eye-holes.

On the roof slates just above their heads a light, summer rainfall began, its *pat-pat-pat* hitting louder than he expected this close. The woman stepped back into the shadow behind Malcolm, whose words seemed half-hidden amongst the raindrops, as they fell almost melodiously into Keith's tired consciousness.

'What are you waiting for? The nights are yours. Throw off your concerns, there's nothing more to be afraid of. Your reign can start immediately, as soon as you have decided to step into the role. Get out and taste the fresh air! We shall see you tomorrow… And you shall be what you choose to be!

'This is your chance, Keith. Now you can become the champion you know you want to be. A king! An emperor! Caligula himself couldn't have had it better! You are free to put all those wrongs to right. You are free to live a life unhindered by silly, petty rules and regulations. You are free now to forge a completely new identity – god, who hasn't wanted to do that at some point in their lives? Refashion yourself entirely, begin afresh, maybe even disappear somewhere new, start from scratch. And all along this new journey, Keith, all the way along, at every step of the way, there you are sorting out the injustices of this world, shaping it in your own image.

'Not an emperor – a god!

'So free yourself of your routines, your manacles! Here comes your moment of liberation, Keith. This very night will see you rise to a higher level, it will witness the birth of a being of a nobler order! For tonight you must begin to throw away the crutches that support you in this crippling state, and prevent you from running wild, running wild among those great spirits from the past who every so often nudge history off-course! Yes, you too will run among them! This is the key, tonight. This is the key!

'What's it to be, Keith? Something which might seem small and insignificant, yet which is to set in motion all the other things you will soon achieve. Something to set you free, something to empower your mind, to show you yourself how strong you are. Do this in the name of whatever you believe in! Do it in god's name, if you want, or to the memory of Karen.

'Or in memory and honour of Caligula himself…

'Why not, Keith? Yes, why not dedicate this first, but momentous, step to the emperor himself, whose name is forever associated with enacting his visions and his dreams, in order to shape the world around him? Go out into the night and cast off the shackles that hold you back, and always have done, and always will do, unless you face up to them…'

It felt like an order. Keith opened his eyes and got up. Looking over at Malcolm, he saw he had not moved an inch. However, there was no sign of the woman. She had slipped away somehow without him noticing. The rain had stopped.

Malcolm leaned forward, and whispered: 'I am right behind you, Keith. Always there, just remember.'

Keith climbed down back into his house. He had to get outside.

Outside, now!

It was what he suddenly needed more than anything else, the fresh air, the cool, refreshing gulps of night air they were talking about. Another of his impromptu night-walks.

He passed his bedroom, and went straight downstairs; reaching the entrance hall, Keith bent down to put on his shoes, not the waterproof boots he would normally wear if it was raining, but just his light, summer plimsoles.

They were sitting just underneath the table which was his docking port. There was his briefcase, his house keys, his spare car-key.

Spare car-key? Why the need for *spares*, really? What they'd just said was so true of him; he was restricted, strangled even, by his own silly habits and worries.

He picked up the key. It felt heavy in his hand, a dead weight of suppressed, unnecessary misgivings and fears. Get rid of it! When had he ever needed it? Here was a perfect and potent symbol of exactly the things that had been holding him back.

He put it in his pocket and opened the door. The damp night air slapped him. He recoiled for a second, then walked down his path and stepped out onto the street.

This was it. This was the start of something big.

He walked and walked, breathing deeply and looking around at the streetlights as if for the first time. Keith Hartman, things are going to change. They really had to, and now they shall.

No more the stifling, constricting life of a little pawn in a big game! No more the whipping boy buffeted by life's events, unable even to control the way he reacted to others around him. No more the dead-end life trapped in a dead-end job with a dead-end relationship weighing around his neck. No, not for him, this restrictive existence that had held him back so long. Life as he had been living it was beginning to be exposed as the lie, the conspiracy he had all along suspected… Time to get out. Time to cast it off. Time to cast off the things that held him back, kept him from flying free and unencumbered.

He reached the centre of town, made his way down New Windsor Street.. He had no idea of what time it was but there was no traffic at all. Stepping onto the bridge, he leaned over to look into the dark, swirling waters of the river below, shaded by high willows on either bank. Fishing into his pocket, Keith pulled out the car-key, rolled it around a couple of times in the palm of his hand, then resolutely raised his arm and threw it out across the water, watching the faint glow of its reflection arc through the dark night.

It plunged with a satisfying *plash* into the water, and was gone.

For a moment or two, Keith stood leaning on the wall of the bridge; then, shaking his head, he raised his back and shoulders, as if quietly throwing something off.

All Quiet on the Western Front.

Stepping back away from the river, he sensed a rightness in what he had just done. Glancing for an instant at the nearby streetlamps, he set off back home. He needed to sleep.

As he walked back through the silent centre of town, his eyes darted this way and that, alive to the newness of how it all felt, and how fresh and exhilarating. Over to his right he clocked another couple of parking meters that needed the Caligula treatment, and down the one-way street was a camera waiting to be blinded. He also set his sights now on a number of roadsigns to be defaced. And one or two shops and cafés where he had been made to feel unwelcome. He would tell people about the mess their dogs made, maybe even post it back to them through their letterboxes. In his car he would rig up a message-signalling device to tell middle-lane hoggers to shift over. Might even begin to signal to bad and aggressive drivers himself, rather than resolutely stare ahead; after all, what could they do to him from their own cars? A serious campaign against the sort of lycra-clad cyclists who ride two or more abreast, as if they now own the roads. People with gnomes and fairies in their gardens. People who adorn loved-ones' graves with wind-chimes and crystals and fairies. Books by worthless celebs. Christmas fayres with nothing but the same tacky products year after year. Bad neighbours and antisocial drivers and space-hogging parkers would have their tyres let down, just enough for it to be an inconvenience.

Various ideas were coming to him now, and he was buzzing with the excitement of it all. And none of it came with any responsibility. No questions asked.

There was no way back now.

Closing his front door behind him Keith knew he wouldn't sleep straight away. He was too wired, too alive. Some drink was required anyway, not least in celebration.

He entered his front lounge.

It was half-empty. The carpet was rolled up, just as it had been upstairs. The pictures and framed prints he and Karen had picked and hung up to make the place their own were gone, piled up on their ends against the far wall. The TV was still there, as was their one sofa, but the curtains were pulled and the ornaments on the shelf were all boxed up, and placed in the corner of the room.

Evidently he'd been busy…

He sat down with a beer from the fridge, and fell asleep to some god-awful, early-morning fodder on the box.

Which mattered not a jot. Not any more.

With the first rays of morning sunlight breaking through between the curtains and round their edges Keith woke with a start, then withdrew upstairs to the comfort of his bed. Now he slept more deeply than he could ever remember having slept. Heavy slumber, too dense for dreams, enfolded him in successive waves, restoring his mind and his body and what was left of his soul.

The afternoon was fading fast when he awoke. He had slept through most of the day, and it seemed to Keith that he had quite simply dropped out of the world of the everyday. Clearly no-one had missed him yet. No messages on his phone. No knock at the door. No connection with the outside world at all. He should phone his parents, he suddenly thought, as if normality still somehow controlled his upturned life.

He dressed and went out to the landing and up the stairs. The loft ladder was still down, the hatch still open, just as he'd left it.

Keith climbed up into the darkness.

Nothing. The attic was empty. As his eyes adjusted to the lack of any light, he began to make out two chairs facing one another, but there was no other sign of life. He climbed back down.

He needed to clear things out. Clear his old life out, get rid of what he didn't need. Kitchen first, the stuff he wouldn't be using any more. Keith opened the drawers and found three bottle openers. One would do; the other two went into the bin straight away, while the good one was employed to open a fine bottle of chilled white. Forks, knives, spoons galore… what for? For all those interminable dinner parties they hardly ever had? A posh set, too, all boxed up and never used… Out with them. Straight into the bin, not even looked at. What a waste…

In the cupboard above, ranges of pots and pans, special Eastern woks and bamboo steamers, a Japanese sushi rice press, bought when Karen was hell-bent on creating Oriental cuisine. Hardly used. A waste of space. Chuck the lot of them.

Old pans, caked with grime and old fat… Just the new ones were worth keeping, surely.

On the walls were a number of framed prints, cool, stylised, black-and-white close-up photos of half-chopped onions, garlic cloves bursting with goodness out of their perfect skins, fresh, succulent tomatoes sliced and glistening… It was strange how a new perspective could suddenly make things appear outdated, stale, unwanted. Onto the pile they went, beside the overspilling bin.

What next? Plates they'd kept just in case. Clever, funny egg-cups. Mugs, oh god, all these mugs: Mugs with smart-arse quips written across them, so very funny at the time; mugs with cute, cartoony figures gurning out at you; mugs which had meant something once, or with pictures of places they'd been together; mugs from previous relationships; mugs which had been used since university. How many mugs do you need?

After the kitchen, Keith made his way upstairs to the bedroom. Karen's stuff was mostly gone, but there were a number of jumpers and cardigans stuffed into drawers that he pulled out and put to one side. Then he looked at his own clothes, and began sifting through things he'd bought on Karen's recommendation but never worn, or never liked. Out they came, swanky waistcoats, funky socks, comedic jumpers and gaudy shirts. Beside the bed were her fashion and sports magazines, strewn lazily around the floor; Keith gathered them up and took them downstairs, together with a box or two of her toiletries and hair accessories.

Now he began to take as much as he could out into the garden, piling the stuff into an almighty stack of junk against the further brick wall. A bonfire was needed. He'd start a bonfire.

Oh god, is this how he did it? Is this the way her body was disposed? Had he done this already, and forgotten? Keith's thoughts suddenly turned to Karen. Was he semi-conscious when he did it, out of his mind, addled with drink and mentally unaware? But he was conscious now, all too conscious, in fact; if he thought too much about it, he could still hear the timbers in the ceilings aching and straining under the pressure of it all.

Like his brain.

Like the awareness of his old life, his new one, his lost girlfriend, his newfound freedom.

He was too befuddled to start a fire now. He went back inside, and opened a beer from the fridge. Drinking straight from the bottle, he went up to the bottom of the loft.

'Anyone up there?' he called up, but the blackness made no reply.

Bang!

Christ! What was that? Keith raced downstairs. It was the front door. Now what was happening? Who the hell was here now?

He turned onto the landings at breakneck speed, plummeting down the steps two, three at a time…

'Ah there you are! God, you look awful.'

Karen stood in front of him. Fuck.

CHAPTER TWENTY-TWO

Keith just stood looking at her. Having let herself in, she brushed past him, and marched into the kitchen.

'Shit, what's been happening here? You're living in a shithole!'

'What are you doing here?' ventured Keith.

'What does it look like?'

'I don't know. I thought you…'

'I've come to collect some more of my stuff. Same as before.'

'Before?'

'Yes,' she continued, paying no further attention to him as she passed in front of him again to go upstairs.

'I didn't expect you back,' he stammered.

'I know. You didn't last time.'

'Last time?' echoed Keith.

'Oh my god, what is wrong with you?' she shouted back at him from the landing. 'Yes! For god's sake, the last time I came round to fetch my belongings.'

'I don't remember a last time.'

'I wonder why.' She disappeared from sight, then she cried out as if in distress, and re-emerged from the bedroom, shouting, 'What the hell have you done with all my clothes? And my boxes of things I had up here?'

'They're down here now.'

She stormed back down towards him. 'They'd better be. Where are they?'

Keith looked sheepishly out towards the back yard, and she stomped out to find where he had pointed.

'What *are* you doing with my stuff? Why… why is it all out here? You were chucking it all out, weren't you? Chucking my personal stuff out onto a pile…' She looked more closely at how it had all been placed, one thing on top of another. 'My god, you're making a fucking bonfire, aren't you! Burning all this perfectly good stuff! You're mental.'

'I thought you were dead.'

'What? I beg your fucking pardon?'

'I thought you were dead. I… I just don't know any more…'

'You're obsessed with me being dead, aren't you? You really need some help! God, what is your problem?'

Keith roused himself a little at this. 'I don't have a problem.'

Karen sneered. 'Do you not think so? How many have you had today, I wonder?'

'None of your business.'

'No, didn't think so…'

She recovered a number of items of clothing and her toiletries bags from the pile. 'Well, why did you think I was dead, Keith? You've clearly thought about this a lot, haven't you…'

'Er, no. I – I thought that you weren't coming back, that's all.'

'Rubbish! You were living a fantasy where I had been killed off, weren't you? I'd been done away with somehow, and you were free to live your own weird existence. Oh my god, just like you said that time Samantha came round for dinner! You're such a weirdo, you really are. Why did I stay so long with you? How on earth did we get so far?' She made her way, hands full, back past him again towards the front door. 'Right. Do not burn any of my things, got it? I shall probably come back again some day soon for the last few things that might still turn up. And we'd better work out when to meet properly so we can sort out bank accounts and the mortgage, and all that. But we'll do that when you're not drunk. No point even thinking about it now, is there?

'Look at you,' she went on. 'You're out of it again. For Christ's sake, just sort yourself out, Keith.' She let her gaze wander over him up and down. 'Honestly, Keith, I do worry about you. I did really like you once, and it's sad to see you like this.'

She let herself out of the front door and left Keith standing at the same spot he'd been standing when she'd arrived.

He noticed this and wondered whether this was evidence enough that he'd just dreamt the whole episode. Perhaps he'd just hallucinated it all? That sounded plausible.

Was he so drunk? Maybe. Who cared?

He went back out to the kitchen, picked up the half-finished beer, and sat down in the front room, turning on the TV and curling up on the sofa.

Who gave a damn what was happening to him?

When he wakes, there in the corner of the room, half in darkness, sits Malcolm. Head still covered. Eye-holes aimed directly at Keith.

'My god!' yelled Keith, jumping back in his seat. 'Oh Christ, you gave me a shock!'

'Sorry. Just checking you're all right,' answered Malcolm.

'I'm all right.'

'You should get some rest.'

'Who do you think you are? My fucking mother?'

'You should sleep properly in your bed.'

'Mind your own business.'

'You are my business, Keith.'

'Bugger off.'

'What's wrong?'

'You saw her. You must have. She was back here.'

'Who?'

'Who do you think?'

'I don't know.'

'Who did you convince me was dead? Who was I supposed to have killed?'

'Karen?'

'Who else?'

'Karen was here?' A note of mild alarm sounded in Malcolm's voice, though there was no telling from his eyes what he was really thinking. 'When was she here?'

'Oh god knows. Hours ago. I must have been sleeping for ages.'

'Keith, she could not have been here. You must have imagined it.'

'That's what I kept telling myself. But it's terrifying when somebody…'

'I know, I know,' nodded Malcolm. 'You must have had quite a shock. But it's a trauma thing, Keith, just a memory of someone that got a strong reaction out of you. I tell you, she's gone, I promise, just as we said. I'm sorry you had to go through that, but then, you're going through so much at the moment, aren't you? And that's all the more reason why you should get some proper rest, sleep off the shock of it all, try to put her death behind you.'

'You're telling me I dreamt it all? Her coming back through the front door, her talking to me? She went out to the yard and took a load of her stuff.'

'No, she didn't. I'm sorry to say, she did not. You go back to that pile of stuff in the yard, and you'll find it exactly as you left it. You imagined her return, Keith, it was all in your head.'

Keith shook his head and closed his tired eyes.

Then Malcolm stood up, walked out of the room and, turning, said, 'I am going to leave you alone now. Make sure you sleep well.'

Keith heard him disappear up the stairs, and then got off the couch, walked into the kitchen, grabbed another bottle of beer out of the fridge, opened it and brought it back to the sofa.

CHAPTER TWENTY-THREE

Malcolm's masked figure leaned forward out of the shadow, and now his tiny eyes peered visibly out from their holes. Keith watched the teeth move up and down, the lips momentarily cover them as they spat out the words.

'The Caligula Club, we call it.'

'Go on… Tell me all about the Caligula Club,' muttered Keith. 'And tell me why I have been invited to join.' They were both sitting up in the loft. Keith was sipping at a cool beer he'd just fetched from the fridge.

'Once Caligula's sister, who had also been his lover, died, it left him with nothing more to prove; it was then that he realised how much he could actually do, how much he could achieve.'

'But Karen hasn't died. I saw her just recently. Oh god, Malcolm!.. What is happening to me? I saw Karen, how could she be dead?'

'You didn't see her, did you? You think you did. You know you didn't. You know in your heart what has really happened to her, don't you? Come on, Keith.'

'Anyway, that has nothing to do with Caligula. Or me. Sleeping with his sister? Come on…'

'Oh dear, it has everything to do with you. You have power now, and the freedom to exercise it. You've even begun to taste it, too, haven't you! And you enjoy it, don't deny that.'

'So I am like Caligula? I can act with impunity? I can do what I want, as long as I keep to the shadows?'

'Absolutely. All normal constraints have now been removed and you are free to explore that idea to its logical conclusion. You can change the world.'

'I can change the world. You're right.'

'All the members you've met so far have been through just the same as you have, Keith. They've all known some kind of damaging change, some tragic loss. But they have all found strength in the pathways that it opens up, and found strength, too, in each other. We created the society in order to effect change. We want to cast the world in our image, Keith! And we took as our symbol the powerful figure of Caligula.'

'Not the nicest of role-models, though…'

'You have to break eggs, Keith, you have to break eggs, don't you!'

Keith didn't answer.

'Having so much to do,' continued Malcolm, 'so very much to do, yet so little time… It's going to be the making of you, now, Keith, and you are already rising to the challenge, you're already making something of yourself. You know this to be the case, you hear your name on the wind, you're beginning to leave your mark on the lives of the people you want to help, as well as on those who deserve to be brought down for their arrogance. That is the way of the world, and that is how you're going to shape it, you know this, don't you… You do know this.'

Keith heard the voice as if it were in his own head.

'So what are you waiting for? Do it now. Go on. It's dark outside.'

And so it was. As Keith left the house clad in black and on his bicycle, he felt an inexplicable elation once again pumping through his veins, around his body. He was on fire. It was the fire of change – *his* change. He was Caligula! He was Prometheus!

This time, he had brought with him something other than just a tube of glue and a spray can. He had a tiny canister of red spray in his back pocket, and this was for something he felt strongly he had to do. It was the sort of thing he knew his old self would have criticised a graffiti-spraying ruffian for doing out of sheer egotism; but Keith was on a crusade – a modern crusade, and he needed people to know it. He would *sign* his work from now on.

All that night and the next, and the one after that, off he went seeking out the targets on his to-do list: a camera here, a pointless and patronising safety barrier there, an advert for a shamelessly exploitative Saturday evening TV show, a car park charging over three pounds for just one hour. All through town he stole, and further afield, staying close to the shadows, shunning the lights and open spaces, leaving his trail of destruction and disruption.

And leaving too something on which he now prided himself: at every site, on every corner where Keith's touch was seen, in sprawling, red spray paint a single name: *Caligula.*

As he was making his way through town he walked past a nightclub. It was late, and youths were spilling out onto the streets towards chip-shops and kebab-vans. One of them caught Keith's eye as he tried to make his way cautiously through the throng.

'Oi! Watch where you're going, mate!' the youth shouted; in the half-light of street lamps and open doors, Keith could make out an aggressive young man in a loose shirt, sweating profusely. 'You almost knocked my glass out of my hand.'

'Should you even have it outside on the street?' Keith heard himself ask.

'What? You takin' the piss?'

Now Keith sensed trouble, and made to move away as quickly as he could. But the youth, with his glass, stepped into his path.

'Poofter,' he snarled.

Keith was suddenly appalled. 'Poofter? You think I'm a gay person? Why?'

''Cos… That's all. Look at you, man, in your black kit walking around, telling me I can't stand on the street 'cos of me havin' a glass in my hand… Poofter!'

Keith warmed to this. 'So because of that, you think I am someone who has sex with other men? Is that what you actually think?'

'Poofter, yeah!' came the keen response.

'You're very funny!' smiled Keith back at him. 'Really funny. You're wasted out here. You should be on stage.'

Bewildered but angry, the youth summoned a few of his friends to his side, but Keith saw new danger in this, and made his swift exit from the area while the other wasn't looking.

Idiot. What idiots there are out there. Who the hell do some of these people think they are, with their prejudices and attitudes?

They need to be taught a lesson. Idiots!

Keith turned and stood on the corner of the street, looking back at where the altercation had taken place. The group of youths had evidently forgotten him and were moving off. Staying in the shadows, as ever, Keith followed them as they headed into the suburbs, each one peeling off until at last only his assailant and one other friend were left. Keith spotted which house the boy let himself into, noted the number, reminded himself of the name of the street, and then turned back towards his own home.

You don't behave like that and expect to get away with it.

'Very impressive,' muttered Malcolm, sitting in the attic with his legs crossed, Keith sitting in the chair opposite him. On Malcolm's knees lay the newspaper, a recent copy of the local *Hillingdon and Uxbridge Times*. 'It seems you're beginning to make quite a splash. Well done.'

In his hand an open bottle of beer, Keith nodded passively.

Malcolm continued, reading from the paper: '"The nightly exploits of the self-styled 'Caligula' have caused a headache for local police, who have as yet failed to identify the culprit responsible for thousands of pounds' worth of damage in and around the Hayes and Hillingdon area." That's nice work – they don't even identify you as coming from Uxbridge. "Police are stepping up their patrols in the hope of spotting the vigilante red-handed, but a source is reported as saying they still have no idea what the perpetrator looks like, despite trawling through hours of CCTV footage from cameras installed by councils and on private property.

'"One young victim, who wished to remain unnamed, claimed that he met the mysterious Caligula outside a nightclub. According to the witness, the black-clad figure verbally abused him for having accidentally taken a glass onto the street below *Temptations* nightclub in central Hounslow as the club was closing. After a brief altercation, in which the young clubber felt threatened and intimidated, the victim was clearly followed home, as two days later an envelope of human excrement was posted through his letter box with a note reminding him of the incident, and signed with the now-familiar soubriquet."

'As I say, Keith, very impressive.'

'Thank-you.'

'However, you must stop signing every dastardly deed.'

'Why?'

'Because… That's all.'

'I thought it was a good idea – I want to show the world that there is somebody behind it, and that there's, I don't know, a purpose to it all.'

'Don't you worry, the world will soon understand that, I promise.'

'What do you mean?'

'Just don't sign the things you're doing.'

'What did you just mean about there being a purpose to it soon?'

'We're going to ask you to do something big for us. We have a task for you.'

'What task? I need to know.'

'You don't need to know yet. But it is going to be big, Keith, and when it starts happening, we'll all be in on it together, we'll all be right behind each other, OK? You're proving yourself admirably worthy of our trust at the moment, with all this activity, and there's a point coming not far away now, when events that you help set in motion are going to make more than just the Hillingdon Times.'

'I don't understand. You'll need to give me a bit more than that.'

'Suffice it to say, we will need your absolute commitment to our cause, Keith, I mean complete trust in you. And don't go getting yourself involved in any Brexit and Europe groups, do you hear? They just cause trouble without actually making any change to things. But the police monitor them so closely, you know that, don't you? You'd be spotted so quickly if you started associating yourself with activist groups, you wouldn't last half-a-minute! And that's why we need to stop mentioning Caligula to the world at large, do you see?'

Keith remained silent. He peered sideways at Malcolm, and narrowed his eyes.

'You want me to kill someone?'

'You've guessed well.'

'Who?'

'Someone big. Someone famous.'

Keith sat back. 'Oh god, Malcolm! What is this? What are you trying to get me into? You have got to be joking.'

'Do I joke? I've told you before that we have long had you in our sights for a task. You are going to be asked to do something very important indeed for us, for our cause. And there'll be plenty in it for you, too. Believe me, Keith, this is only the beginning.'

'I don't understand. You'll need me to bump someone off? For a good cause? What are you, mad? This is bonkers, you know that? How can I even begin to agree to killing someone? I'm no hitman.'

'You will be, you will. Honestly, Keith, there is going to be such a lot of upheaval soon, you have no idea; and you are going to have your part to play, an unbelievably important part.'

'Not sure if I want it.'

'Oh dear, Keith, really!.. Do you think we'd have let you come this far now, without knowing that you have everything you need to play this role? The anger, the frustration, the balls! You're perfect, and nobody will suspect a thing, not a soul! You've proven that already, and you've killed too…' Malcolm broke off for a moment. Then: 'But you cannot sign your name to a single thing any more, do you hear me? Nothing. From now on you're incognito.'

'OK,' answered Keith, and draining his bottle he climbed out of the loft, leaving Malcolm to himself. It was time for bed. Keith was exhausted. He would not be going out tonight.

CHAPTER TWENTY-FOUR

No, no! Bring out the crazies! Bring out your dead, why not! There is nothing more scary than not knowing where your control stops and someone else's takes over. But the taking over is only a part of it, oh my god, who would have thought I could be taken over?

It's all about sex in the end. It must be, it must! The mad, raving lunacy of sex and orgasm! Bring out the dead, maybe; but they can't tell you how it actually feels to find someone next to you, all over you, all around you. Even if it's only for a couple of months, or days. Hours even.

The Blonde, she must be on the table still. Up for it. Knows what she wants, knows what she likes. God, she looked good last time I saw her. Smelt amazing, too.

What strange lives are lived, though. A tangle of possibilities, all these lives of ours! We could be away off into the sunset by now, disappearing into the obscurity of adventure.

Away from it all!

So it's the sex, as well as the oblivion, that attracts me to this new existence. Well, good to get that out of the way. Darwinian superman…

A glance in a café, knowingly returned. A taxi driver's wink. A fleeting touch of the hand, that's all that would be needed to start it off. A nonchalant invitation to meet up.

What about Kitchen Woman, though? Kids, yes – but more mature, more interesting. More experienced. Mind you, a life spent juggling school-runs, holidays with the kids cooped up in the house, difficult exes to contend with… She'd be less fun after a while, and have way more baggage.

How fast it goes, this concertinaed future, this daytrip to eternity.

Anyway, the only reason it's all about sex is the lack of it. It must be. We've always known that to be the case, haven't we? The louder they shout, the less they're getting. Go on, shout away! My time will come.

My time will come.

In the meantime I'll keep on hunting for it, that elusive little temptress.

I'll have her, whoever she is.

The Blonde is within reach, though. That's next week's task.

Where do all these wires go? They come out over the door and sneak back in somewhere… Pipes and wires, pipes and wires.

Have they been there all along? I haven't noticed them before. They are a manifestation of something. Or someone.

The whole house, oh my god, has been slowly rearranged for this. There are wires and pipes going up into places I hadn't seen them going before.

Things become so clear once you have this level of seeing.

Not for everyone, though, this point of view. Is it just that I'm at a higher vantage point now? The clarity is almost enough to dazzle. A dizzying round of visions, a visionary cascade! That's what it is: a cascade – extraordinary! It just doesn't stop. Just doesn't…

Doesn't stop. Doesn't stop.

Perspective contracted till it's painful, so painful.

It's like you're lying in bed as a small child and seeing the wallpaper getting closer and closer and closer, until the pattern's so big that your whole vision is filled with just this one thing and it seems to be silently filling your head with its screaming, a screaming-out of nonsense – until you pass beyond it, beyond what was reality and then you can see what is really there… What is really there? A presence in the whiteness. A blank presence and an unknowing awareness of everything that's out there. Never go too often to this place… It's deafening, blinding.

What is Malcolm preparing? What have they made out of me? Am I their project? No bad thing, I guess. What did they have before I came along for them? And what did I have before they came along? What was I? A worthless pen-pusher, a cog in a dreadful system, a poor, deluded fool. What was it I was looking at? Not this view, I can tell you, not these visions. Oh no, just a worthy pen-pusher, nudging lives this way and that – a nudger. A plodder. A desk and a computer for a view, paper coming at me from all sides. A boring life, a boring girlfriend. Blondie may be boring. Kitchen Babe may have kids. But they'll be different, my path will be different, at least for a little while, till I get tired of them.

Then on to the next! How modern. How liberating. That's because I am now beyond the norms of acceptable. I have moved out of that life into my own construct!

A work of art, that's what Malcolm is creating. It's a whole fucking work of art, this pact. This whole shebang is being designed around what they plan for me. And why not? I deserve it.

This world needs a new voice, someone to put it straight.

I'm here! I'm ready! Bring it on…

Bring what on?

What are you going to be from now on? A messiah? You, Keith Hartman, a messiah? A god? An emperor for the modern age?

Caligula Keith.

Sounds good. Bring it on. Bring on a murderous reign, it can't be any worse than what's out there now. I'll dispense all the justice and providence they need. I'll take on that particular burden, leave it to me. I'll take care of it all. No need to worry now. Caligula the Just is born… Ready to go out into the world and put it to rights.

All the jobsworths and the idiots and the youthful pricks and bullies and the officious and the worthy and the pompous… God, you'd better look out from now on! Caligula the Just! I'll be a Caligula they'll remember for the right reasons, not the calculated evil done by a madman – this will be the calculated wisdom of the everyman, the little man, the unjustly treated, the walked-all-over, the poor, the beaten, the ignored.

Caligula Keith!

It really could come to happen as he saw it. He really would be the hero who could change things for the better. A better Caligula. He would launch himself into project after project after project… This was his calling. No more pen-pushing, no more nudging. No more roll over and smile.

Caligula the Just.

A murderous reign… A murderous reign, though.

Murder to set free? Actual murder in cold blood? Reduce a family by a father? A mother? A child?

Keith turned over and moved across to the other side of the bed. It was cooler here and the pillow felt fresher.

Kill in order to save? A murderous saviour? Is this how it starts?

What the hell was up with him?

A pact with a faceless madman who'd been summoning him into the attic? And with a death on his hands already… Was he going to be happy killing someone else? Maybe more than one person, too? Maybe lots.

The emperor Caligula? Manifested here on earth all this time after the original? Is this how it starts? What the hell was he thinking?

Am I mad?

Chapter Twenty-Five

It had taken Keith a long, largely sleepless night to come to this decision, but on getting up the next day, he realised he had to go through with it. Malcolm's revelation the night before had shocked him. Now he was thinking hard about this role he was playing within the Caligula Club. What was he playing at?

Nothing about the whole affair was right. And this latest twist had to be reported. More murder was a horrendous idea.

He was going to have to take it to the police.

But, he winced, what on earth was he going to tell them? Where to begin? They would have so much on him, especially if he revealed himself as Caligula. And that he believed he'd killed Karen…

Keith picked up his car key from the docking port, opened the front door and savoured the coolness of the morning air. He was sober, he felt more clear-headed than he had done for days. There was a clarity in his vision today. He took a deep breath and made for his car.

When he reached the police station, a large, postmodern pile with a wide, glass and red-painted metal entrance porch, Keith carefully drove his car into the public car park behind, made his way round to the front entrance, and finally marched up to the man sitting behind the reception desk.

He swallowed hard. He must have looked pale.

'Good morning,' he started. 'I've come to confess something.'

'Good morning,' answered the police officer, looking up at him curiously. 'And what is it you'd like to confess?'

Keith paused, then he heard himself say: 'Murder. And conspiracy to murder. Oh my god…'

At this the policeman stood up, called out to a colleague in a back room, and turning back to Keith, said: 'Sir, would you please follow DCI Bayes here; you'll be able to explain everything to him.'

'Thank-you,' said Keith, numb.

Bayes came out and approached Keith, who recognised him immediately as the male officer who had come round to visit after Samantha's death.

'Hullo again, sir.' Bayes evidently recognised Keith too. 'This way, please.' Keith was taken along a nearby corridor to a small, plain room. 'DCI Bayes here,' the policeman spoke into the walkie-talkie attached to his collar. 'Can we have some level two interrogation back-up please, room four.'

A moment later, a second, unfamiliar officer had joined them in the room, a recorder was switched on, and Bayes spoke clearly into a nearby microphone, stating his name, the date, the time, the place and finally asking Keith to confirm his own name.

'Keith Hartman.'

'Now, what is it you'd like to tell us?' asked Bayes.

'I think I've killed my girlfriend.'

'You think?'

'Yes. I'm not sure.'

'Do you remember killing her, sir?'

'No. That's the problem.'

'But you haven't seen her for a long time?'

'Kind of…'

'Kind of?'

'She's been round to collect some stuff once or twice. I mean… she left our house, and she has appeared now and again, but I don't think she has, if you know what I mean…' Keith broke off, recognising the stupidity of what he was saying.

'Sorry, sir, let's get this right, shall we? Your girlfriend has left you, she's been back a few times to collect some of her belongings, and yet you believe she's actually dead? And that you've killed her?'

'Sorry,' muttered Keith, 'I know it doesn't sound right, nothing sounds right at the moment. But I just don't have a better explanation for it, I really don't.'

'Right. What's her name?'

'Karen Davies.'

Bayes wrote down the name. 'We'll do a check for you, if that'll put your mind at rest. But it doesn't sound quite as though she's dead, does it now, sir?'

'No, I suppose not. But there's more.'

'Go on.'

'I've been asked to commit a murder, too.'

'Have you now? By whom, if it's not too much to ask?'

'By… by a man living up in my…' Keith trailed off. He had never regretted anything as much as coming here now to the police.

'Sorry, sir, I missed that. Somebody living up in…?'

'My attic.'

'Your attic?'

'I've been asked if I'd kill someone, someone important, and…'

Bayes leaned over and turned off the recording device: 'Let's say we stop there, shall we, sir? Otherwise…' he was still smiling, but only just. 'Otherwise, we might be talking about your good self being charged with wasting police time. Now, unless there's anything else you'd like to get off your chest, and unless you've got anything concrete to back it up with, maybe you should get yourself back home, get some rest and start again tomorrow morning.'

Keith looked into their faces, unblinking and unbelieving. This had been a bad idea. They must have been laughing at him, and they'd certainly have plenty to joke about with their colleagues once he had left.

'Sorry,' murmured Keith, feebly. He stood up. 'Thanks for your time. You're right. I need some rest.'

'Take a holiday, Mr. Hartman, get away from it all.'

How ironic, thought Keith, as he walked ahead of them, down the corridor, out of the police station and back to his car. This was already the most memorable holiday he'd ever had.

CHAPTER TWENTY-SIX

It was high time to phone mum and dad. Keith took a deep breath. He always wondered how much longer he would manage to bear these interminable conversations that wended and wound their way around nothing in particular, and ended with him feeling frustrated and unfulfilled, in spite of his parents' evident delight at hearing from him.

'Hello!' he started, cheerily. 'How are you, mum?'

'Keith, oh hello, love. Your dad and me have just come back from a morning out at the garden centre. You know the one round the back of the old Rec?'

'I think so.'

'Yes you do, *Harveys*, it's called, I think. Or is it *Harrisons*? No, *Harveys* .. Tell a lie, because *Harveys* is the name of the new discount shop that's just opened in the centre of town where *Howards* used to be, remember?'

'No. Not really sure.'

'Yes you do! *Howards* the little hardware shop, where granny used to get all her doilies from. She used to buy four of them for two-pounds-fifty. Ever so cheap, but really lovely quality, really well made. They used to last her for years. When she died we had to get rid of them for next to nothing – a pity, really, 'cos we were sure they were worth something, but there you go… But going back to *Howards*, it had been going for donkey's years.'

'Where I once bought an old Brownie camera from?'

'Oh, I don't remember that. Maybe… Anyway, we always used to wonder how that place ever made ends meet, and now it's gone anyway,

I blame all this intranet shopping, nobody ever goes out into the high street any more, they just sit at home and list all the things they want (or don't want – it seems to me that consumerism's gone mad, if you ask me), and anyway Mr. Howards who ran it died eventually, and he'd never married, not the type, so people said (though you can't trust everything you hear, can you?), and I never went in myself because of how he treated his customers – you remember how he spoke that time to Mrs. Fenton?'

'No.'

'You remember Mrs. Fenton?'

'Not really.'

'She was the old lady who lived two doors down when we lived at number twenty-three. Towards the school-end of the street.'

'Oh, Mrs. Fenton, yes…' answered Keith dishonestly.

'So after that time we hardly went in, and now he's gone anyway, and it's *Harrisons* now, which does all sorts of cheap, discount stuff. *Harveys*, not *Harrisons*… Just done it again, didn't I! Anyway–' she came momentarily up for air.

'Well!' exclaimed Keith, as he hoped he might now veer the conversation towards his own downcast mood. But he was too late.

'– as I was saying, your dad and me went to *Harveys* – no, *Harrisons!* – this morning, just to have a look at their displays. We hardly ever buy anything, do we, love? Ever so expensive, you could spend a fortune there…' Keith heard his father grunt in the background, as his mother continued: 'And do you know what? You won't believe who we bumped into.'

'No… Well, go on then.'

'Mr. Tomkinson,' announced his mother triumphantly.

'Go on… Mr. Tomkinson?'

'You know, Mr. Tomkinson who used to own the garage where your dad would take his car for servicing and MOTs and repairs. He had a funny eye; never knew if he was looking at you while you were talking, or over your shoulder. One eye on the fire, the other one up the chimney, as your uncle Gerald use to say. Anyway, there he was, right as rain.'

'Why shouldn't he have been?'

'Oh your dad and me thought he'd passed away a long while ago, and we hadn't seen him around at all since he'd retired. Then there he was all of a sudden in the garden centre, buying some summer plants. He wanted them for his garden – he lives on the Howelands estate now, in a bungalow with a garden out the back – and he said he'd had such a lovely show all spring with a wonderful display of primroses and primulas. You see, he'd only just moved in last year, he said, and he didn't really know what was in the garden, so you're supposed to wait a year and see what comes up and then you know what you've got and where all the gaps are, and he said he'd had such a lovely display of primulas and daffodils and all the trimmings, when spring came, but now they'd all died off and there wasn't any other colour any more – it's just like when we lived at number twenty-three, you remember? The whole lot came out for spring, then we didn't have anything at all for ages. But actually–'

Keith's mother tended to start the next sentence of her pontifications before pausing a second for breath, so as to prevent anyone from spotting a chance to interject.

'– if you think about it, a lot of gardens have that problem. How's your little back yard doing? Have you made anything of it?'

'Not yet.' Keith wondered about telling her he was on the point of setting it all alight.

'Primroses and primulas are lovely, when they come out, and I know they go on and on, being perennials, but once they're gone, they're gone.'

'Mmmm.'

'Here's your dad. He wants a word.'

Keith's father came on. 'Hello, son.'

'Hi, dad. How's things?'

Keith's father was a man of few words on the phone. After a comment or two about the neighbours' dogs and their leylandii, there was an uncomfortably long pause.

Then: 'Here's your mum back. All the best, son.'

'Bye, dad!' Keith was used to the brevity of conversations with his father. They both understood that not much else needed or was wanted to be said.

Then his mother came back to the phone and chatted about Roy and Sheila Bernards who live at the top of Burgess Avenue; Roy had just had his knee operation. She went on to describe their walk to reach the Bernards' house in minute detail, including the current state of the park, the druggies sitting around, the lack of English being spoken, the way even his father felt threatened. Keith heard in the background his father's disgruntled rebuttal of this last fact, but his mother went on regardless.

Eventually Keith cut in, exasperated by the straying into right-wing territory. 'Well,' he said, 'I'm glad Mr. Tomkins is alive and well, anyway.'

'Tomkinson, Tomkin*son*,' she corrected him. 'I suggested he get some crocosmias and red hot pokers, they'll add some colour, I told him. Lots of red and yellow if he puts them in. And you can get them ever so cheap, too, four for ten pounds, and they looked OK, not too droopy, either – a real bargain, and who doesn't love a good bargain? But we said we'd pop round to see him in his new place at some point, and he wanted to show us his garden, so that'll be nice, won't it? Probably wait till he's got something put in, now, there's no rush. Might leave it till the spring, and then we'll be able to see all the lovely spring flowers, otherwise no point going, is there? I do love primulas. And I love the name, too, don't you? Such a lovely ring to it. Must be Latin. *Primulas…*'

Keith heard her say the word, he even vaguely registered her final musings on its unusual sound, all the while realising it was unlikely he would now be able to chat in any useful manner about his own strange predicament, or about how he was feeling. What would he have said, anyway? After all, she would hardly be receptive to the basic idea that he was sinking into a madness, a dark, depressed place. And that he'd killed Karen.

It would have to wait. Maybe he should go and see them for a few days.

That'd be fun.

'Mum, I've got to go now. I am needed in the kitchen. OK?'

'How is Karen?' asked his mother, belatedly. 'You both doing well?'

'Yes, I think so. Right, well… Good to speak to you, mum. All our best!'

'OK, love. Bye! Bye!..' Her voice tailed off into Keith's empty silence.

Let's not prolong it…

Then he put his phone down. He always came out of such a conversation feeling exhausted by the pointlessness of it all.

But this time, there was something else that had struck him.

He wasn't sure what it was, but it was not just the fact that he himself was feeling out of sorts at the moment. There was something else she'd said which troubled him.

Or, at least, which had struck some sort of bell deep within him.

Now, what on earth was it? He would struggle to remember what ground exactly she had covered.

He always did.

But there was a knot in his memory of what they had been talking about, a node of information which internally he must have noted, but which was just out of reach now. He was striving for it, reaching for the apple on the branch above, just out of reach. Perhaps he should ring her back, ask her what she'd been going on about, relive the whole conversation…

He balked at this, and decided he had to find it himself. It would surface, things like this always did for Keith. Many a time he would suddenly have some detail or name from the past leap brightly into his head, as if it had never gone away. This would be the same, he knew it.

Out of reach, out of reach. Not an apple above him; rather a dense, knotty twist of recognition that he'd noticed subconsciously while she'd been chatting about… About what? The old hardware shop? The new discount store? Garden centres?

Mr. Tomkinson coming back from the dead… Parks… Drunks and druggies…

Any of this stuff would have chimed with plenty of familiarity for Keith at the moment.

Roy and Sheila Bernards. Knee operations. Burgess Avenue. Dogs in the neighbours' garden. Mr. Tomkinson.

Mr. Tomkinson…

It *was* something about Mr. Tomkinson.

His bungalow, his garden? His flowers?

The flowers!

Keith suddenly sensed himself getting closer now. It was in the flowers, it was something to do with Mr. Tomkinson's flowers. What the hell had she said about the flowers that made him flicker with some vague recognition? Come on, what was it...

Keith couldn't even work out what he was hoping to chance upon. But it was niggling him so much now. He knew there was a subliminal kernel of revelation he had noticed, and there was nothing else to do but find it.

He delved deeper into his memory. It was a similar process to when he'd lost keys or documents around the house – you needed to track every place you'd visited meticulously.

Flowers… Spring flowers… Red hot pokers…

Bungalow garden.

Not much colour during the summer.

Lots of colour in the spring.

Daffodils, primroses, primulas.

Primulas!

It was *primulas*. He had it. And in that very instant he knew why, too!

A rush of shocking recognition hit Keith as he stood there. A recognition of a new and changed reality which was about to wash over him and inundate his whole existence. Again.

Not only did Keith realise that finding this word was a harbinger of unknown consequences, probably dire and dangerous; but if he was right, if what he had just remembered was true, then this was about to change the whole balance of what he thought he knew, and the implications were enormous, truly momentous…

Keith checked the calendar on his phone. It was Sunday, the last day of his holiday. So he was expected in at work the next day. Perfect. It could not have worked out better.

What a holiday. And what dreams and nightmares he had been through.

No drink, nothing tonight.

He had to have a completely clear head. That had been half the problem. Keith was beginning to see it all now, the whole affair had just made a shocking move into focus. Not everything made sense by any means, but maybe, just maybe, he had found a thread which might lead to unravelling one or two of the big knots that had been tying him up.

He felt he was on the cusp of a new knowledge for which he would have to adapt himself once again. But this time, change would be coming from somewhere within himself – there'd be no gentle nudging from a demon hiding in his attic.

Chapter Twenty-seven

First day back at work. He had not been looking forward to this at all.

The small talk. The questions about the holiday. The knowing stares at his unkempt appearance. The difficult silences. How would he cope?

Passing through the embracing, semi-circular entrance into Uxbridge station, peering up momentarily at the bright colours of the civic shields in the stained glass above the ticket hall, Keith saw his train sitting there on the platform and climbed on board, briefcase clutched unusually tightly to his chest. He scouted round for a seat and found one that would look out to the Kitchen Woman at Barons Court. Old habits die hard. He settled into the upholstery as other places around him started to fill up. His breathing became calmer, it was a familiar routine once again.

The train slowed down at a couple of places where the ubiquitous fluorescent-yellow-jacketed workers were standing around beside the tracks, peering at cables, discussing the work they were carrying out. How much do these lines really need repairing all the time, wondered Keith. Is it so necessary? They seem to congregate for months on end in their white vans and their cordoned-off areas.

It was a bright day. Hot and intense after a recent shower. Too bright to see into the kitchen today. Anyway, it was school holidays; no daily routine for this young mother, who was probably enjoying something of a lie-in, maybe even a bit of quality time with her husband or partner or illicit lover before the kids started bounding around, demanding her attention.

He emerged blinking into daylight at his destination and set out across the park to his office. Past the usual checks, into the lift, along the corridor.

'Hello, old man!' beamed Carter. 'So, the adventurer returns… And not even a tan to prove it! Where did you go, again? Cleethorpes?'

'Very good,' sighed Keith, raising a smile at Carter's bold greeting. 'So how's it going here, then?'

'All very good, matey, all very good.'

'In other words?' smirked Keith.

'In other words, nothing to report. Nothing at all. Happy? I know I am.'

Keith sat down at his place behind his partition and started sifting through his in-box. Piles of reports were dutifully waiting for him, and he knew that the way he was feeling would best be served by putting his head down and getting on with it all. Toad-like work, that'll get him through.

'What happened with the Mahanu Brothers you were working on?' asked Keith half-way through the day, not long after they had both come back from lunch. 'Did you get them?'

Carter's disembodied voice wafted over from the other side of the partition. 'No such luck. They were let off on a technicality. Bloody bureaucrats. And bloody lawyers.'

'Unlucky. Still, you gave them a run for their money. Something to think about. Especially if they are thinking of doing it again.'

'That's my boy. Positive thinking, eh?'

'Does the Home Office think positively, I wonder?'

Carter's forehead and eyes poked over the top of the partition. 'Well, your guess is as good as mine. God knows what they are thinking half the time…'

'No. I reckon some of the boys at the top need taking out, don't you?'

'Maybe,' answered Carter, before disappearing again, and going silent.

'You know,' Keith pushed on, 'it seems to me that there are too many people at the top doing absolutely nothing for us here down below. There should be a cull.'

'Christ, you've had a refreshing holiday, reflecting on the world's ills, I must say. What's brought all this on?'

'Oh, nothing,' answered Keith nonchalantly. 'Forget it. I was just having a frustrated, revolutionary moment. Sorry.'

They both carried on working, in silence. Then Keith said: 'You know, I think Karen, my Karen that is, might be having an affair.'

'Really?' came a surprised retort, before Carter himself appeared in person and leaned over the partition. 'Why?'

'Phone calls with nobody at the other end. They put theirs down when I answer. Texts in the middle of the night, or while we're watching TV together, which she then deletes, saying they're from her wayward brother or her parents or friends. And she's always out. Especially in the evenings and at weekends.'

'Oof, poor you,' muttered Carter in sympathy. Only it wasn't sympathy, was it, thought Keith. It was curiosity.

'And she seemed to be getting so close to Samantha. Do you remember Sam Taylor, the policewoman I told you about?'

'The one you'd had a fling with?'

'Yes. And the one who was killed in a car crash a month or so ago. Do you remember me telling you?'

'Ah. Yes. Her…' Carter paused, then resumed the conversation in an almost imperceptibly eager tone. What was this, wondered Keith, as he continued laying the trap.

'And you reckon your Karen was what? Too close to her? Gallivanting around with her? I don't understand.'

'Well, not having a fling with her, that's for sure. I don't think she was that way inclined.'

'OK.'

'But they did meet up surprisingly often, her and Samantha, which is weird, seeing as Karen knew all about my time with her in the past. I reckon they were up to no good, maybe going around town with each other, nightclubs and bars and stuff. I mean, what else were they meeting up for? Why would my Karen, who does some sort of office work in a consultancy on the outskirts of Slough meet up so regularly with a police officer? It just doesn't make any sense to me.'

'No. Strange…' concurred Carter. 'And you say she deletes her texts all the time?'

'Exactly, that's weird, isn't it?' murmured Keith, warming to his theme. 'It's a bit suspicious, isn't it…'

'Isn't it just.'

'Sorry, Carter, I don't mean to put all this onto you.'

'Don't be silly, fellah. Don't mention it. Problem shared, and all that.'

'Thanks.'

'Don't mention it. I'm just sorry for you. But it's good that you got it off your chest.'

'Yes, I think so too.'

As five o'clock approached, Keith finally began to feel that he was making some inroads into his pile of work. It had absorbed him completely, that sense of aiming to chip away at something that might appear less of a burden by the end of a period of consistent and relentless activity.

It took his mind off his task too. He had done what he needed to. When Carter left, the seeds sown would begin to germinate. Thoughts would give rise to ideas which would give rise to suspicions.

God, this was good. It was the most in control he had felt for months.

So what was next? Wait and see?

Surely not. That couldn't be Keith's style from now on. He would have to take a risk, no matter what the possible consequences.

So what was it to be?

Carter got up and put on his jacket. It was five.

Then he took it off again. 'Too hot. Just remembered how stifling it is out there at the moment.'

'Too right,' agreed Keith.

'Right, young man. I'm off. Don't stay too long, will you?'

'To be honest with you,' answered Keith, 'I've got myself into a bit of a rhythm with these here, and I'm seriously tempted to stay a bit longer, just to get on top of them all. Look, I've cleared this lot here and if I could knock these ones on the head I'd be a happier man when I got home.'

'OK.' Carter looked as if he was about to mention Karen's infidelities again, but clearly thought better of it. 'See you tomorrow, then.'

'Bye. Don't you worry about me,' replied Keith cheerfully.

There was no clever retort from Carter. Keith must have given him some cause for concern.

Keith being Keith, a leopard trapped by his spots, he genuinely did see the value in getting on with the work in front of him. However, it gave him the perfect excuse, too, and would have him beavering away for a good hour or two, well into the evening. Security never minded, and it would ensure Carter had well and truly gone home, by the time Keith decided to act.

The moment came. It was gone half-six, after a couple of interruptions from Barry in Security checking he was OK, when Keith finally scattered a number of reports across his desk and over his keyboard; a scene was created of somebody looking for more answers than his own computer could give.

He stood up, went around the partition and switched on Carter's computer. A blue screen flickered on the monitor as it warmed up. The space appeared for the password.

Keith leaned in and placed the cursor onto the blank space. This was where he'd find out if he had made the right connection, after all. He'd remembered seeing the last three letters when Carter had typed them in before. There are not many words ending with those three letters. *Primula* was one, that's what had struck him when talking to his mother. That unusual combination of letters, how often does that occur? Only in one other case had he ever seen it. And given recent events, there really could only be one possibility for this password.

c – a – l – i – g – u – l – a

And he was in!

Carter's screen flickered into life, along with his desktop, all his icons and apps.

As a further precaution, Keith brought round some of his papers and reports, placing them around the desk he was now sitting at, with one or two on the floor. It looked like he was deep in some conundrum. Looking over his shoulder at the office door, he froze dead still for a second or two and listened out for any noises, any footsteps. Nothing. Barry had evidently been quite reassured that Keith didn't need any more interruptions tonight.

He now scanned the various icons on the screen. Nothing out of the ordinary. He opened up a couple of folders and files relevant to his own work, so it would look like he had a genuine reason to be in here. Then he started looking for something else. Anything else which might give him more of a clue.

A clue to what?

That was a big question…

But there had to be something here which could lead him onto another path. After all, no further proof of Carter's own involvement was now needed. That password alone was watertight evidence. How stupid of him to have used that as his password – who else would choose that, unless they weren't somehow wrapped up in this whole affair?

Keith looked down at his hands. They were trembling. He could hardly put the right fingers on the right keys. He suddenly realised how far he had ventured. His entire body was at this moment flooded with adrenaline. He needed to stay calm. He needed to find something. Something concrete. Some clue as to what he should do next, or where he should go.

None of the icons looked out of the ordinary.

Keith clicked on the Start icon. Up came all the computer's apps. He ran his eyes over them as he scrolled down.

What was this one? *Henf.*

Henford, maybe? He clicked on it.

For a couple of seconds the screen went black. Then it flickered on again, this time with an entirely different-looking desktop.

This was it! It was another system altogether. He was no longer on the same network. Suddenly Keith found himself within Carter's own area. Or was it the dark web? Or a network for the Caligula Club?

The door opened.

Keith froze. Barry poked his head into the office.

'Didn't see you there! Sorry. Thought you'd gone.'

'Just doing some cross-references with Carter's records,' answered Keith, sounding shrill and shocked.

'I'll leave you to it. Bye for now.'

'Bye. Thanks.' Keith breathed slowly in and out, in and out, in and out…

Eyes back on the screen, Keith feverishly peered at all the icons now sitting there, all in orderly lines, some marked with symbols and unfathomable names or codes, others with clearly recognisable references to what had been unfolding for Keith over the past months: *Caligula*, *Henford*, *Police, Sam T, Leslie T, Karen D…*

Keith H.

There was his name sitting there in front of his eyes.

Keith double-clicked on it, hardly daring to breathe.

Up flashed a window, bright green with a large *PROTECTED* across the top. Below was the space for a password.

Keith tried *caligula* again. Then with a capital. Then with all caps.

Nothing.

He tried a few more ideas. Still no luck.

Keith closed this window and tried to open *Henford.*

PROTECTED.

He tried a few more. *PROTECTED.* Every time.

OK, thought Keith. So be it. But at least I know now. Carter is in on it, after all. I've been duped, horribly. But I do now know who's behind it. And it isn't me who's going mad. It is not me.

I'm not going mad.

This sudden realisation, this sudden reassurance felt like an invisible arm reaching round to console Keith, and for a moment or two he allowed himself to slump in Carter's chair, putting a hand to his brow, almost suppressing a sob. He closed his eyes.

Then he jumped up. Quickly, he had to move now! Everything had to be put back in place. Was there any way Carter would know he'd been fishing around in his computer? Keith swiftly went into the general history folders and spotted his use and the time spent on it had all been logged. He deleted it. He logged out, too, and shut the whole PC down correctly, so as not to leave any incriminating trace.

Mind you, Carter might be monitoring all this remotely anyway… Who knows? Or he'd spot something tomorrow…

Never mind. At least Keith was on to something now.

This was enough. At last.

He carefully looked around one last time to see that he had left everything looking the same as before. Then he picked up his jacket and briefcase, and headed through the empty corridors out of the building. A cheery *good evening* from Barry closed the bolt on the whole experience, and he felt the weight leave his shoulders as he headed for the Tube.

Previous nights wandering the streets alone, all the while avoiding cameras or witnesses, had set Keith up well for this one, special night. He arrived home late. It was not long now till it would be dark. He flung his briefcase against the wall inside the hallway and ran upstairs through the clutter of his empty house and went into his bedroom to get changed.

A black, long-sleeved T-shirt; thin, black gloves; stretchy, flexible jeans, again black; finally the balaclava, tucked into his pockets, so as not to look too weird on the streets of West London. There might have been a whole month of padding the streets of Uxbridge behind him, but this night there was only one place he knew he had to get into.

He was tired, though. It had been so hot all day, and he'd worked flat out long into the evening. He would have to have a rest first. Keith stretched out on his remaining sofa and tried to get some sleep into him; he had a feeling he'd be needing all his energy later.

He woke with a start. For a second he couldn't remember why he was here in the lounge, then it flooded back to him with a flutter of excited panic.

Too late. He'd wanted to tackle this, and if it was going to be without the help of the police, well then he would have to be strong. And prepared. He picked up some heavy-duty wire-cutters from the shed, grabbed his pocket torch from under the stairs, a penknife in case he needed to defend himself, and opened the front door.

No. He shut it again. Too obvious. There might be somebody watching. Leaving lights on, he opened the kitchen door and crept out to the back yard, then through the gate leading out to the private alley which ran behind the whole terrace. Once on the streets he breathed the night air. It was cooler than it had been during the day, but was still stifling. A half-moon lit up the clear, starry sky. Keeping to the shadows and the smaller streets and suburban routes, Keith made his tortuous way across town and away towards Henford.

The strange, abandoned military base held the key to it all, he was sure. Tonight he would finally get to the bottom of it.

Here he stood, crouched right into the dense shadows close to the outer fence. The undergrowth seemed to crowd around him protectively. It was the dead of night now. Absolutely silent, except for the occasional distant car over on the main bypass. Keith looked along the fence towards the entrance where he had seen the ambulance on the *street view* image. Nearby, just behind him was the little track that led to the hole he and Karen had sneaked through.

Keith found the track and came to where they'd crept in. As he had guessed, the wire here had been replaced and reinforced. Keith moved along, further into the dense undergrowth now, pushing back nettles and brambles away from his eyes. Now was the time to put on the balaclava. He pulled out his wire-cutters and made for a part of the fence which stood behind a wall belonging to a low-lying building providing cover.

Snap! Snap!

Before he knew it, he was in. Bending his body through the gap, Keith took careful note of where he had made the hole. Then he headed out into the heart of the base.

Shadows were everywhere. The empty, shattered windows and the hollowed-out buildings created deep crevices of darkness between which Keith moved stealthily. A rusty antenna cast an intricate pattern of criss-crossing shapes over the cracked and weed-covered tarmac track that led to the centre of the base. Keith turned right and clung to the backs of the buildings that lined the track.

There were no lights, nor any sign at all of recent human activity. What was it about this place? Why should Carter have a whole folder dedicated to it on his computer? Why did Samantha think it was so important that she mentioned it to him in code?

Deeper and deeper he ventured. Some of the buildings here at the centre were larger. There were communal halls now, a gym, the officers' mess, administrative offices, a sentry box or two, a three-storey block, a tall tower presumably for climbing or rescue practice. The whole area was still cloaked in utter darkness and silence.

A door hung open on one of its hinges. Keith went in. Turning on his torch he warily threw the light briefly around the inside. Rubbish littered the floor and some nearby shelves. Steps led up to a corridor, which Keith followed. Doors opened off into abandoned offices. Behind a desk in one of them stood a filing cabinet. Keith opened its rusty drawers. Empty.

He went back out along the corridor. At the end were double doors, which he pushed tentatively open. He cast his torchlight into the vast darkness beyond, and found himself in a high dining hall. Along the edge were the remains of serving areas leading off into kitchens.

A rat scurrying away from the beam of light made Keith jump momentarily, and he turned off the light. Now, apart from the thin moonlight entering from windows on the far side, he stood in total darkness. The silence was deafening.

But it confirmed, as did the rat, that nobody had been here in a while.

Keith breathed with relief and made his way back outside.

He moved round to the back of this complex of buildings, careful to stay as hidden in the shadows as possible. Cutting alongside an area of tussocky grass, he turned to follow a narrow passage between the back of the dining hall and the gym. He peered in here, as he passed a gaping fire exit, and looked out into a grim void.

So there really was nothing here, not in this part of the base. He looked around for what other buildings might be still in use, but only moonlit dereliction gazed blankly back at him.

There must be something more to this place, he thought. There *must* be.

Is it underground? Is that it? Could there be a hidden entrance to some vast, cavernous, evil HQ right below his feet? Perhaps the way in is inside one of these inconspicuous barracks? That'd take ages to find.

As he made his way further from the entrance he'd made, Keith remembered the area he'd seen on the satellite images when he'd first looked up Henford – a blurry, nondescript part of the base at the further end, where it wasn't obvious whether there were even any buildings or tracks. He was approaching it now.

There it was ahead of him, an open space, bounded in the distance by a low building with a tall chimney, and beyond that the trees near the boundary fence.

But what was going on? As he got closer, Keith saw that the whole area was itself fenced off; high, forbidding gates blocked the track he was on, and from these gates a serious wire fence ran off in both directions. Not only this, but just beyond this heavy-duty fence ran another. Both rings of fencing were bristling at the top with the fiercest-looking barbed wire.

There were no security lights, though, and still no sign of activity.

In the air hung a sweet smell.

Keith kept to the shadows, still. He was sure he was getting close, and couldn't afford to take any risks now. Moving quickly away from the gates he made his way right around this perimeter fence. All the time he was trying to see what it was that this area contained, why it might be so well defended. All it seemed to be was an open area of bumpy, tussocky grass with a number of low bushes and shrubs. Vague shapes glimmered faintly near the middle.

He was now almost opposite the gate that led into this compound, and he was well hidden, since the trees on this side came almost up to the edge of it, casting deep shadows over the ground beside the fence. On his belly Keith crawled to the fence and pulled out his cutters. This wire was tougher, much tougher than the earlier stuff. It took real effort to crack through first one, then a second, then a third strand. This was going to take a while, he realised, trying to remain as still and silent as he could. He was trembling again, which he felt was hardly surprising. *Come on, let's keep going… Don't let's get caught now!*

He was through. That was the first fence. He crawled through slowly and folded the wire back on itself, should he need to get out quickly. Now he was creeping through the no man's land towards the inner perimeter. As he neared it he saw it was made of the same thick wire as before.

Here we go again.

Keith silently got to work. He had completely lost any sense of what time it was, and was committing himself to the sole task of getting inside this fortified plot of land, as well as getting back out again.

Snap! Snap! Snap!

Finally it was done. Heaving himself through on his stomach Keith pulled the heavy wire back as he had done just before. Then he got back down flat on the ground and lay still again. For a good while this time, just to make sure there was no chance at all of being seen. He would let the night settle again, allow the darkness and the silence to take back control.

He lay there with his head on the ground, looking up at the stars, then out over the compound he'd broken into. The night had definitely cooled down, he only just realised, though the air was as still as ever.

And there was that sickly, sweet odour lingering around here, too. What was that, he wondered. It was pungent and penetrated deep into his lungs.

Enough time had passed. He stayed low and started making his way towards the centre of the area. Kneeling up a little, he took stock of what there was to see.

Low bumps and ridges, occasional bushes. A small tree here and there. Posts, too – he hadn't noticed these from afar. They were small, wooden posts, with little signs clipped onto them. And all around, small shapeless forms, each with a post. Some seemed to be under tarpaulin or plastic, glinting in the moonlight, others were black with the night.

Keith crawled his way towards the nearest.

The smell was getting stronger.

He raised himself slightly on his feet, crouching low. This one had a plastic cover over it. It was about the size of a body.

Surely not?

Keith pulled back at the cover. It gave way and the contents below swung out.

Shit!

The empty sockets, gleaming in their decay were the first things that greeted him. Then the gaping jaw, responding to his intrusion with a grin. The stench hit Keith as physically as a punch.

He shrank back from it in disgust, turning away. It was all he could do not to cry out, but his mouth filled with a reflux, and he covered his nose to try not to be sick.

What the hell was this place?

Keith sat still and looked around. He moved quickly over to the next form he could see in the darkness. This one was covered in a blue tarpaulin. Holding his nostrils still tight, he crept up to it and pulled back the corner. Skeletal feet poked out, the flesh coming away with the cover. He jumped up to the other end and pulled it back. Staring back up at him was a revolting sight, the remains of a face, eyes largely gone, hair falling away in rotting clumps, skin pulled tight over the cheekbones, visibly black with ripeness even in this light.

Oh my god, oh my god… What on earth have I come to?

It was a charnel house. He crept over to another, then another; this one was just laid out to the elements, the next was under a metal frame, bloated and oozing juices out onto his white shirt. Another had become almost entirely a pile of bones thinly covered with a skein of leathery flesh; the muscle had mostly disappeared and the whole human form seemed to have sunk into the ground.

A white shirt! Keith went back to the body he had just seen. It must be! It was the man who had jumped from the motorway bridge. His build was the same, the sweep of white hair too; but now, exposed like this throughout the summer's heat, his face was bloated and blotched, his sinews pushed through the tight skin around his neck.

Keith was beside himself, and could hardly breathe. He had spent the last few months wondering what was real and what was being fed to his imagination, and this latest twist was now beginning to make his head reel again. He felt nauseous. Moving over to another figure he started to realise just how many bodies there were out here. At least thirty, thirty-five? Thirty-odd corpses lying out here in various states of decay. He almost tripped over one, vivid red and purple in the moonlight, its eye-holes white with putrefaction and the mouth peeled back in the grim parody of a smile; Keith's feet retreated swiftly from the messy puddle of juices that it lay in.

He had to get out. This was becoming too serious now. Time to go.

As he made his way quickly back to the holes he'd made in the surrounding fences, a sudden, tragic thought hit him, and caused him to stop in his tracks for a moment.

Samantha!

Oh no… What if this is where she ended up? There still hadn't been a funeral, after all; red tape and post-mortems, apparently. Could it really be that she had been bumped off, just to end up in this… this…

A far-off clang of metal brought him to his senses.

It was not so far-off that they wouldn't be here any second now. He had to go, they must have noticed he wasn't at home.

Keith raced at full pelt now to the holes he'd made, pulled himself through the first, even turned around to pull it back roughly into place

– in this light it would be difficult to see that it had been tampered with. Then a mad dive across to the second hole, a frantic fumble through to the other side, and again just enough time to pull it closed, as headlights swung into view on the other side of the compound.

Keith retreated well into the shadows as the vehicle approached the gates to the compound. He crouched, hardly daring to breathe, and watched as two men climbed out of the 4x4, one of them with a large dog on a lead. Keith remained so utterly still he could hear the blood pumping around his head and inside his ears.

The two men opened the gates and walked inside with torches flashing in all directions. He was too far away to be picked up by them, but the dog would almost certainly sniff him out any moment now.

Various options were racing through Keith's mind: Once they were well inside the compound he could risk going round to its gates, closing them in, even locking them in if they'd left the padlock behind; he could get in the 4x4 and physically bar the gates with it. But he wouldn't get far. The dog would bark furiously, he'd be noticed, they'd have guns, too, surely. He might be able to steal the vehicle and make a getaway; no, they'd have taken the keys with them, and they'd have locked the outer perimeter gates, too. They're not bungling idiots, these guys – Keith sensed he was up against something or somebody quite extraordinary.

So it was best not to give his position away at all. That's how he'd survived all his night-time activities so far, by staying in the shadows, by doing nothing extravagant that might have revealed him. He'd have to do that now, but quickly, damned quickly.

Staying low but moving fast Keith raced through the shadows all along the outer fence, until he was able to leap across a tiny stretch of open ground. Once he was behind a row of barracks which led right up beside the central complex of buildings, he was able to dart from shadowy block to shadowy block, right back out to the other side of the base.

He had now reached the hole by which he had first entered, and crawled through it. He had done it! Keith sighed with relief, and as he crawled out through the undergrowth, he pulled off his balaclava, and threw it up high into the tangled branches of a tree surrounded by a thicket of brambles.

They're bound to spot the break-in eventually, he thought, especially when light comes. The dog will find the scent, and then hopefully follow it to this point; maybe that'd put them off his trail for a while.

Then he ran like never before, back towards his house through the deserted streets and suburbs, as if all the demons and devils that were haunting him were snapping hungrily at his heels.

CHAPTER TWENTY-EIGHT

All the time he was running he heard himself under his breath gasping words, almost as if in a fever:

Police. Police station. Must tell someone. They'll have to believe this.

He had to get to the authorities before anybody got to him.

Go straight there. Just keep running. Run right in, they'll have to believe you. Tell them everything.

It'll have to be everything, too. Not just about the bodies. They'll need to know the lot, the whole lot. The texts from Samantha, the Caligula code, the Caligula Club, his nightly missions…

The first signs of day were appearing ahead of him, a thin greyness outlining the roofs and chimneys of suburbia.

Keith's thoughts began at last to assess more rationally what had just happened. So they were definitely onto him. They must have been looking for him – why else come out there in the middle of the night with torches and dogs? This was it, now; he'd broken his cover for good.

That was why he would have to go to the police. They'd have to believe him this time.

He should get changed.

No, just rock straight in and tell them, for god's sake.

If he looked in any way dishevelled…

Better to be dishevelled.

Anyway, what if the police are in on it too?

Don't be daft.

Everybody seems to be in on it.

Just get to the station.

I should get hold of my passport as ID.

Just get to the station.

I really don't want anyone getting hold of my passport. I won't be able to prove who I am, otherwise. Heck, I've lost my identity several times already in this whole affair… Couldn't bear to lose my passport to them. I know where it is, it'll be safe still. Just need to pop in, get my ID, put on another top, get into the car and drive.

Five minutes. Five minutes, that's all.

Five minutes!

Keith arrived at the end of his road. It was very quiet. The darkness of true night was beginning to dissipate. He stood stock-still for a good ten seconds, to listen for anything untoward. Nothing at all. He walked briskly along to the street behind, up the alleyway to his back gate, and found his way back in, arguing fumblingly with the gate latch, then with the back door key, his trembling hand hardly able to hold it up to the lock.

Once inside, standing again to listen for intruders, Keith was sure he was alone. He ran now into his study, opened the drawer with various documents and bills stuffed inside, put his hand right to the back, and withdrew it triumphantly holding his familiar maroon passport.

Then he dashed across the landing to his bedroom. Grabbing a shirt from the chair at the foot of the bed, he pulled off the black top that was torn and dirty from the night's exploits, and put on the shirt, looking out of the window as he dressed.

The 4x4 was pulling up opposite. Its lights were off. Its engine was silenced as soon as it was stopped. They were here.

Keith's heart missed a beat.

He had to get out. Where was his car key? In the kitchen? In a pocket? God knows.

Shit! Where the fuck was it?

He ran downstairs to grab the spare one before they got to the front door.

Oh shit! Damn it! Brilliant!

Keith ran back up to the bedroom, and stood for a second, contemplating his next move. There was only one way out of this.

He ran up to the top floor, climbed the ladder that now hung perpetually down from the attic, and hauled himself upwards as quickly as he could. He hoped there was no-one waiting up here for him too, but he was in luck. Sort of.

They were downstairs instead, entering through the front door. Their light footsteps echoed around the empty house as they fanned out to check all the rooms of the ground floor, before clattering noisily up the stairs. They were moving fast now.

Keith pulled up the ladder behind him. He closed the hatch.

Now he pulled out his torch and switched it on. As quietly as he could he moved across the attic space, climbed over to his neighbours' attic, pushed his way through all their junk, made his way finally over to number forty-four, and lifted the hatch.

No other option. He finally felt a pang of regret, of pity.

There was no time for a ladder even. He lowered himself through the narrow space, leaning on his elbows, then allowed himself to hang down, swung for a second or two, and then knew he had to drop.

Bang!

He was heavier and louder than he'd imagined.

It was bound to have woken him up.

It had. A door on the floor below immediately creaked open, a footstep was audible on the stairs.

'What the–?' The old man's face seemed contorted with shock and fear.

Keith screamed at the top of his voice, in order to keep the advantage of surprise: 'Get out of my way! Out of my way! *Move!*' He threw himself bodily down the stairs towards him, and almost comically raised both his arms to make himself bigger.

The neighbour recoiled, terrified. Keith ran past him, hissing at him not to follow. Downstairs now, all his instincts kicked in, all his inculcated, meticulous attention to detail, as he raced towards the front door. Passing into the now familiar cluttered hallway, Keith stopped at the trestle table near the entrance, picked up the spare car keys, opened the front door, ran out into the cool early morning air, looked around for the very car that so often was parked inconveniently in front of his own front door and clicked the button on the key. Spotting the giveaway orange flicker of lights further down the road, he ran towards it, keeping a nervous eye on his own house, and reaching the car he tugged furiously at the door handle, climbed in and was moving off down the street before his neighbour had even had time to get to the street to look out.

He parked the car right in front of the police station this time, at a jaunty angle on double yellow lines.

As he left the car the station's automatic doors slid open, Keith ran inside, raced straight towards the man sitting behind the reception desk. The man recoiled and made for a door behind him.

Immediately from either side came three figures, covered from head to toe in enormous protective suits. They looked like they were straight out of a sci-fi film, or worse, Chernobyl. One of them grabbed his left arm, while another, a woman to his right, slid the car keys from his grasp, taking them straight off back outside. He could see her out of the corner of his eye as she climbed into the driver's seat.

'Don't worry, sir, we'll sort that out. You'll have to come this way, with us please,' said a third, while he and the one gripping his left arm led him forcibly out of the reception area, through a number of security doors and into a small room.

'What's going on?' shouted Keith. 'You don't understand.'

'Just come this way, please!' came the reply. 'This way.'

He was ushered into what looked like a sports centre's changing area, with benches and cubicles. His three assailants peered at him through the wide plastic visors, and one of them shouted and pointed at the opening ahead of them.

'Take all your clothes off. We'll bring you new ones. Get in there and shower. Shower really well. Do this now. We cannot help you until you have showered really well! Go!'

One of them left the room to stand guard outside, while the other waited by the door and turned obligingly to the side. Keith took his cue, threw off his clothes and walked into the shower area. There was soap here, plenty of it, and shampoo, so he did as he was told. Things were weird enough now for him to realise he had to stop asking too many questions. He was beginning to feel that it was not worth it anyway, and, having made the decision himself to come here, he needed to accept his fate and swim with the flow.

When he emerged, his own clothes were gone. In their place was a neatly folded pile of clean jeans, a shirt, pants, socks, shoes, all of them roughly in his size. Once again, Keith sensed that others knew more about him than he did himself.

'All done?' asked the man by the door. He banged with his fist on the door behind him and it opened. The other figure, still clad in his plastic suit, entered with a contraption resembling the hand-held scanners one sees at airport security. This one was bigger and attached with wires to a heavy box he was holding in his other hand. He ran the device over Keith's naked body, the front, then the behind. A couple of swabs were wiped over his skin. Various bleeps sounded from the big box, and eventually the first man asked:

'Can I ask how you're feeling, sir? Are you feeling OK in yourself?'

Still perplexed, Keith answered: 'Fine. Really. Just fine.'

From a pouch, the first figure now produced a small torch, and said: 'Stand still. I need to have a look in your eyes. With his rough, plastic-clad hands he opened Keith's eyelids and shone a bright light into his vision, peering from as close as he could through his visor. Then out came a plastic container, from which the other took a swab. 'Open wide,' he ordered, and proceeded to take a full sample of the inside of Keith's mouth. The other man did something similar with his own swab over Keith's hair, the back of his hands, his arms, then quickly, over other parts of his body.

'We'll have these analysed out the back, but it looks like he's all clear,' said one of them. 'OK, get dressed as quickly as you can, and come back outside.' He turned around, as the other man began unstrapping his helmet and taking it off. They closed the door behind them, and Keith began to get dressed.

As he came back out into the corridor, there were three of them waiting outside for him. A duty officer was clearing away the suits, while the man who had scanned Keith smiled and said, 'This way, sir. Follow us.'

They walked along the corridor into a side office.

'Sit down here.'

The room was bare but comfortable.

This was no interrogation room or cell. There was a sofa. A pot-plant.

'What can we get you, Mr Hartman? A coffee? A mug of tea?'

Keith sat down. He put his hand to his head, unable to answer.

The police officer answered for him: 'I think a nice mug of tea, please Tom. Make it a strong one.'

Then: 'What is happening?' asked Keith. 'How do you know my name?'

'We know what's been going on, Keith, so you don't need to worry any more. I hope I can call you Keith?'

'That's not my car, you know?'

'We guessed as much. Relax. We'll get it back to its right owner. My colleague is just moving it round the back out of the way. We've got to move fast, and make sure nobody knows where you are.'

Keith looked around at the kindly faces surrounding him. 'I don't think you understand the danger I'm in. Sorry, but you honestly have no idea what I have just seen.' Keith was beginning to panic.

'Keith, my name is Detective Inspector Mark Wilson, and these are my colleagues, Inspector Gareth Knowles and Sergeant Paul Burrows. I'm afraid we're going to have to ask you to come with us immediately to somewhere away from here. You're going to have to trust us.'

Keith looked suspiciously at them, and was about to ask them why, when suddenly the office door opened and a tall, thin, clean-cut man in a plain, tieless pale blue shirt and brown corduroys entered brusquely. He stood in the doorway, looked around as if taking stock of what was happening, and said:

'Good. So he did come to us, after all. Let's get him out of here now. We leave from the back gates in five minutes. Give him his tea or whatever, get him to the car, and then we're out! I'll go ahead and meet you at you-know-where.'

He turned to leave, but swivelled round to address Keith: 'Morning Keith. You've had an interesting night, I hear. Again…'

He was about to go, but at the last moment he turned around again and asked Keith: 'The password. What was the password for Carter Henry's computer?'

'Caligula.'

'Thanks.' Then he was gone. As he left he brushed hastily past the policeman bringing in a mug of tea for Keith, who now sipped at this as if in a daze. It began to bring him back to his senses. He opened his eyes wide as if waking from a long sleep.

The policeman called Wilson leaned towards him: 'As he said, sir – perhaps it would be best if you sipped up fairly swiftish, like. We've got a bit of a journey ahead of us.'

'Yes, of course.' Keith was coming to the conclusion that he was better off throwing his lot in with these, and allowing himself finally to trust that they were what they were supposed to be. He stood up. 'I need the toilet.'

'Just along the corridor, second on the left.'

Still unable to say very much, Keith nodded in acknowledgement and thanks, opened the door, and went off to the bathroom. This was, he realised, his last chance to get away if he really wanted to. Quite where he'd go now he had no idea. He washed his face in cold water, and stared for what felt like a long time at his reflection in the mirror above the sink. His drawn features gazed balefully back at him through bloodshot, tired and uncomprehending eyes.

He dried himself off, went back to the office, and forced a smile at the upturned faces.

'Right, Keith, you're coming with myself and Inspector Knowles. Let's go.'

They walked not into the reception area again, but through more corridors, down a short flight of stairs, out to a parking area beneath the building, and into a car. Its engine was already running, and in the driver's seat sat the young policewoman who had relieved him of his neighbour's car keys. Keith sat in the back beside Knowles, while Wilson climbed into the passenger seat.

'This is Sergeant Susie Haynes,' said Wilson, nodding at the driver, who turned and smiled.

'Hello again, Mr. Hartman.'

Keith murmured a confused hello, then asked: 'My neighbour's car. You're going to return it to him?'

'We'll explain later,' she answered. 'I think that for the moment you just need to get some rest. You're safe now, and in a couple of hours you'll be even safer. Sit back and enjoy the journey.'

A reinforced steel gate opened automatically and their car nosed out, joining the main road, where it now put on some speed and raced out of town.

A sudden tiredness hit Keith, and he felt his eyes becoming heavy with sleep as they pulled away from London. His head nodded forwards and backwards in fitful snatches of dream. He noticed at one point that they were passing through a service station, then along a hidden slip-road onto the M40 before welcome sleep finally overtook him completely.

Chapter Twenty-nine

He woke because the car had made a number of bumpy twists and turns, indicating that they had come well away from the smoothness of the motorway and were working across country. He opened his eyes and looked blurrily out of the window.

Green countryside and occasional limestone cottages suggested they'd been travelling for quite some time.

'Good morning,' said Knowles beside him.

'Morning,' answered Keith.

Haynes turned her head slightly from driving, towards Keith: 'Is he awake? Good! We're not far now,' she continued to Keith, 'you'll be pleased to know.'

'Thanks,' he mumbled. Then he added, almost apologetically, 'I've been asleep for a bit.'

'You certainly have,' chuckled Wilson. 'I reckon that's to be expected, to be honest.'

Knowles leaned in and said: 'If you're wondering, sir, you'll probably be getting quite a few answers about things in just a short while.'

'Good. I'm glad to hear it.'

'In fact,' continued Wilson, 'I'd be prepared for a few shocks.'

'I think I've had enough of those to be fairly used to them by now.'

'I hope so,' Keith heard Haynes mutter.

They drove into a built-up area and passed through a town centre filled with parades of charity shops and cafés, newsagents and hardware shops, a scene of bustling but hapless youths and young mothers. Then their car drew into a nondescript suburban estate of bland, seventies bungalows, houses, front lawns, and pulled up onto one of these driveways; they were on a small road that led to what looked like a number of smart, middle-class cul-de-sacs. It could not have been more anonymous.

'OK, here we are,' chirped Wilson. Haynes turned off the engine, the doors opened, they all climbed out. Keith was struck by the heat. It was hot again, today, and it must have been getting on towards mid-morning. He hadn't even thought about work, but then maybe that was utterly insignificant now.

It was hard to adjust to yet another reality, thought Keith, but he hoped this might be the last time. It was too traumatic; like being present at one's own birth each time.

Haynes came round to Keith's side, and put an arm at his elbow. 'Listen, you must take your time in here. Don't freak out, now.'

Well, that was it, wasn't it, thought Keith. How not to worry someone...

'Go on… You can't leave it like that. Tell me more…'

But instead, leading him by his arm, she coaxed him through the plastic and glass front door, behind Wilson and Knowles. Keith heard one of these shouting: 'We're here! Anybody at home?'

They walked through a hallway and turned into the main room. A number of figures sat around on sofas. Two men and a woman.

The woman was Samantha.

There she sat in plain-clothes, hair tied up. Alive.

Keith had had enough people coming back from the dead recently, what with the Nigerian, Karen, even Mr. Tomkinson, that there was almost a sense of rightness to it. But it still did not prepare him for the sudden rush of feelings that flooded his mind when he saw her there. He swung round to look for a chair, and finding one he slumped down into it and looked around.

How many more shocks like this could he take, he wondered.

'Hello, Keith. Sorry.'

'Sorry? Why sorry?'

'Sorry for putting you through all this. We feel awful. I feel awful.'

'Putting me through all this? You mean this is all your doing?'

'Sorry. I really am.'

Keith rubbed his eyes and sat up straight. This time he needed to be in control, not like before. He had no drink in him, no dizziness, nothing. He could take whatever was being thrown his way. *Let's hear it, whatever it is.*

After all, it couldn't be worse than what he'd witnessed at the disused base the night before.

Suddenly a thought occurred to Keith: 'Oh god, you do know about the bodies, do you? At Henford?'

'We do now, thanks to you. We followed you last night.'

'What? How could you have done? I was really careful.'

'It's our job, Keith.' The other man in the room now spoke up. 'Let's do this properly, shall we?'

He stood up, leaned over to Keith, and shook his hand. He was grey-haired, with a thin, stubbly beard and strangely wide, rimless glasses. 'My name is Thomas Erwin, I am leading this investigation. This is Graham Morell.' It was the same, thin man who had put his head around the door at the police station. Erwin continued: 'Graham is also from MI5, so I guess we're all actually colleagues, Keith, though we probably haven't met. Samantha you know, and you've already been introduced to the other three, Mark Wilson, Gareth Knowles and Susie Haynes. Let me explain…'

Keith heard himself ask: 'Am I in some kind of trouble?'

'No, not with us.'

'So where are we?'

Samantha answered: 'It's a safe house. In every sense. Nobody except us knows you're here. You will not be found.'

'Thank god. I think you need to tell me everything, please. I can't take any more. I promise I'll tell you everything, but you need to tell *me* everything too.' It sounded like a prayer, a final pleading coming from somewhere deep inside him. It sounded like this was going to be the last time he could ask this of anyone.

'Well, we've brought you here,' continued Erwin, 'for your own safety, and because this is serving as our base for a particularly difficult and complex operation, of which you have now become a major part.'

'I feel as if I have been a part of it for a long time.'

'You have. Longer than you realise.'

'So you were never even involved in a car accident?' he asked Samantha.

'I am so sorry, no. But it had to look as if I had.'

'Why?'

'So that they thought I was out of the way. And… so that you kept up your suspicions that something was going on.'

Morell took over: 'We've been following a particularly vicious little group of terrorists or anarchists, call them what you want, who have been planning something quite big.'

'Terrorists?'

'Yes, but not the jihadist, islamist sort. These are insiders, real political idealists who are plotting some serious upheavals within the state. Desperate fellows, but not your normal thugs and blunderers. No, these have real clout, especially as we knew that one or more of them must have been embedded within MI5 itself.'

'Carter?'

'Exactly. But we didn't know that until now. You clearly had your suspicions, though, and indeed you found something that led you to the body farm at Henford?'

'Body farm? Is that what it was?'

'Yes,' said Samantha. 'A place for testing decomposition on human bodies.'

'What? Is that even allowed?'

'No,' she answered. 'It's still illegal here. Some countries do it for forensic, scientific purposes, to work out how long a body's been dead, or to gauge human responses to certain types of disease. That's what we think this one had been set up for.'

'But you don't just set one of those things up, do you?'

'Precisely,' answered Erwin, 'that's the point. This is why we need to take this very seriously indeed; they have set up one hell of an operation. After all, where do you get bodies from? Or the land to set aside for it? You have to have plenty of friends in high places, as you can well imagine.'

'So you knew about the body farm?'

'We had our suspicions. We guessed something might be going on at the base.'

'Which is why,' interrupted Samantha, 'I texted you the clue about Henford. I knew you'd get the bit between your teeth.'

'And sent me into the lions' den? Thanks.'

'We knew they wouldn't do much to you; they'd just try to frighten you off. We had to keep our own involvement completely invisible. Sorry, again.'

'But why on earth are they experimenting on dead bodies? What do they hope to gain from it?'

'Well, we believe the group is planning a major biological attack,' said Erwin. 'Not just wiping out a pavement-full of people, not just a mass-bombing or plane-crash to take out a building or two. We have intelligence leading us to believe they are planning to release a nerve agent of some sort, a dirty device or a biological weapon. And not just in one place, but in several big cities at once. A serious wiping out of swathes of the civilian population and maybe the social infrastructure with it.'

'Christ. That is serious.'

Wilson, sitting beside Keith, added: 'As well as agents in the government and civil service, they clearly have friends within the military, who will be able to see a lot of the logistical side through, and who obviously helped them to acquire the secret use of Henford base. There they have been looking at the varying degrees of exposure affecting bodies, in preparation for the big day.'

'Shit! I was all over those bodies! Am I all right?'

'Yes. That's why you had the reception committee waiting for you when you arrived at the station this morning. But you're fine.'

'You knew I was coming?'

'It was a fairly good guess, Keith. You'd finally chanced upon something at Henford that was going to be big news for someone.

We'd seen you enter the place, we guessed you'd find the bodies, after hacking into Carter's computer.'

'How do you know I'd got into his computer?'

'Barry from Security.'

'Barry! From Security. Of course…'

'Once we realised you had followed through your suspicions, we tracked you to Henford, knowing you must have made a crucial link with what you'd seen on his PC. We had an inkling that they were doing something with bodies somewhere, and presumed you'd find something out, then come and tell us.'

'And if they'd have caught me? They came after me, you know?'

'We'd have taken them in there and then. Don't worry, we weren't going to expose you to any more danger.'

'Thanks. That was kind of you. But hang on – why didn't you just arrest them then, anyway? You had your chance.'

'Well, Carter was not one of the men who came after you. He is bound to be on the run now, and we do want to catch up with him. And… we wanted to keep you clean from any contamination with us, if you see what I mean.'

'No. I don't.'

Samantha butted in: 'If they still think you did not come to find us, then they might be happy to deal with you still.'

'You want me to go back to them? Into their arms? To catch Carter?'

'Carter, and the ringleaders with him. We still need you, Keith.'

'You must be joking.'

'We aren't.'

'Surely they know I came straight to the police?'

'No. They only know that you stole your neighbour's car.'

'And,' added Samantha, 'that car has now been left on a roadside and burnt out, as if you have abandoned it.'

'You've burnt out my neighbour's car?'

'I'm afraid so. We had no other option. There was a risk of infection, too.'

'Oh my god!' Keith again felt a pang of dreadful guilt.

'So now, as far as they are concerned, you are on the run. And you probably have decided not to come to the police. They know you think you won't be believed. That is why we made sure it seemed fruitless the first time you came to us. What better reason not to risk returning to the only people you thought you could trust? In their eyes you have gone to ground, all on your own.'

'Bloody hell, you've played me good and proper,' muttered Keith.

'I'm afraid both sides have. Sorry, Keith,' admitted Morell, smiling.

'But why did they bring me in on all this? I mean, I don't have anything to do with chemical attacks or terrorism.'

'You were a perfect fall guy. You were for us, too. For them, though, once they realised you'd accidentally stumbled on inconsistencies with the invented records of a dead Nigerian, at first they tried to shake you off the trail. Then, when they saw how susceptible you were to conspiracies and plots, they decided you'd be perfect for doing their dirty work for them.'

'So the Caligula Club… Was that all just for me? A way to make me do what they wanted?'

'We think it was. They've done it to others, too, we believe.'

'But… Oh god, they wanted me to kill someone.'

'We know. As soon as you mentioned that to us, the first time you came to the police station, we knew you were onto something. From that point we were keeping a really close eye on it all. The more we saw, the more we realised they'd found a brilliant way to convince you of a different reality altogether.'

'Like Malcolm coming down into the room and talking to me.'

'Malcolm?' asked Knowles.

'The man in the mask. His face is covered with a bandage of some sort. He is the one who seemed to be living in my attic.'

Knowles nodded. 'Ah. Malcolm, is it? His real name is Nicholas Tyte, and he is someone we'd really like to get our hands on. He is one of the developers of the nerve agent they want to use. During the course of earlier experiments he was contaminated in his own lab, and so his face is pretty disfigured. Maybe he prefers to hide it by wearing a mask, though – perhaps he thinks it's more dramatic.'

'Well it works,' sighed Keith. 'Really freaky to see. Not what you want to find waiting for you in your attic.'

'He's a nasty piece of work.'

'He must have been up in my attic for ages?'

Yes and no. They'd set it up nicely by occupying number forty. We've been watching them for months. They went up through the shared attic space from there.'

'Oh god, of course! Number forty was all barred up and closed off. We'd thought they were renovating it. So that was where they were operating out of. Now I see.' Keith was beginning to feel a massive weight falling almost physically away from him.

Erwin leaned forward and spoke again. 'Listen. Let's put our cards on the table, Keith. You need to understand how serious this is, and why you are still involved.'

'Go on.' Keith returned with a jolt to his present circumstances.

'We have uncovered a plot to use chemicals or nerve agents or something across several theatres, and it is imminent. Very imminent. The ringleaders have no idea we're onto them, and they might still believe you're willing to work with them.'

'I see where you're going with this. I'm not sure I like it.'

'I hardly see you have much choice, do you?'

'But they'll be suspicious that I got into their body farm and then ran away from them.'

But less suspicious if you tell them you've started to understand what they're really doing, and that you're willing to join their cause. What have you got to lose? You're holding some good cards now, and they don't even need to keep up the pretence of the Caligula Club. You can tell them you know them for what they are now, you agree with their principles and you want to help them. You're still an attractive proposition for them.'

'It's a risk.'

'It's a bigger risk to hope they don't carry out their plan.'

Keith shuddered.

'I still have some questions. Who was pushed off the bridge? I am sure I saw his body at the Henford base. After all, if it hadn't been for seeing him, I would never have even got involved in the first place – I wouldn't be sitting here now, would I?'

'We're not sure who he was,' admitted Wilson. 'Obviously someone they didn't want recognised. Hence Carter fished out a useful, but inconsequential identity from a mass of identities going back years. A Nigerian terrorist who'd long since gone back home and as good as disappeared. Then somehow they tied up their witnesses' statements to match the story.'

'But not Leslie Trent's.'

'Not Leslie Trent's, no.'

Keith sat back in his chair. 'Well, I can't believe all this. It's still just too much.'

'We understand. And we know you must still be very much in shock. But it's absolutely crucial that you know you can trust us, and that we are on your side, Keith,' said Erwin, earnestly.

'I do. It's fine. It's beginning to explain things. Thank-you. And thanks for rescuing me.'

'Our pleasure,' beamed Samantha.

'Just one thing,' he replied to her smile. 'You knew of the Caligula Club when you texted me that riddle, along with the chicken crossing the road. So the name was already known to you?'

'Kind of,' she admitted. 'We had the name already in our sights, in a manner of speaking, and I wanted to know if it would ring any bells for you. Same with Henford. We hoped to work out if you'd come across anything at all in your own field.'

'Actually,' interjected Morell. 'you see, *Caligula* was one of the codewords they'd been using for their group, which kept coming up in our intel. So, of course, we knew we were on the right track once you also started using it as your signature tag, as it were.'

Keith looked down, suddenly ashamed. 'Maybe it's my turn to apologise now.'

'We'll be turning a blind eye to all that, given the unusual circumstances,' retorted Erwin with a knowing glance at Knowles. Keith spotted this, but pretended he hadn't noticed.

CHAPTER THIRTY

'Come with us.' Erwin and the others all stood up and, uncertain, Keith followed them towards a door that led into the back room. As they entered, he caught Samantha by the hand, and whispered:

'God, it's good to see you're OK. How are you?'

She smiled warmly back at him. 'Fine. Absolutely fine. I'm so happy to see you again, too.' She gave his hand a couple of tight grips, then turned fully towards him and they hugged. The warmth of the moment enveloped them both.

Keith now looked around and found himself in a large and cluttered room. Heavy curtains were pulled tight across the wide window which must have looked out onto a small suburban garden. The middle-class, little canopied lights all around the walls were on, but in the centre a large table had been set up with four computers whirring quietly away on each side. At one of them was a young, uniformed officer who stood up and greeted Erwin, as he entered, with a *sir*. Then he glanced at everyone else, and said:

'Good morning, everyone.'

'Morning, Harris. Sit down. How's it going?'

'Good, sir. We're starting to get quite a lot of info coming through now.'

'Keith, this is Sergeant Daniel Harris. He's manning the IT at this end of the operation.'

Harris nodded towards Keith. 'Morning, sir.' Keith returned his nod, taken aback at the scale of the operation, the glowing screens, the files of paper all over the table, the phones and webcams set up around the room. On the far wall a large screen was set up. This was a hive of activity, a mini-NASA hidden out here in bleakest Suburbia.

Morell cleared away some of the files and pulled a chair up to the table for Keith: 'Sit down. We need to know what it was they've asked you to do. What can you give us?'

Keith racked his brains. 'Malcolm said that now I'd tinkered around with the petty stuff I'd wanted to deal with, they now had a bigger job for me to do. He was reluctant to tell me at first, but when I guessed it was to kill somebody…'

'Who was that somebody? Did he give you any idea?'

'No. He just said it was someone big. Someone famous.'

'Famous? As in a celebrity? Or someone big, a politician?'

'No idea. Sorry. Nothing more was said.'

They were interrupted by Harris, who was staring intently at the screen nearby. 'Here come the first documents from Carter Henry's computer. They've managed to break into the ones on Mr. Hartman and they're sending them over now.'

'You won't be surprised to learn,' explained Erwin, 'that Carter Henry did not turn up to work this morning. We have had our lads working on his computer, using all sorts of cunning methods to hack into all his various *Henford* files. We're getting some of the contents coming in now. Look…'

They all immediately gathered round the large screen fixed to the wall. On it was now appearing a number of files and all manner of data.

'Here's one called *Keith H.* Let's find out what Mr. Hartman was intended for.'

'Good idea,' muttered Morell. 'Let's see… A whole CV here, Keith – all your life and contacts and friends…'

Keith was staggered; they had gathered so much information on him. It was all there on the screen, documented with chilling accuracy. Loves, likes, dislikes, hates… Important connections with friends, his family details, addresses, facebook habits, computer habits, clothes, typical purchases, financial details… on and on it went, all the dates and times logged and commented on down the right-hand side.

'Here, this is interesting,' said Samantha, spotting something in the margin: '*Useful for Operation INC. Use Mark Lane – has good links with Westm. and BBC.*'

'Westminster, presumably,' suggested Haynes from behind. 'Who is Mark Lane?'

'Mean anything to you, Keith?' asked Morell.

'No. Never heard of him.'

Morell turned to Wilson. 'Do a check on who Mark Lane is. Maybe someone connected with a government official. Get in touch with the BBC too.'

Keith gasped. 'So I was going to be persuaded to assassinate someone in the government? That's crazy… An assassination?'

'Possibly. The assassination of a top politician, maybe several, maybe right the way up to the top – the Prime Minister even.'

Keith did not respond. The full impact of what he had become involved with was beginning to hit home at last.

Morell continued scanning the file on Keith, speaking as he did so: 'Looks from this here like you'd be used to sow chaos and confusion just as they were implementing their plan for mass killings. Look… The country would be paralysed, the whole system would be decapitated and convulsed with inaction, while they imposed some kind of martial law in the name of stability and civil order. Nobody would have been looking for *you*, of course; you're a lowly civil servant, completely under everyone's radar. All they had to do was convince you that you were doing something as part of your own crusade, fulfilling your own potential, as it were. So they encouraged you with stuff you wanted to do, like speed cameras and the like, until you'd convinced yourself that whatever they asked you to do was for your own good as well as the greater good.'

'We think they were helped by Karen, I'm afraid,' added Samantha.

'Ah, god, yes! Karen!' exclaimed Keith. 'What on earth was all that about? Is she alive or not? And who the hell was she, if she wasn't actually my girlfriend all along?'

'I can see you're confused,' admitted Morell. 'Well, she certainly wasn't on your side, I can assure you that. We've analysed some of the glasses and cups we found in your house, and a lot of the ones you used showed traces of ketamine and GBL. Do you remember her pouring drinks for you, without you seeing her doing it?'

'Yes, all the time. But…'

'Well, she was almost certainly spiking these drinks with the drugs I just mentioned. They would have knocked you out and caused hallucinations, making you accept all the things you were being exposed to.'

Keith was both angered and saddened at the thought: 'How could she have done that to me? How come she was so involved against me? I even thought she liked me,' he ventured.

'Sorry,' said Samantha sympathetically. 'She was not at all as she seemed. What with her working on you downstairs with drugs, and them haunting you from the attic, you were very easy to manipulate and convince.'

'And to think, it was you who introduced me to her.'

Samantha looked shamefaced: 'Sorry.'

'But why? Did you know then she was…?'

'Yes and no. She was someone I knew through friends. To be honest, she was always... well, a bit weird and full of fairly extreme opinions. I was never that close to her. I think a few of us brought her along to one of those parties in Streatham. But then, as she strayed more and more into activism, she remained in our sights. I never felt I could warn you, though – what business was it of mine?'

'But it was you who got in touch with us, or with her, recently.'

'Yes, you're right. And that wasn't altogether for social reasons, if I'm to be honest.'

'Where is she now?'

'Actually, we're not entirely sure,' answered Samantha. 'She's fallen off our radar, I'm afraid. But we're not sure just how heavily involved she was, or whether she knew the big players. I'm afraid she's not anyone you'd really like to be associated with, Keith. She was in our sights a few years back as an activist and member of an anarchist group…'

'Anarchist group? Karen?'

'Maybe she'd put some of that behind her, but we think the Caligula Club got to her once they realised she was living with you. A perfect opportunity for them, and another reason to hook you into their plans.'

'Which is where you come in, Keith,' Erwin took over: 'We're going to hook you into *our* plans now.'

'God, that sounds good,' retorted Keith, exhausted.

Samantha put a hand on his arm. 'You mustn't worry. We're going to make sure this works. I promise.'

'Fine. Fine, honestly,' said Keith, straightening up and turning round to face the others with a smile that almost didn't feel forced. 'Come on, then. What's to be done? What's the plan, boss?'

'To find out what their actual intentions are, and to stop them in their tracks. To catch those responsible and bring them to justice. And we begin by finding Carter.'

'He's the key to locating the rest,' added Wilson. 'We need you to get in touch with Carter, and then we'll have more of a handle on where they're all working and what exactly they're doing.'

'Go on,' persisted Keith, doubt rising perceptibly in his voice, 'you've obviously worked it all out…'

'We have. And we're going to start with a funeral.'

'*My* funeral,' interjected Samantha.

'What?' exclaimed Keith. 'Oh god, that's a bit weird, isn't it? Why?'

'I'm supposed to be dead, aren't I? You believed my death was part of a wider conspiracy – well, it was. But this is *our* conspiracy, not theirs. They still believe I died.'

'And that's a good thing?' asked Keith.

'Of course,' beamed Erwin. 'It's an ace in our hands, if you think about it. They'll not be looking for Sam at all. We can use the opportunity of a funeral – if there is ample evidence of it, and they can see that an actual funeral and committal has taken place, then we've got a whole extra operative who can work under their radar.'

'How clever. And when exactly am I to attend this macabre event? And where?'

'We've got it all planned…'

'I'm sure you have.'

'It's going to take place in an out-of-the-way little church in the West Country, where some of Sam's relatives on her mother's side apparently hailed from.'

'Apparently?'

'Yes, all part of the cover. In fact, the congregation will be filled with members of the local constabulary whose faces won't be known at all to anyone watching. We've booked out a slot in a remote village in Gloucestershire. And a slot in the local crem, to take the coffin away to.'

'You really have thought it all out, haven't you…'

'We have.' Erwin leaned forwards, and lowering his tone, he almost whispered, 'Keith, I need hardly remind you again of how seriously we are taking this threat. Our futures are at stake, and the future of the whole nation. Something very big is going down. I hope you're fully on board? I hope we can rely on you? You do understand, don't you?'

'I do,' affirmed Keith. 'But really, how is a mock funeral going to help in all this?'

Morell took over: 'We are pretty certain it'll lure one of them out to see if you turn up. They know you were fond of Sam, they'll want to know if they can still contact you, check on whether they can still use you – or need to get rid of you…'

Keith shivered. 'Really?'

'Of course. And that's why you'll need to play an extremely careful game. You see, you'll need to appear angered by what they've put you through, of course. But if they're going to take you back to finish the tasks they've obviously got in mind for you, you're going to have to persuade them you're still in.'

'And somehow,' added Erwin, 'get them to tell you more about their plans. After all, if they do want to use you to take out a big cheese, they'll have to reveal quite a bit. You're going to find that out. And bring it back to us.'

Keith nodded, but said nothing. The clarity in his mind echoed like a solemn knell. He knew they were right. And he felt there really was no way out of this. After all, perhaps he *was* now the key to the whole mess. Perhaps there was finally a destiny awaiting him, bigger and much scarier than the supposed destiny he'd sensed when he was Caligula Keith. This was altogether more serious. He'd have to man up. This was indeed, as they say, *it*.

Samantha's voice cut through his thoughts.

'We'll need to make it look as though you've been living fairly rough for a few days, by the time the funeral takes place. We have to have a completely watertight and believable backstory for you to take with you.'

Morell continued in the same vein: 'Some clothes you might have picked up cheaply from a charity shop. You took enough money with you when you escaped from your house, and you've been surviving and keeping your head down, wondering what to do, and whether to get back in touch with them. The funeral you had already heard about, and you decided you'd wanted to get out to attend that, before making up your mind… This was your chance to get your head clear once and for all.'

'So I abandoned my neighbour's car. I set fire to it, presumably because… Well why *did* I do that, exactly?'

'Were you determined to leave no trace of where you'd gone?' suggested Wilson.

'Or were you hoping to confuse them? Make them think you'd died?' asked Samantha.

'No,' answered Keith, 'they'd look for the body. And they know a thing or two about how bodies decompose, don't they.'

Erwin said: 'You were in no frame of mind to think logically. You simply wanted to get away from it all, you needed to efface the memory of what you'd found at the body farm – in short, you wanted to get everyone off your tracks, including the police, since you don't trust them at all, either. You took it off to a remote lane which you knew well from your walks with Karen, set it alight, and headed off in the early morning across tracks and fields in the hope that you would shake them off for long enough to gather your thoughts.' He turned towards the woman police officer who had taken the car away: 'Susie, where did you take the car to?'

'Patch Farm Lane,' answered Susie, 'just the other side of the industrial estate.'

'Good. Very remote. Nice one.'

Keith looked puzzled. 'Did I actually sleep rough? Or did I hole myself up in a little B&B somewhere? I'd brought enough money and my passport with me.'

'Good idea. A little B&B in Gerrards Cross, let's say. And you've been trying to avoid getting cash out of the wall, in case you can be traced somehow; after all, you're very paranoid at this stage. You don't know who you can trust.'

'How do you know they'll come out to find me in deepest Gloucestershire?'

Knowles leaned in: 'We'll get you to Gerrards Cross, and you can use your card a few times – a jacket for the funeral, the train ticket, a taxi booked from the station to the village, stuff like that. They'll be looking for this kind of thing, and they're not daft, this lot. They've got the gizmos for it all, you'll light up like a beacon, believe me!'

'And we'll put out a fair bit of online chatter, too, about the funeral, and link it with the local station's name,' said Morell. 'It's going to be Kemble where you arrive, and the church itself is at Wyncombe Parva.'

Erwin joined in: 'It's planned for this Friday. Today's Tuesday. By the time you arrive in Gloucestershire they'll be all over you, I guarantee it.'

'You know,' suddenly ventured Keith, turning to Samantha, 'I am finding it really hard seeing you again, alive like this. And now to be talking about your funeral… It just feels like I haven't been able to rely on anything definite at all for ages. I actually don't want to risk losing any of this now I've finally found you again. And now that another, new reality has been opened up to me.'

'I know,' smiled Samantha, reassuringly. 'It's been tough for me, too. If I'm honest, I didn't really want to go through with it – I did wonder if it was the right thing to do at the time. But I knew we had to do it in the end, and I can see now how right we were to make them believe I was dead.'

'You think so?'

'I do. It was a powerful way to convince you that something was going on. And, painful though it was, you might never have wanted to believe in a plot if it hadn't affected you deep down.'

'This is not what I want to hear. Not right now.'

'I know it's not.'

'Never mind. Let's get on with planning your funeral.'

Chapter Thirty-One

The small church sat among guardian yew trees behind its high, Cotswold wall of lichen-covered stone, set slightly back from the road that ran through this tiny village. A lych-gate led the eyes up past neat, gently leaning gravestones towards the shadows hanging heavy over the entrance. Here among these recesses of ancient stone stood a number of figures: a vicar in robes, the earnest family patriarch, a stooping mother seemingly unable to stifle her sobs. They welcomed Keith as he approached. The father took his hand, muttered something inaudible, and motioned for him to enter.

Keith marvelled at the tableau set up in front of him. It was impressively authentic.

The interior was a scene of perfect Anglican sobriety. Wide gothic arches spanned the aisles, supporting the oak beams of the roof. Just above the heads of the congregation, carved stone memorials attached to the whitewashed walls, immortalised in bad, clerical Latin the worthy lives of local notables and dignitaries. Modern, brightly coloured banners hung down from some of the pillars, spiritual remnants of the recent trendiness associated with the Church of England, and now inexplicably integrated and accepted into the fabric of every church.

Keith took his place near the back of the nave.

Ahead, in front of the altar, stood the coffin already on its stand, covered in lilies and bearing a wreath of faintly gaudy flowers.

Keith glanced around to see if there was any hint of someone watching him, anybody who looked as if they didn't belong at this sombre event. He was to be disappointed; every face appeared lined and dented with genuine grief. This was a good show, it really was.

The service started. Wise words were uttered, prayers were poured into the air which hung thick with sadness; opinions and memories were pronounced with wistful solemnity. Keith actually felt tears at one point well up in his eyes, in spite of the emptiness of everything around him, the empty hymns, the sermon, the memories. The coffin, of course.

Eventually, this was raised onto the broad shoulders of brothers and uncles, and carried past him out towards the doorway. He loyally let a grief-stricken gaze linger in its direction, then allowed others to process slowly towards the daylight streaming into the church. Finally he stood up himself and made to leave.

He stepped towards the porch. Outside, a chill had settled on the air and it had become overcast. Around him, faces reflected the inherent sadness of high summer. As he left the church, Keith turned round to glance back inside; there had been nothing here but a beautifully staged funeral, the mourners in place, the grief almost tangible.

'Goodbye, and thank-you so much for coming,' he heard someone say nearby.

'Thank-you. Lovely service.'

'God, we'll miss her.'

'So sad. So young.'

Keith let his gaze wander round the leafy, nature-filled graveyard. The brilliance of the foliage in every corner of his vision, the hopping blackbirds, the furtive squirrels. Bright, carefree flowers wafted and bobbed among the dead.

Suddenly, Keith noticed a face among the trees. A woman in black, away from the rest of the congregation. He peered into the shadows and saw her move away at his glance.

It was not curiosity that made him utter his platitudes to the vicar and the others nearby; it was the certain knowledge that someone had at last made contact. He wandered as nonchalantly as he could away from the path and towards the edge of the graveyard.

Behind the trees where he had seen the face, a little track led to a kissing gate, and beyond that a weathered, public-footpath signpost pointed out to a small, open field. Keith pushed the gate, which squeaked on its hinges, and found himself following a woman, disappearing through the other end of the field, where a low, stone stile led over into a short slope to open land. Keith pursued her intently.

A light breeze had turned into a gusty wind, and as he passed out onto the wilder, more open heathland beyond, Keith saw that the woman had slowed down, turned around to face him, and was letting him get to within shouting distance.

He approached. She lifted her hair and looked directly at him.

It was Karen.

Keith stood stock-still, his feet rooted to the wild, tussocky ground.

'You!' is all he could cry out.

'Yes. Me.'

'You've got a nerve. Why have you shown up here?'

'Why not? She was my friend too.'

'How dare you?'

'What? Impinge on your grief? The grief of a lover?'

'You shit! Why did you do what you did?'

'Shut up, Keith. You deserved it.'

'How?' Keith was not in control of his feelings, and felt he had too many strands to hold onto. He was a rag-doll with puppeteer strings to his left, other strings to his right. Which role was he supposed to play now? Her presence here confounded him. She was making him feel nauseous.

He stepped towards her. Her features shone quite clearly out at him, her so-familiar face, the face he had had beside his own so often on his shoulder, in their bed, on his pillow…

'What the hell are you playing at? Where have you been?'

She looked away. He went on: 'What do you think you're going to achieve? Are you in league with them, then?'

'I am someone with principles, unlike you.'

'But what principles? Do you think you'll change anything?'

'Yes, I do!' she suddenly shouted, fiery and angry. 'Don't you want things to change? I know I do!'

The wind blew around them both standing on the high ridge. He watched her hair swirling.

'Did I mean so little to you?' shouted Keith.

'There was nothing there, was there… Not at the end. God, it was awful.'

'But I did love you.'

She turned away. 'Sorry,' she said, barely audibly.

'Why are you here, anyway?' asked Keith.

'To check you out.'

'To see if I still want to do your dirty work? I take it you're working with the Caligula Club?'

'Kind of.'

'Why check me out, then? What are you hoping to see?'

'Do you want to work with us?' Karen stepped towards him. 'You know you have the perfect cover. You've played your part brilliantly.'

'This is ridiculous,' sighed Keith. 'Is that how you found me here? Did you use your shadowy friends in the secret organisation?'

'We found out where you were staying. So we decided to get in touch with you.'

'Why? To carry out a murder? You are mad. I've had the first few good nights' sleep in ages, my head feels clear. And I reckon I know why, too. Thanks for all the drinks, Karen, thanks a bunch! I've no job, I've nowhere to go back to. I don't know who to turn to. And you want me to throw my lot in with you? What do you take me for? Do you think I'm mad?'

'Carter sent me.'

'Carter?' Keith's expression darkened. 'What did he say?'

'Meet him, at least.'

'Meet him? Where? I take it he's currently out of office, is he?'

'Meet him in London. I have an address and a time.'

'Oh my god, you're all so fucking cloak-and-dagger! What *is* your game?'

'Here.' Karen handed him a piece of paper. Keith took it and unfolded it. He read the address on it and the date. It was for a few days' time. A hotel bar in London, near the Tower.

'And he'll say what? "Join us, old fellow. Be a part of our great, reforming project!" Or does he want me out of the way? Are you leading me into a trap?'

'For god's sake, Keith, just go, will you? You've done all the hard work now, they know you're trustworthy. Go and see what he has to say.'

'When did you change?'

'I didn't. I always wanted to do what I'm doing now. And you've enabled me to do that. If you want the same, deep-down, you'll be able to see that I've enabled you, too.'

'And what is it, exactly, that you want?'

'A change of system. A fresh start for everyone. A better, fairer world.'

Keith raised his head back and laughed. 'Well good for you. You're mad, you know?'

'Not as mad as the millions who just keep on going, with their heads down, never asking if things could be different, better…'

'Do you actually realise what you're doing? If you break things up, they never get put back together again.'

'That's right! And what's wrong with that? We don't want things to go back to how they are now. It's got to be a clean break. A total break with the past. The system is fucked. This country is rotten, completely rotten. Don't you see?'

'I see you talking as if you're in control… You have the madness of all anarchists!'

He turned to go.

Karen shouted after him through the wind. 'Will you go to London? Will you meet with Carter?'

'Maybe,' he answered as he disappeared into the lower field. 'See you.'

Keith wondered if he would actually ever see her again. She had switched within the space of a few weeks from a lover in a stable world to an anarchist obsessed with an unstable world. Via a faked death.

He wondered if he could trust anything ever again.

CHAPTER THIRTY-TWO

Out in the middle of the tussocky field, half-hidden in the dip of an old ditch or furrow, the device was positioned and whirring almost inaudibly. Surrounded by brambles and long grass, a passer-by would not guess it was even there, set back away from the public footpath that ran along one side of the field's boundary. Beyond it, in a further dip, lay another, similar machine, matt black and glinting occasionally with a small, orange light. Three small funnels ran along the top of both machines, pointing upwards like pre-industrial cannon.

The field was not a site of outstanding natural beauty. There was nothing nearby which counted as dramatic or breath-taking. There was no scenery bright with expectation for ramblers or hikers. One thing alone made this route across the Sussex countryside worth exploring both for enthusiasts and non-enthusiasts alike.

Just on the other side of the boundary hedge glinted long lines of lights disappearing away into the distance. The summer's heat reflecting off the tarmac and piling layer upon layer of hot air in the way of one's sight made the whole runway shimmer with an unreal dreaminess.

Standing here, the passer-by needed to wait only minutes before the next metal leviathan started roaring towards them, its jet engines adding to the waves of hot, distorted air, before taking to the skies and flying directly over them.

As they pass, leaving Gatwick for distant climes, they look so near, it's almost if one need only raise a hand to touch them.

Chapter Thirty-Three

Given the seriousness of his mission, Keith had decided to take a taxi onwards from Marylebone – this would give him time to gather his thoughts, prepare his words, perfect his role. But he was having second thoughts. He had climbed into a black cab, and now sat checking his phone-map for the state of the traffic, confronted by a screen criss-crossed with bright, red lines. Perhaps the Underground might have been better.

Roadworks everywhere.

Roadworks clogging up all the main arteries into and out of the capital, roadworks seeping like an infection into the side streets. Keith stared balefully out onto a city increasingly in the grip of the hi-vis brigade. It was still early in the day. Where do they all come from? What the hell are they all doing?

'Bad traffic this morning...' he ventured, as his taxi came to another standstill.

'Bloody dreadful, ain't it, mate. Absolute gridlock...' His driver seemed immediately cheered by being given the chance of a good moan. 'Seems to get worse, don't it? I dunno, they're every-bloody-where today!'

They were. Slowly Keith edged through the centre of London towards his destination in the City. There was much more traffic than normal, he thought. In fact, this was crazy.

He checked his phone. A notification had popped up from the newsfeed.

Both Gatwick and Heathrow now closed due to interference of runways and flightpaths, believed to be deliberate disruption of flights into and out of UK.

Another one popped up.

Massive surge in traffic jams in major cities across UK. Expect delays of up to several hours.

What was going on? This wouldn't do, thought Keith. They were not too far away now, so he thanked his driver, paid and climbed out onto the pavement. He knew this area fairly well – he'd make the rest of it on foot. Past cars and vans, buses and lorries idling in the motionless queues he raced on towards the Tower of London. Just at the first glimpse of its ancient walls and towers, with the grand, mediaeval elegance of All Hallows church opposite, Keith found the hotel and entered.

It was a light, airy, first-floor room he found himself in, with a high, classically patterned ceiling and elegant chandeliers. The quiet buzz of the affluent at ease, of backroom business being done, hummed in the air about the waiters as they wended their way between the cloth-draped tables and velour chairs.

Keith saw Carter sitting at a window table as soon as he entered, and noticed him almost immediately raising his gaze to meet his own. A waiter glided over to Keith, who brushed him aside with the words: 'Thank-you. I have a meeting with the gentleman over there.' The waiter backed away and Keith strode across towards Carter's slightly hunched figure. He pulled the high-backed chair out from under the table, and settled himself down into it, all the time with his eyes fixed on the man he'd spent most of his weekdays with, hour after thankless hour at the same office desk.

'Keith.' Carter's voice was calm, betraying nothing.

Keith decided he needed to play the same, hard game. He echoed the greeting: 'Carter.'

The waiter arrived, lingered.

Carter looked over at Keith. 'What'll you have?'

Keith turned to the waiter. 'A soda and lime, please. With ice.' The waiter placed a menu in front of him, and turned to fetch the drink.

'So,' began Carter. 'Here we are…'

Keith did not reply.

'After all this time, we meet at last in full possession of the truth.'

This rattled Keith: 'Not quite, though, Carter. I mean, I don't know half, really, do I?'

'Well, you know a lot more than you did.'

'I know I've been played like a fool.'

'It's true you've been treated badly, but really, Keith, how else could we have done it?'

'I know about the body farm.'

'We know you know. How else do you think we realised you were onto us?'

'Come on, then…' Keith warmed to his theme, and felt the confidence in himself growing. 'Why have you got a body farm? What's it all about, Carter? What more do I need to know?'

'Where have you been, Keith?' Carter's voice remained calm, but Keith could detect a hint of menace and frustration in it. 'We've been wondering what happened to you these past few days…'

'It doesn't matter where I've been. Away from your prying eyes, that's all that matters to me.'

'It is very hard indeed to disappear from our radar, Keith – let's just say that, shall we? But you seem to have managed it for quite a few days now. Been having some help, have you?'

'What do you think?'

'I think you might be playing with fire, my old friend, if you think you're going to pull any wool over our eyes.'

Keith stayed tight-lipped.

'So why don't you just tell me where you've been hiding out, Keith.' Carter paused. 'I take it you wouldn't be so stupid as to come here with a wire on you?'

'Again, what do you think? But you're more than welcome to check me out if you wish.' Keith made to open the collar of his T-shirt.

'That won't be necessary.'

'I disappeared. I hunkered down away from home for a few days. I needed to get my head clear.'

'I'm sure you did.'

'Well, I can't tell you how much better I now feel. Want to know why?'

'I think I can guess.'

'How exactly did you get Karen to drug me?'

'You're quite the regular drinker, Keith. We made sure your lovely and cooperative other-half was supplied with the right potions, as it were, to drop into your various tipples. Or to spike the bottles before returning them with their caps back on into the fridge'

'You are bastards.'

'We are! I shall take that as a compliment. Thank-you.'

'And now you have me here.'

'I do.'

'So what are you planning?'

'I'm sure you can hear it unfolding right now, outside.'

Keith listened. From the street below was coming an endless honking of car horns, shouts and occasional crunches as some drivers were evidently trying to scrape past stationary vehicles into side streets to escape the gridlock.

'It's beginning right beneath our noses. The revolution has started.'

A glint in Carter's eyes betrayed an excitement at long-planned events unfolding at last. Keith's phone buzzed as another newsflash popped up. He looked at it.

All major UK airports closed until further notice as government declares major terrorist incident.

'What the hell is happening out there?' asked Keith, now suddenly aware of the momentous timing of this meeting with Carter. 'You planned it deliberately to have me come here at this time, didn't you?'

'Oh, come on, Keith! Everything over the last few months has been meticulously planned. Hadn't you noticed?'

Keith looked around at the others in the room. Some were getting up and going over to the windows, peering down at the growing chaos on the streets. Others were reading the latest headlines on their phones, trying to digest what was going on. Keith was beginning to realise that events really were running out of control for him – he was in very deep.

Here in this elegant room, though, everything was strangely calm. Surreal and disturbing. Outside there was incipient chaos forming on the streets – in here, nothing. The drinks would be brought over as if nothing was wrong.

Keith decided it would be best now for him to find out as much as possible about what was happening.

'Are you responsible for all that outside?' he asked outright, 'And the airports?'

'You have it in one. We have placed a number of military-grade devices in the approach paths of all the major airports, to fire flares intermittently, and that alone is causing chaos for people travelling. We saw a few years ago how just a drone or two could bring Gatwick to a standstill… The motorways are also becoming completely jammed up even as we speak, thanks to the strategic placing of roadworks and road-closures.'

'All this planned chaos, and just the plucky little Caligula Club behind it all? That sounds unlikely.'

'We have hundreds working with us. Hundreds and hundreds, believe me. It's much bigger than the plucky little Caligula Club, as you so disdainfully put it.'

'So I wasn't imagining it when I felt there were so many barricades and men in hi-vis – all these roadworks everywhere…'

'All part of our plan.'

'But flares near an airport? Surely you'd be spotted…'

'There are public footpaths all around them, you'd be surprised. They are patrolled, but very unevenly and poorly. It's easy to hide a device in a thicket – and difficult to spot where a flare's come from, once it's in the air.'

'When she found me at Wyncombe, Karen talked about bringing the government down.'

'Absolutely. That is fully our intention.'

'Why?'

'Why not? The country is in a truly parlous state, nobody knows what they're doing, we have been drifting along like a third-rate, third-world, petty fiefdom, in hock to Europe mainly. But there are people in power who want to do something about it, want to achieve so much more. We're taking back control.'

'Sounds familiar. And how are you going to achieve that exactly? And why drag me into it?'

Carter chuckled. 'You've dragged yourself into this, not the other way round. There's no way back now, I'm afraid. Either you commit yourself to seeing this through, or we end it here, now. There's just too much at stake, you see. And too many people involved now. It all depends on whether I think I can still trust you.'

'You are joking? After all I've been through?'

'Go on.'

The waiter suddenly arrived and put down Keith's drink: 'Are we ready to order, sir?'

Carter leaned forward, putting down his menu. 'Actually,' he replied with a winning smile. 'We'll not be eating right now, I think. Is that all right with you, Keith?'

Keith was caught off-guard. 'Er, fine by me.' The waiter disappeared again.

'So who do you think I'm going to turn to, then?' hissed Keith, leaning forward now. 'Do you really think anyone will believe me about this whole sorry pantomime? They didn't believe me before. Why should they believe me now? Anyway, who would I turn to? You've probably got people everywhere, haven't you...'

Carter paused. Then: 'I suppose you know how serious this is? This isn't just some crackpot idea cooked up on the back of an envelope.'

Keith nodded. 'I've lost everything. I have nothing else to lose. I am in, I tell you. I just wish you hadn't put me through all that. It was terrifying and I am still bloody furious.'

'I know. I can imagine. Fair enough.'

Keith tightened his lips and clenched his teeth. Then he said: 'I have some questions, though.'

'Go ahead. Can't promise I'll answer all of them.'

Keith paused. He had a lot of things on his mind. But maybe he should start with some of the finer details; that way, he might manage to piece together some of the bigger picture himself.

'The dead Nigerian, the one who triggered this whole thing off. Where did he fit in?'

'Oh, that's easy,' smirked Carter. 'A useful identity, long since finished with, since his return to Nigeria. There was no black man at the scene of the accident, you were right.'

'But the witnesses, the two doctors, Hawes and Smythe? Were their statements faked?'

'Absolutely faked.'

'Oh my god, they weren't even at the scene, were they? They knew each other, didn't they? They were colleagues, so… Bloody hell, they raced out to the scene and posed as witnesses, is that what happened?'

'They were at the scene already, actually. Just needed to run down the banks to the motorway, and there they were on the carriageway amid the wreckage, shocked, dazed, dishevelled and unable to easily identify their vehicles in the crash at first, made their very believable statements from their very believable, blood-smeared mouths and ripped shirtsleeves, before disappearing back into the undergrowth and away from the mêlée…'

'Who were they?'

'Two of the scientists we have working on our little project. At the time, they were chasing a third scientist of ours to bring him back into the fold.'

'The man in the white shirt? On the bridge?'

'Yes. Richard Selwyn. He was threatening to go public with our work, and had decided to make a run for it. Unfortunately he fell off the bridge. Or threw himself off.'

'He was pushed.'

'No he wasn't, actually. You made that up yourself. We found out later that he had been infected with a certain amount of the stuff he was working on, and so he may have chosen to kill himself.'

'Which is why you took his body straight back to the body farm? You didn't want anyone finding that stuff in his system?'

'Correct. His reactions to the substance could be monitored along with all the others we had there.'

'Who are they, all those bodies rotting away for your experiments?'

'Losers. The homeless, the missing, the unwanted.'

'Where do you get them from?'

'Anywhere there are people in dire straits. Britain's an ugly country now, let me tell you. There are plenty who drop out of the system completely. All you need to do is know where to look.'

'Are they contagious? I crawled around amongst them that night.'

'No. You're fine. It's contagious when airborne and agitated. But once inside us, there's not any danger, it seems. But you shouldn't have gone back. we tried to scare you off with the Google-patch over Henford – it didn't work.'

'The witness, Leslie Trent, though – she was real?'

'Yes, which would have been fine, if you hadn't decided to go and speak to her.'

'Mind you,' mused Keith, 'the unluckiest part of it all was having me driving past the event on the other side of the motorway. Just as it was all happening. Now that *was* unfortunate, wasn't it?'

Carter sucked on his teeth. 'Yes, a major fly in the ointment. We had to get you in on our plans, because you were a risk.'

'That's why you got me involved, is it? And to do that, you all had to make me think I was going mad, losing it completely… Oh my god, you took me in, hook, line and sinker.'

'It's true.'

'How on earth did you manage to convince me that Karen had died?'

'When we finally got you up into the attic, you were so far drugged that we were able to clear your house fairly comprehensively. What we didn't finish then, we sorted out while you slept it all off the next day.'

'Bastards. Again.'

'Sorry.'

'Are you?'

Carter bit his lower lip. He seemed to smile, though not pleasantly.

'I spotted your password, too,' continued Keith, 'which should have been more original.'

'Again, a schoolboy error on my part, still using that particular name. My boss was not happy.

Malcolm?

'Well, its not Malcolm. His name is Nick.'

'Nick, then. Who is he exactly?'

'Never you mind. Too many questions.'

Keith paused for a moment. He still needed to know more.

'What about Karen?' he ventured.

'What about her?'

'She never was interested in me, then?'

'God knows... Maybe, once. Sorry, fellah.'

'And you managed to persuade her to join your cause?'

'Not exactly difficult, to be honest. She had always been involved in various underground activities. Not the sweet little bunny you thought her to be…'

'I'm beginning to realise that now. But I take it she wasn't meant to march back into our house, after she'd supposed to have died?'

'You're right. She was a fool to do that. She knows better now.'

Keith shuddered at the sinister tone.

'So you want to stick with us, then?' asked Carter suddenly. The question came out of nowhere, but Keith could see that, underneath it all, Carter was still trying to gauge where Keith's loyalties lay.

'Yes, but I still can't believe you want me to kill for you.'

'Don't think of it as killing. It's a political assassination. A necessary assassination.'

'Call it what you will. I am scared at what you're turning me into.'

'Oh, come on, fellah. Let's think about it, shall we? You've had your fun putting straight a few petty things you didn't care for in society, but now you have the chance to make a real difference, a complete change in the order of things. Are you really going to turn down that opportunity, now you've got a taste for doing this? I hardly think so. You are the least likely person to be bringing down a government, anyone looking for the archetypal anarchist is going to completely overlook you, no offence intended. And you have the total support of the Caligula Club – I mean, you couldn't ask for better friends in high places, covering your back, dusting over your tracks, setting the authorities on all the wild goose chases we can devise. This is your big moment, Keith – just think about it.'

'What's in it for me?'

'A seat at the table. Or just wealth. Or both, if you want.'

'I am with you in so many ways,' sighed Keith. 'I'm fed up of the way things are at the moment in the country as well. I hate what we've become… I know why you're wanting to shift the whole place onto a better footing.'

'But?'

'But is this the right way to go about it? And am I really capable of killing someone?'

'We think you are. We *know* you are; you've proven it already. And the way it has been planned, well, there are a couple of high-level players, and then a big one.'

'I don't understand.'

'You will. You see, it's not just the timing of your coming here that was important today. This particular venue happens to sit right on top of the grenade that is about to explode in everyone's faces today.'

'There's a bomb?'

'You could say that, yes.'

'I still don't see what…'

'Right below this building is an old Underground station. Nothing left of the original furnishings, of course, and only one of the platforms still standing. But it sits right on the lines that link Westminster and various other key points in the capital. Mark Lane, it was called in its time. It is now our HQ. Nobody else knows about it, though half a million people travel past it every day without realising. So if you're still interested in helping us, Keith, you'd better get yourself ready to come down there with me. I happen to be one of only a few people with the key…'

Keith couldn't believe his luck! So this was Mark Lane, then – a place, not a person, after all. How often had he been thrown off course like this?

'You're going to get into the Houses of Parliament from the Underground?'

'No, Parliament is coming to us. And then we are going to London City Airport. We need to get out of the city, to put our plans into action. *Operation Incitatus*. It means *swift* or *stirred up* in Latin. And it was a famous horse, too.'

'Caligula's?'

'Spot on. The horse he made into a consul. Today we're making our own tribunes of the people. Today we're going to be the king-makers!'

The waiter had brought over the bill for the drinks. 'Are you coming, then?' asked Carter, as he placed a substantial amount of money on the table; the waiter returned and took the money as Carter waved away any hint of change.

'I need the toilet,' said Keith. He stood up and marched over to the gents.

As soon as he was inside, he feverishly reached for his mobile. God, this was risky. He'd have to be really quick. Send it out quickly to Samantha, where he was and why. They still thought her dead, after all. Otherwise, who would he be texting so urgently? And why at this particular moment?

Actually, on second thoughts, perhaps it would be stupid to keep his phone on him now, just in case they did check it out later. He would have to explain why he'd been writing. And to whom. *Shit, he'd be in trouble…*

Once he had written this message, that would be it – he'd have to be out of touch. There would have to be no way of seeing he'd contacted anyone. After all, Carter was suspicious enough as it was. And if they were going underground they'd be out of signal, anyway,.

Mark Lane disused undergr stn. Cclub HQ. Am going with Carter to Lon City Airport. BBC and Parl.mt. involved

Send.

Checking it had sent, he hid the incriminating phone on top of the cistern, pressed the long flush, washed his hands, leaving them visibly wet, and went back out to join Carter.

'Follow me,' said Carter, and they walked out of the room, leaving behind them an increasingly agitated crowd of affluent City-types looking out of the window as if they were the Russian bourgeoisie peering down onto the streets of St. Petersburg.

Chapter Thirty-four

Carter took him outside. They were on Byward Street, All Hallows directly opposite them. On the pavement, people were walking in every direction, talking animatedly into their phones.

'Not a clue, not a bloody clue.'

'No idea. The whole system's down.'

'I'm heading back on foot. Everything has stopped.'

'Just stay at home, will you. Mummy's on her way.'

Nearby car horns were still being honked, but many of the cars themselves now looked abandoned, and some even had their driver's doors hanging wide open. From the direction of the City a group of burly protesters were heading towards the Tower, placards raised, repeated slogans chanted.

'*CRIMINAL CLASS! CRIMINAL CLASS! CRIMINAL CLASS!*'

Keith followed Carter down into the subway that would take them to the other side of the busy, but blocked road. They descended the steps that led towards the underpass, but then, just as their path turned, Carter stopped, took out a key, turned it inside a keyhole, pushed the numbers of a code into a tiny keypad and then pulled back a screen Keith had hardly noticed at all. It was part of a massive grille that lined this part of the underpass; there was nothing remarkable about any of it, but like so much of London it was part of the fabric of a city that had been reworked, remodelled and altered until the passer-by couldn't even recognise what had once been there. Here, side-by-side with the 70s or 80s brick and tile-work was the old entrance to Mark Lane Station, long-since abandoned and forgotten.

But not now.

As soon as they were through the doorway, Keith found himself following Carter into a well-lit stairwell leading into the depths of the Underground. Behind him Carter locked the entrance. They went down onto the platform.

The place was humming with activity. Serious-looking men and women strode purposefully here and there. Boxes and files were everywhere, and partitions had transformed the whole platform into an open-plan office. Keith could hardly believe his eyes.

The largest screen by far blocked off the length of the platform from passing trains, presumably so that no-one would see any sign of all this activity from the adjacent lines. Anyhow, it seemed to Keith, after all that had been happening to him recently, that people don't tend to look around half as much as they should; it's *heads-down* and carry on…

Above his own head and on the walls were still all the signs of an abandoned tube station: Pre-war posters and scraps of 1960s advertisements called out from an earlier age, and murky, cobwebby corners revealed old brickwork and Victorian, iron girders. Dank, black patches clung to the flaking walls and grimy stalactites of dripping substances hung at the joints of pipes running along the ceiling.

But there were new pipes, too, and wires and cables everywhere. The whole place hummed with frenetic activity, computers and large megaservers in groups of twos and threes flickered and buzzed and clicked beside every desk. People were sitting earnestly at screens, others wandered round checking on different screens. A number of wide TV screens were also fixed high up for everyone to see, showing the 24 hour newsdesks as the day's events were unfolding. Keith noticed a number of military types marching back and forth, then he spotted a familiar face from the world of politics, then another. There was the Shadow Home Secretary, he was sure of it; and over on the far side there were a couple of junior ministers that turn up in the media every so often.

This was in every way bigger than he had imagined it was going to be. There were people in here who had opted for a particular outcome, and had clearly thrown everything in with this potential version of history. Keith could not believe what he was looking at. This operation had been years in the planning, years and years…

'This way,' motioned Carter. A thin, humourless man approached Keith and frisked him thoroughly and intimately.

'Phone?'

'No' answered Keith, relieved at his decision to leave it behind.

The man looked at Carter. 'All clean.'

Now Carter led Keith into the thick of all the activity. They walked between the carefully placed boxes and filing-cabinets, Keith peering into each compartmentalised office-space at the blueish tinge of screens showing maps, charts, statistics, Skyping, emailing. The atmosphere was electrifying. There was loud talking from all sides. There were occasional shouts, even cheers.

One cheer went up when the TV showed that an attempt to reopen Heathrow had been blocked by the arrival of the military. Quite what was happening was not at all clear to Keith. It was weird for him to be so unaware of their exact plans, yet to be at the very heart of where it was all being masterminded.

He needed to know more.

'You're controlling everything from here?'

'At the moment, yes.'

'It's the perfect place.'

'Isn't it!'

'Won't all this eventually be spotted when a train passes?'

'There are no trains running.'

'Of course not…'

'We have hacked into the entire system, and have complete control over what goes where. We've manufactured a number of small but critical collisions at key places on the network, blocking certain routes, and we have also switched most of the trains off the main lines we want to use and onto other routes, where they have either been taken on further by drivers in on our plan, or will simply be brought to a stop at the next station by a confused driver anxious to get everyone off.'

'It's brilliant!' admitted Keith. He was astounded by the amount of thought and planning that had evidently gone into it. And appalled. He was stuck here without contact to the outside world, unable to stop these madmen from sowing chaos and destruction, the like of which had never been seen. He had never felt so alone.

'And you're going to use the link with Westminster to go and take control of it? And the BBC too?'

'Ah, no. Wrong way round. As I said before, Parliament's going to come to us. So is the BBC.'

Before he could explain, another cheer went up. It was being announced on the big screen that the authorities in Birmingham had declared a state of emergency. Shocking footage of tanks and military vehicles rolling past the Bull Ring flickered across the screen.

As they were watching the news a train pulled into the station, stopping on the other side of the main partition that blocked off the platform.

'I thought you said there were no trains?'

'There are two. And this is the first.'

A number of the people milling around opened the partition to meet the passengers disembarking from the train. They sounded like journalists and political pundits as their conversations came within earshot. The train had arrived from the east, and though Keith's knowledge of how the tube lines here actually fitted together was slight, it was soon clear that they had come directly or indirectly from the BBC on the Circle Line. There was all manner of earnest chatter, as they came into the main office area, and spilled out to greet various figures waiting for them. Suddenly Keith realised that things around him were beginning to move fast, as he was dragged along by the currents of these events.

'It was easy, honestly. No-one even batted an eyelid.'

'A couple of old dogs complained here and there, but, you know…'

'I had to let go of Farleigh in the end. She was adamant.'

'The phones were down anyway, so there was nothing she could do about it.'

'Was the train waiting when you got there?'

'Punctual as a German on speed.'

'The Westminster train is on its way here, Carter.'

'Excellent! Do you want to move that one back, then, out of the way? Everyone, this is Caligula Keith.'

'So, this is Caligula, is it?'

'Congratulations. You've been doing a very brilliant job, I hear.'

Keith nodded and shook some hands offered. Then Carter continued: 'Make way for the Level Two's, would you.'

'Listen,' asked a face familiar from the TV, 'shall I go up now and start broadcasting?'

'Why not? Mention Birmingham.'

'Has Birmingham gone?'

'Looks like it has, along with Bristol.'

'That was quick. Especially Bristol. Troublesome lot, normally.'

'And we were hearing before we left the Beeb that the Scottish Parliament was threatening to blockade themselves in Holyrood.'

'Too late. There are already riots up and down the length of the Royal Mile and Princes Street. The powers-that-be won't stand a chance once the militia take over.'

'Someone needs to check on HM. Is she going to fall into line with COBRA?'

'Is COBRA going to involve her anyway?'

'Doesn't really matter, to be honest with you. And if we're coming down the M4 and in from the west, we'll pick her up on the way in if we need to!'

'Looks like the folk at Aldershot have made their move.'

'On to Phase Two, then.'

'Is the whole of the motorway clear?'

'Don't worry, we've sorted it. James has just sent me a clip of armoured vehicles roaring down the M40, it's a hell of a sight, I can tell you.'

'No mistaking what's going down now…'

Another train had just pulled up at the platform, this one coming from the west.

'This is ours,' said Carter enigmatically as he led Keith by the elbow. Most of the people on the platform were already beginning to move towards the open doors of the newly arrived train, and as he stepped onto it, Keith spotted more familiar faces from the world of politics: There was the Shadow Defence Minister; the Shadow Foreign Secretary; the Education Minister; the Home Secretary; a government spokesman for the Chancellor. This was extraordinary. Did these people realise what they were involved in? Did they all understand the kind of organisation they'd thrown themselves in with?

There was an out-of-place *Mind the gap!* as the doors closed, and then they were off, going back westwards, the way the train had come.

One stop. Monument. *Everybody out.*

'The goods have landed at City Airport.'

'That's good news. God, let's hope that is enough for us.'

'Simpkins has overseen the preparations for the docklands embarkation. The boat is ready.'

'Who is taking us out?'

'Miles.'

'I thought he was in Glasgow?'

'He's back. It worked.'

'And Canary Wharf? Are all three lines now blocked?'

'They are. With hundreds waiting on the platforms for their trains to start up again!'

Carter interrupted this conversation suddenly. 'All right, folks. Not too much, hey? Careless talk, etc. He looked sideways at Keith: 'Follow me.'

From the platform of an eerily quiet Monument Station, the whole group, forty or fifty politicians, journalists, hackers and traitors, all made their way down an escalator that had stopped working. Keith found himself going with the flow in an odd, passive manner which did nothing to dispel his fears. He looked up at the signage. They were going deep down now, towards the terminus station of the Docklands

Light Railway. Well, that made sense, given what Carter had said about the City Airport. Clearly they were going to take a train out east.

Sure enough, there waiting for them on the platform was a train, doors open. New faces had joined them now from another platform. Keith remembered that these stations were all interconnected with Bank Station. So here was the money coming, the financiers, the brokers, the bankrollers…

They climbed aboard.

'Henry. Glad to see you made it.'

'We had trouble, Alex. Bit of a scuffle in the end.'

'Fatalities?'

'No more than we'd planned for.'

'Did Alicia make it out?'

'Yes. She's gone to ops point twenty-one.'

'Good. We'll catch up with her once she's done her thing.'

'The Beeb have just gone off-air, too.'

'Have they now? That's interesting.'

'What are they showing? Stirring old footage of World War Two or something from the 2012 Olympics opening ceremony?'

There was laughter.

'Is anyone following Radio 4?'

'They've gone quiet too.'

'Cue the Archers Omnibus!'

More laughter.

'There's the little question of Trident Submarines, though.'

'Surely they have more to go on than listening out for Radio 4, don't they?'

'They do. Don't worry about them. We've turned enough of the top brass for them not to overreact.'

'Recent orders have made sure they're well away at the moment. Far out in the mid-Atlantic. By the time they think about how to react, we'll be in control.'

As the train rattled through the darkness and emerged into daylight, a figure who had been on the platform back at Mark Lane stood up and cleared his throat for attention.

'Ladies and gentlemen,' he called out, as the conversation all around him hushed to silence and faces turned in his direction. 'Ladies and gentlemen, welcome on board this very special service!' There was a ripple of laughter. This was certainly a good-humoured revolution, thought Keith. How very British. The man continued: 'In a short while, we shall be at London City Airport, and from there you all know what you have to do. I wish you well. The story of the century has begun! Good luck to you all!'

There was applause and a cheer or two.

Beside him, Carter turned to Keith. 'Exciting times, Keith.'

Keith nodded. 'Yes, I suppose they are.'

'What a pity you won't be able to savour this amazing event.'

Keith stared back. 'Why not? I thought I was going to be a part of it?'

'So did I, fellah. So did I…'

CHAPTER THIRTY-FIVE

'I don't understand.'

'Oh, don't you? Really?'

'No, I thought you wanted me in on your plans. Christ, Carter! Do you want me in or not? You're just fucking about with me again…'

'Not I,' Carter hissed back. 'Not I, fellah. It's you who's fucking people about.'

'How? How am I doing anything other than what you've asked?'

'Come off it. You had a phone on you back in the hotel.'

'I did?'

'You checked the latest news at one point on it.'

Keith sighed. 'I did?'

'And now you don't.' Carter echoed Keith's sigh. 'I had half-hoped you'd be on-side. Thought we had convinced you to work with us. But, guess what? Suddenly, when checked over, fancy that – no phone, nothing. Wonder where that went… Vanished into thin air, did it, Keith?'

'I – I don't know. I guess...' stammered Keith. But he knew he'd been caught out.

'I shall see in a short while whether you did betray us,' hissed Carter.

'Damn you!' Keith retorted. 'So why bring me along this far?'

'Because, I might have changed my plans for you but, my god, you still have a job to do, old boy. One hell of a job. And you won't be shirking this one, I can tell you that.'

A buzz and a hum took his eyes away from Keith for a second. Carter reached into his pocket and spoke into his phone: 'How many? Keep them away from the strip. We'll be there in twenty.'

He turned to Keith. 'There we are, then… Proof of your treachery, it seems. Turns out the police are at the airport. How interesting. Wonder how they could have known? Only one person could have possibly informed them of our plans today, wouldn't you say, Keith?'

'Could have been anyone,' muttered Keith, though he could hear in his own voice that he didn't sound at all convincing. 'Surely there are people in your operation who might not be all they say?'

'Keith, you have no idea how committed these people are. Just look at who we've got with us. Can you imagine how much they have had to put on the line for this day?' Turning away to look out of the window, Carter continued: 'We shall resolve this, anyway, Keith. And I think someone with a wild imagination like yours will enjoy, perhaps even savour, the creative thought that has gone into the planning of your final moments. I hope you're ready for a surprise. We did have these contingency plans at the ready, just in case.'

Their train emerged from the underground lines. Above the roofs of East London, as their train sped along its raised tracks, Keith could see the signs of chaos gradually overcoming the capital. To the north, not far away was a big plume of smoke, another smaller one in the distance. In the streets below was further gridlock, empty cars and people running around in all directions, some out of panic and fear, others thriving on the excitement of the moment, looters and muggers, gangs and marchers.

The whole place was going mad.

Keith felt it keenly. Somehow, his own madness seemed to have been leading all along to this point, but he had no idea how this present clarity of his could bring him through to the other side of the chaos now encroaching all around.

A distant explosion somewhere out in the suburbs of the city sent a massive, black cloud of smoke into the air. The boom of the crash followed seconds later, and inside the train all eyes turned towards the sight.

'A plane.'

'Brought down?'

'Run out of fuel?'

'Oh my god! A plane, just like that?'

'There'll be more. Hold tight.'

'That can't be right.'

'Today, anything is right.'

'Just hold on. We're almost there.'

'There's a reception committee. You've all heard? Get heads down. Make for the HQ block across the other side of the platform. We'll get you out.'

Keith grabbed Carter's arm, and looked into his eyes, fixing him with a stare. 'Carter! Come on! What are you thinking of? You can't take over a whole country just like that!'

Carter's reply was icily calm. 'Just watch us.'

'Does everyone here know what you're about? I mean, the body farm, the virus?'

'There are different levels of access to the relevant information. As with any organisation. Don't you worry yourself about it.'

'Don't worry about it? Christ, Carter!' Keith was looking around for a way to escape. But it was hopeless. 'Oh my god, this is so out of control now.'

'You'd be surprised how much under control it actually is.'

Keith looked over Carter's shoulder at all the politicoes and journalists. These were all die-hard revolutionaries sitting here, they had invested too much. How would he manage to get away from them? At this late stage, there'd be no way at all of persuading them to change their minds, either… Look at them all – this was a nightmare he was living. An unreal nightmare of madness and impending catastrophe.

Once again Keith was living through a nightmare.

Or maybe it was destiny.

Are we back to the Messiah thing again, Keith?

Keith had to know what was about to happen. At least then he might be able to nudge events in his favour. Maybe even help the authorities get one step ahead. How else could there be any way out of this mess…

'Are you bringing everyone out via the airport? Is that your plan?' he asked.

Carter looked at him for a moment. Then: 'Not quite. You see, it did look, didn't it, as though we'd be taking a flight off somewhere just outside of reach to form our interim government.'

'And you're not?'

'No, it's simpler than that. A boat is sitting waiting to take us downriver to the M25, where we'll make a swift move over to the west of the capital to join forces with the military that has gathered on that side of the city.'

'In this traffic? You'll be lucky.'

'Hard shoulders all the way. We've set up roadworks and traffic blocks around the M25 for all the stretches we'll need. Before you know it we'll be arriving in the west of London at the head of a force ready to impose martial law.'

'A state of emergency? But you're the cause of it.'

'Well, that's not quite how the public will see it. All the trouble will be coming from this end of the city.'

'How so?'

'The reason we hold London City Airport is not to get any of us out. It's to bring something in.'

'What, exactly?'

'Have a guess, come on, Keith.'

Keith looked blankly at Carter.

'Oh well, you'll see soon enough…' Keith did not like the sound of this.

The train rattled past the glass and steel giants of Canary Wharf, round the meander of the River Lea snaking into the Thames, then clunked over switch points as it turned onto the tracks leading further east still, towards the airport.

They had arrived. The splutter of gunfire sounded across a deserted platform, and everyone in the train crouched down. A nearby explosion rocked a building and windows were heard smashing.

'Doors opening now!' someone close by shouted. 'Get out and run to the left. Get across to the HQ. Keep your heads down. The fighting is over the other side!'

Keith was bundled along to the doors that were sliding apart. A harsh, high-pitched rattling of automatic gunfire lashed against his ears, a window nearby burst into a terrifying fountain of glass.

Someone nearby screamed, then one of those beside him tripped and fell beneath the sudden stream of people running. Keith was dragged away with the crowd. Carter was next to him again, gripping his arm, and he found himself pulled through a door and along a passageway. The platform was strewn with glass and plastic, a bloodied hand clawing for a hold on the railing, a body lying in a pool of deep red.

Another scream, then more shouting, and with the shock of someone who hasn't fallen over in years, Keith stumbled and staggered to the tarmac floor. He put out his left hand, was further jostled by somebody behind him, forcing him onto his side, loosened from Carter's grasp. But he was up again within a second, hearing the whizz of bullets nearby. Then past figures looking like snipers as they knelt behind the platform benches and makeshift screens, firing out at their attackers. Finally, crouching beneath tiled walls now chipped from shrapnel and bullets, Keith was pushed down a couple of steps and then back up again and onto another train waiting on the opposite platform.

Where was everyone else? They'd gone round the other corner and disappeared into the depths of the airport, but Carter had brought him here. The firing had stopped abruptly. Keith found himself inexplicably on his knees.

He got up. It was an empty train, except for two men. One was Carter. The other was a familiar figure to Keith, though he had never seen the pockmarked skin until now; the eyes surrounded by weeping, red sores; the hairless eyebrows; the lips ringed with scars from an experiment gone wrong.

'Malcolm!'

'Keith.'

As Keith stumbled to his feet he felt Carter's hands grabbing his own. Before he knew what was happening, he felt his wrists and arms being yanked forcibly behind his back. He caught a glimpse of plastic hand ties.

'What's going on?'

'What's going on, dear Keith, is that you have reached your final act.' Malcolm's familiar voice wormed its way into Keith's head, the soundtrack to a breakdown, the commentator on his descent into madness. 'As they say, this is the end of the line for you!'

Malcolm chuckled at the cliché, as did Carter.

'You're crazy! The lot of you!' cried Keith. 'How on earth do you think you'll get away with all this?'

'Oh, but we will,' answered Malcolm. 'I'm only sorry you're not going to see how well we laid our plans.'

'It really is a pity,' added Carter, pushing Keith violently down onto a seat and tying his binding around one of the vertical hand-holds that ran down the length of the carriages. Keith sat trapped and motionless.

'What's going to happen, then?'

'You are going to carry out a major political assassination, Keith. As planned…'

'I don't think so. Not like this, tied up and helpless.'

'Helpless, but not useless. You see, on your final journey you are indeed going to rid the world of a political activist who has been in the news a lot lately.'

Behind him, near the front of the train, Keith saw boxes being wheeled in, light, plastic canisters with valves and hoses. Then three operatives started working on placing wires around them. A fourth came in after them and placed a device gingerly into the midst of the pile.

There was no mistaking what was happening.

'Yes, Keith,' confirmed Malcolm. 'Detonators and explosives.'

Further down the train Keith could see the same happening again, and yet more beyond.

'Is this the virus?'

'Of course it is,' whispered Malcolm.

'Oh my god. You really are going to release it!'

'We're not. You are.'

Carter interjected: 'Mad Keith's final act. A defiant attack on the public, a lone-wolf's sadistic act of terrorism, an outrage the world will not believe, and which the public will not tolerate.'

'You're going to blame me for all the day's madness?'

'Not all of it, no. But we'll make sure you're seen as a key figure.'

'By the end of the day,' continued Malcolm, 'the world will be rid of Caligula Keith, whose group has been so determined to bring anarchy to the streets of our capital, and to so many other cities and airports all across the country. With our help, order will be re-established.'

Suddenly there was a commotion behind them. Keith turned to see a couple of black-clad thugs dragging a woman into the carriage. They hurled her to the floor.

'Thank-you, boys,' Malcolm smirked. 'We thought you'd like a companion, Keith.'

Keith stared down into the bloodied face of Samantha, who was having her hands tied behind her back by Carter.

'What a pretty couple,' sneered Carter, as he pulled Samantha to her feet and sat her down opposite Keith. 'I'm sure you've got plenty to talk about. Coming back from the dead entails so many good stories, I'm sure.'

'Let's go.' Malcolm caught Carter by the elbow, and they made to leave.

'Malcolm!' called Keith as the doors were about to close.

Malcolm peered back in. Carter was on his phone and grabbing Malcolm's arm, he said: 'The boat's ready. We need to be out of here. The police have been neutralised for the moment.'

'Malcolm!' The urgency in Keith's voice stopped the two men in their tracks. They turned to look back into the carriage. Keith paused just long enough to formulate his words. Then: 'Just one thing: What was Caligula's motive for this final act? I need to know what the story is going to be. What drove my madness, my anger against the world?'

Without hesitation, Malcolm said just one word.

'Money.'

The doors closed with a hiss and before Keith had a chance to say anything at all to Samantha, the train began to move with a jolt. It was on its way, wherever that might be.

'Shit,' cursed Samantha, wiping some of the blood dripping from her upper lip onto her shoulder. 'What is all this?'

Keith stood up. 'We have to act fast. Really fast. Are you attached to anything?'

'Yes. This pole.'

'I can get you off that. Hang on.' Keith was hampered by his own attachment, but with a stretch he could make his leg reach the bottom of her pole, where it was attached to the floor. Kicking with all his might, he loosened it a little.

'You're almost there,' she gasped, leaning further away from his aim. 'Do it again.'

A second kick. A third. A fourth, and with a sudden shock it was free of its bolts which had secured it to the linoleum-clad floor. Samantha swiftly sat down to pass her plastic hand-ties under it, and she was moving freely. Now it was her turn.

'A good kick near the base,' muttered Keith. 'Right at the bottom, near the screws…'

Crack!

He was free. 'Thanks!' he cried, delighted at her strength.

'Good. Get up.' Samantha was looking around earnestly. 'We should get to the front of the train to stop it.'

'We don't have long,' Keith sighed. 'Anyway, what happened to you?'

'Ambushed. They took us on as soon as we got to the airport. I guess they realised you'd warned us. Quite a lot of injured. They isolated me, and made a grab for me from behind. Bastards wanted to get their own back for my disappearance to the underworld!'

'We should contact your team.'

'Who's driving this thing?'

'No-one. The whole line is automated. They've hacked in and programmed it to crash somewhere in the capital. Have you got your handset on you?'

'Yes, but let's try to get these things off us first.' She tugged furiously at the plastic cuffs.

Keith looked around for something sharp and glanced at the floor. Shards of broken window lay scattered nearby.

'Here!' He bent awkwardly down behind him and picked one up. Manoeuvring himself round to Samantha's back, he began to use it like a knife to sever the plastic cord tethering hands together. He immediately felt it slicing into the soft flesh of his own palm and into the roots of his fingers.

'Careful what you're doing.' She retreated jumpily from a sudden slip which nicked her flesh.

'Sorry. I can't see.'

'Try again. Hold it lower.'

'I'm trying. God damn it! I can hardly hold the thing, I've got no grip on it.'

He felt the trickles of blood running down his wrist and saw them beginning to form a dense constellation of crimson drips on the lino flooring. As the train jolted from side to side, her boots smeared them underfoot.

Keith pulled his sleeve down over his hand. It seemed to work.

'Just a bit more. Hold on…'

Snap! It was done. She was free. Now it was her turn. In a matter of seconds she had wrapped a sleeve round her own hand and sawn with the glass at Keith's cords until they too snapped open.

'Well done! Now let's get word out.' Samantha reached a hand to the walkie-talkie strapped over her shoulder, and with the press of a button it crackled into life.

She shouted into it. 'Samantha Taylor here. I'm with Keith Hartman. Over.'

A distant voice responded: 'Morell here. We've had to retreat. Where are you? Over.'

Samantha replied: 'We're on the Docklands Light Railway, heading back into London. The train is packed with the virus, plus detonators and explosives!'

Keith interrupted. 'They're wanting to crash it somewhere publicly. They want to blame this on terrorists and take control.'

'Over!' added Samantha.

'Where are you heading? What's the target? Over.'

'Money. He said money,' answered Keith.

'Over.'

There was a pause. Then Keith pressed the device again and shouted into it.

'Hey! I heard them talking about Canary Wharf. They said they'd blocked all the lines and the platforms were filled with commuters. And there's a branch on this line which goes right through the centre of Canary Wharf. That's it! They're going to crash us there! They're all going to be contaminated.'

'Over!'

Looking back, Keith could see London City Airport now disappearing from view again, as they passed high-rise buildings, offices and luxury apartments; below them sparkled the expanse of the Royal Victoria Dock .

Morell's voice suddenly snapped back.

'Good! We've identified the spot. You're right. They've got trains at a standstill over at Canary Wharf. Over.'

Samantha shouted into the walkie-talkie: 'Get everyone out of there! Evacuate the whole site now! Over!'

'You get off the train somehow. Over!'

'We'll try to stop it first. Over.'

'Wait!' shouted Keith. 'You need to know! Carter and Malcolm – Nick Tyte… They're on their way to the M25 Dartford crossing…' Keith was trying to remember all the details Carter had revealed about their plans. He continued with his garbled regurgitation of the information. 'They're driving right round the M25 to meet their military supporters who are coming in from the west. Over.'

'Thanks, Keith. Now get yourselves off that train. You've only got a few minutes before it turns off into Canary Wharf. We'll clear the place of people. Over and out!'

'Where are you going? How are you going to stop it?' screamed Keith, as he watched Samantha running down towards the front of the train. He followed her through the carriages, his hands leaving thick, gooey prints of blood on everything he touched, as he clambered over the canisters and edged nervously past the piles covered with snaking wires. As they got closer to the cabin at the front, one of the precarious piles fell into the gangway, clattering noisily at their feet.

'Oh god! Oh god… What are we doing here?' rasped Keith, his heart beating so hard he could barely make his voice audible now.

'Look, we're at the controls.' They were at the front of the train, and out of the window ahead they could see the tracks leading over the River Lea, then out over the big roads below, where all the traffic still stood in unmoving queues. To the left ahead rose the shimmering, silver towers of Canary Wharf, the heart of the financial district out here in the east of London. In the sky helicopters were heading over towards the area.

'Look. These are the controls under this lid.' Samantha pointed at the plastic-covered box to the left of the doorway in front, which faced out onto the tracks moving directly beneath them. 'Can we prise this open?'

Keith kicked at the top of the console, trying to dislodge the lid. It was heavy-duty, designed to withstand vandals and hooligans. He tried again, to no avail.

A whirring noise and a shuddering jolt made them both jump and look at each other.

'It's getting faster.'

'They've pre-programmed it to speed up for the crash.'

'Come on!' screamed Samantha with renewed fervour. 'Get it open! Now! Try again!'

Keith sat down on a seat to get better leverage, and kicked again at the panel.

It flew open at last. In front of them was a bewildering array of switches.

'Can we slow it down at least? We're definitely speeding up even more.'

Ahead of them the tracks split off to the left and into Canary Wharf.

'I don't know what is what. Do you? Can you read any of the labels?' cried Keith. He was ready to turn one of the knobs or pull down any switch. Samantha looked paralysed too.

'Oh god!' she shrieked. 'Oh god! I just don't know.'

The train rattled over its points, racing through Blackwall and Poplar stations, their platforms full of confused commuters staring up at the helicopters. From these platforms, police were moving them away down to safety.

Now travelling uncomfortably fast, the train began its final, headlong turn to the left and towards the grand canopied station at the centre of the district, nestled between the great towers at the heart of Canary Wharf. Ahead of them now they could see trains sitting at all three platforms under the steel and glass canopy, one of which was the ultimate target of their own makeshift missile.

'Look! *Doors – Emergency open.* We can jump into the water. Quick!'

He looked to where she was pointing. Seeing a red lever labelled *override* he pulled it right down, hoping it would cancel out the safety mechanisms for when the train was moving, and then he flicked a large switch. Then another similar one next to it.

The door in front of them opened up, causing a flood of warm, summer air to swirl into the carriage, then all the side doors eerily slid out of their anchored positions, filling the whole train with terrifying currents of air.

'Come on!' shouted Samantha. 'This side! It's our only chance.'

Keith leaned out and saw the gravel and the railings racing below. Steel trusses and concrete supports and girders blurrily criss-crossed his field of vision. 'We really have to jump out here? My god!'

'When you hit the water, get under the bridge if you can, because of falling glass. Then swim away from the crash site! Quick as you can! God knows how far this stuff will spread!'

In its final, frantic approach to the station the train was rattling noisily over a bridge. Emerging from under the canopy of the evacuated West India Quay station, as it raced to enter the gap between the high-rise offices of Canary Wharf, a brief, shimmering glimpse of water below was their only cue.

They each leaned out of a doorway, watching the platforms and bridgework rushing below their feet.

'Now!' shouted Samantha as the water of the docks appeared on just the other side of a safety barrier attached alongside the tracks. Pushing with all his might from the running board, Keith felt his body arc into the air, high and clear of the barrier. Out of the corner of his eye he saw Samantha had made it too. They fell down into the gap between two branches of the tracks, tumbling, so it seemed, in slow motion through the shadows of girders and pylons, until they hit the water with a crash.

The darkness enveloped him. He kicked furiously with his feet and pulled himself up with his arms. Light above him felt just out of reach still. Bubbles swirled like crazed fish all over his head and around his eyes.

Then he broke the surface at last. Daylight streamed into his senses. Gasping at the air, he was just aware of another head bobbing in the water under the bridge, when a *crack!* broke above them. Then a boom, followed by the sound of shattering glass.

'This way! Take deep breaths, hold your breath as much as you can… Whatever you do, try not to breathe in too much!' shouted Samantha.

He followed her head, staying under the safety of the bridge for a while as huge shards of glass fell from the buildings above. Finally, they headed out across the open water to the other side of the dock.

In the sky a helicopter appeared.

CHAPTER THIRTY-SIX

It was homing in on them. The two bobbing figures thrashing furiously in the cold water squinted up at the bright sunshine being intermittently blocked out by the noisy machine hovering above them, its blades pushing the water round their heads into wild, swirling and incomprehensible patterns. They could make out a gas-masked figure at the end of a cable, harnesses, straps… The figure came closer, within reach now.

And suddenly they were being winched up into the helicopter, first Samantha, then Keith. A crazy yank through an air now acrid with the smell of burning. As he disappeared inside, Keith just caught a glimpse of the fires raging across the other side of the dock, before the pilot tugged at the controls, lifting them high as quickly as he could. Wrapped up in metallic blankets, surrounded by the noise of radio chatter and the deafening roar of the rotors, they sat back and relished the welcome sense of safety at last. Someone wrapped Keith's hands in makeshift bandaging

A familiar figure appeared and sat down in front of them both.

Keith recognised him as the policeman Knowles.

'Gareth!' screamed a delighted Samantha. 'Thank god you're all right!'

'Hello, you two. Well done. You were amazing.'

'Did you get everyone out of Canary Wharf?' asked Keith.

'We think so. Not heard anything yet, but thanks to you we just had enough time to get announcements out on the Tannoy. The whole area's now clear.'

Samantha asked: 'When will it be safe to go in?'

'We reckon it's an airborne virus, which is why they put explosives on the train. Maximum effect, and people running away from the scene would have taken it with them, maybe spreading it wider. But once it's inside, it stays inside. It was all done to get the greatest impact, and for them to be able to storm in and take control, while everyone was in confusion and terrified at the idea of it spreading. We'll go in with protective gear as soon as we can.'

'And what's happening at large?' asked Keith.

'We intercepted one of the cars on the M25. We're still looking for the other one. It evaded us for a while in the lanes around Potters Bar. Carter's in our hands.'

'And Malcolm?'

'Tyte, he means,' corrected Samantha.

'Tyte is still on the run. But there have been a number of high level operations against the military who rebelled, and it seems that order is being gradually restored. We've whisked HM off to the West Country, as you'd expect, and taken over Westminster and the BBC.'

'Oh my god, though!' mused Samantha. 'There were so many people involved in this. You're going to be making so many arrests, aren't you?'

Knowles grimaced. 'Hundreds. I tell you, this is going to be a difficult time. But thanks to the files we've downloaded from Carter's computer, we have access to all their names, and it's given us a massive pre-emptive advantage. We've got a good idea of who is on our side, and who isn't.'

Keith leaned forwards. 'Who was actually behind it all, then?'

'Far-right alliance backed by American alt-right groups. Once Britain was out of the European Union, they saw this as a way of getting their men into populist positions within our government. Sold it as a clean-sweep for politics, a new, vibrant nationalism, with hands held across the Pond.'

'Crazy…' muttered Samantha. Keith nodded. Pulling his arm out of his blanket, he reached for her hand. She smiled through her still dripping hair.

Turning back to Knowles, she asked: 'Where to now?'

'Hospital for a check-up. Just in case.'

'Broken bones?' ventured Keith.

'And virus infection.'

'Oh. Fair enough.'

Chapter Thirty-seven

The walk home from hospital was everything Keith needed that afternoon. He had been kept in overnight, while he was checked over. Within himself he felt fine – never better, in fact. His back ached from the gymnastics he'd had to perform while jumping off a moving train, and his slashed hands hurt like hell. He dutifully took the various supplements the nurses had told him he needed.

He had half-slept through a night full of dreams punctured with gunshots and warnings shouted from around darkened corners. And on the occasions he had woken up, disturbed by the real noises all around the ward, he could hear the hospital trying to cope with the rising numbers of people wounded in attacks or by masonry falling from burning buildings. It had been a day and a night of terrors right across the country, and the capital was especially hard-hit by the unfolding events.

But by the next day, Keith, who was more than ready to leave, happily gave up his bed and got ready to make his way home.

Checking out at the reception desk, with people swarming all around in bloodied bandages and on makeshift crutches, Keith was informed that a letter had been left for him. The receptionist foraged around on the shelves behind her and then handed over a brown envelope with his name scrawled hurriedly on the front.

'Thanks,' he smiled, as he turned towards the automatic doors of the main entrance. Outside, he was greeted by a bright sky hung with brilliant blue, a few wispy clouds straying just above the roofs on the horizon.

With his now carefully bandaged hands, Keith opened the envelope. It was from Samantha.

Hi. I have left you resting this morning. I understand you're fine, and seeing as I am also fighting fit I have gone back out with the others to mop up some of this mess. I'll get in touch very soon. We all will. In the meantime, get home and relax. You deserve it. xxxx

Smiling still, Keith set out towards the front gates of the busy hospital, and started along the main road. This was the Royal London Hospital. He knew roughly where he was. It was miles from Uxbridge. It would be hours and hours of walking. But he had no choice. There were no buses running, or trains. Not today. And all along the road was the detritus of the previous day's chaos, cars empty and open, some of them burnt out. This would take days to clear, maybe weeks.

So off he set, purposefully but taking his time. He breathed in deeply. The air was fresh. The day felt different, very different from any other he had known. The whole place felt as if it had been reborn, after a trauma.

Heck, Keith knew what that felt like. It would take time, for sure.

The walk would do him good. And tire him out – he would get a better night's sleep when he did finally get home.

And so he walked. And walked.

The sights he saw were astonishing.

At first, as he made his way along the main arteries into the centre of the East End, Keith found himself stepping over the broken glass and debris of a night of rioting, similar to the scenes from the 2011 lootings. Shop windows, the front doors of houses and blocks of flats. On the other side of the road a whole shop-front was still smouldering from the fires that had destroyed everything inside. Acrid fumes hung heavy over this part of the East End. A burnt-out police car stood nearby, then a number of temporary tents set up with ambulance crews still tending to the injured.

'Hey!' shouted someone on the other side of the road. Keith looked, and saw an altercation between two of the local residents over some incident earlier that morning. 'I've been watching you! Hands off my…'

On and on it went, a nation of broken communities struggling to make sense of what had just happened. More broken glass, a lamp post bent right down to the level of the road to block it, a tangled mess of empty cars and puddles of oil. A bonfire burning on a traffic island. A fire-engine spraying a building which was now just a grinning façade, plumes of dense smoke adding to the ash already drifting over the scene from other quarters.

Then a gang of angry young white men shouting across the street at an equally angry gang of young black men, crossing towards each other just as Keith was passing. Their angry women-folk now also getting involved. A police patrol of two young officers on foot clambering over the debris of the night to get to them, before knives were drawn.

Suddenly he was at the edge of the City itself, as the smaller-scale shops and Victorian terraces began to give way to the vast glass and concrete skyscrapers rearing up in London's financial heart. Still the cars lay strewn all around, still there were signs of the previous day's battles. At the entrances to the big institutions and offices stood armed guards, people in suits running in and out, an audible buzz of chaos-control. Everywhere he looked Keith saw people on phones, many of them standing frustratedly waiting to be connected as the systems gradually began to come back online. Above him the glass frontages of the massive blocks were scarred with missing or shattered windows. Out of a few, smoke still rose. Paper was everywhere, on the roads, the pavements, wafting around in the air.

Reaching the Tower of London Keith paused to savour the sight of the army guarding the entrances and standing at the roadside, moving ordinary folk on by. Two small, armoured vehicles squatted like unblinking, protecting demons on the forecourt in front, and there were signs of further activity down beside the Thames, where he could glimpse the top of a military frigate or something similar. Walking on, Keith could not resist taking a peek at the entrance to Mark Lane, which he knew the authorities must have descended on with full force once they'd received his message.

The whole street here was completely blocked off. Wire fencing stopped him from getting close to the subway where he had followed Carter only the day before – god, it felt longer…

Military types were bringing computers and machines out from the subway into makeshift tents set up on the street in the spaces amongst the abandoned cars and vans. Keith thought he spotted Erwin amongst them all, but before he had a chance to shout, a soldier in full fatigues and brandishing a brutish-looking machine-gun moved him on.

'Come on, mate. Move away from here, thank-you. On you go…'

Keith knew that his old self would have wanted to tell this soldier who he was. But this was no longer the old Keith. Smiling, he wound his way into the side streets that led northwards towards the centre of the City and ever westwards on his long journey.

It struck him now how many other people were also out walking. It felt like the whole city had been filled with curiosity about what a revolution, or the aftermath of one, actually looked like. Is this how it was after the Blitz, he wondered, or on the day after the war ended? A sense of childlike fascination with a newly ordered world, a faint relishing of the wild horror that had been unleashed…

Anyway, nothing else on the roads was moving today. No buses at all, no vehicles – there was no space on the road for driving, anyway, what with all the immobile cars and vans, burnt-out or otherwise. Instead people were wandering, strolling even, through a strange landscape of familiar places altered by events into something almost unrecognisable. It was like seeing a relative after many years, hearing their voice, their opinions, their ideas all unchanged and just as predictable as before, but now seeing all this emerging out of an old person's face, the features at odds with how you had always remembered them. As Keith passed them, people were pointing up at damaged buildings, tutting at the wreckage of the previous day's madness, shaking their heads at the weirdness of it all.

He walked past the Bank of England and Mansion House. So many police, so many armed guards; every side street bristled with the presence of the authorities keeping a lid on the situation, while helicopters kept watch in the skies overhead. On the streets, cordons kept the curious at a distance, as black-clad security men talked earnestly with officials. A number of ministerial black cars sat parked in front of the Bank's entrance, evidence of the previous night's panic now marooned amid the unmoving chaos.

Passing ever westwards along Fleet Street and the Strand, Keith began to see his first camera-and-bag-laden tourists, looking every-which-way like wide-eyed pheasants, and wondering what on earth had occurred on their visit to the capital. He realised he was now getting close to the West End, Theatreland, Covent Garden. Still the abandoned cars, though some were being reclaimed now, and their drivers attempting to scrape them past others in the way. The shells of a number of office-blocks and a few looted shops poured their fumes into the air, tents set up by the Red Cross and St. John's Ambulance were in evidence on some of the street corners. There were fewer injured now, maybe it was a lot later in the day.

It must be. Keith must have been walking for at least three hours. He hadn't been rushing – just taking in all the sights and sounds. He was, after all, as curious as the rest. Why not? he thought. Then he remembered his own part in it all, and like a bolt of thunder, a force stopped him still in his tracks.

Christ! How the bloody hell did I escape that? I almost died. It was actually happening around me. I was actually there…

For it felt, as had so much recently, like a strange, dislocated dream.

Not only was Keith viewing these reverberations of chaos as if he was just an outsider looking in, he was finding it very hard to understand that he had only yesterday been at the heart of it all as it was unfolding.

He shuddered.

How easily he could have been injured, how close he had been to death. Even the jump off the bridge might have been fatal if they had not timed it just right. He knew he was so lucky.

But here he was now staring dispassionately at the carnage, as if he'd been away for a while and just returned. He had even been moved on from Mark Lane; he was now once again utterly divorced from the action.

Keith shook himself free of these confusing thoughts and pressed on. He was genuinely relishing the walk, and not just for the momentous history he was seeing all around him. It had been a long time since he had done such a long journey on foot just for the sake of it.

He had reached Hyde Park. It was completely closed off and secured with wire, clearly being used by the authorities as their HQ. The whole park as far as the eye could see had been commandeered and was criss-crossed with tyre and track marks, helicopters swooping in and out, people hurrying in all directions. Tanks and smaller armoured vehicles were rolling out of the gates, a few fenced off areas deep inside were filled with people who were protesting their rights, orders were being barked to units of soldiers who were then running off to carry out their duties somewhere.

The roads all around Hyde Park had been forcibly cleared, cars were literally piled to the sides and on the pavements. A few foreign news channels were broadcasting from a safe distance, though a close eye was being kept on them by patrols of soldiers in jeeps. This was no place to be, reasoned Keith, and he began the long hike along the north edge of the park out away from the centre of London, and making his way finally towards his home.

The abandoned traffic began to thin out and the usually crowded roads beyond Shepherd's Bush were showing signs of moving again, albeit slowly. Ahead, the streets and roads and lanes which Keith knew were leading him home stretched out into late afternoon. His feet were beginning to hurt, though he suspected he was barely half-way along his route. He had no phone for checking his route, just an instinct of where he was headed, and a willingness for complete submission to the day's unfolding.

Slowly, through suburban townscapes that now felt more normal than the centre of London had that morning, Keith emerged into the leafy suburbs he knew so well. Some of them had even been the targets of his recent, snook-cocking incarnation as Caligula, and on one stretch of road where a speed camera still stood defaced by his hand, Keith marvelled at the destruction that had since been wrought on it – the lens showed signs of his black spray, but the rest of the mechanism had been left a mass of warped, soot-covered metal; the pole on which it was positioned had been yanked to a jaunty and useless angle. The anger of the masses, once unleashed, made his own efforts appear like mere scratches on the surface. As he progressed along the roads, more evidence was visible of genuine, maybe middle-class violence lying just below the veneer of suburban good-manners: more speed cameras, defaced road-signs, parking restrictions, traffic-flow barriers, petrol-station forecourts.

Keith was on the other side of these frustrations now. He was no longer sure where his sympathies lay.

Uxbridge at last began to appear on road signs. He was getting close.

The blisters on his feet were starting to hurt. He was by now seriously tired. Not long now, thought Keith, before he would turn into his street, get into the house, start putting things in order, maybe even begin to work out what to do with the place. It was going to feel peculiar for a while, he realised.

He would sleep well tonight, though. God, he would sleep like a babe.

In his own bed again, at last.

Keith arrived at his street, and stood on the pavement looking up at his house. He breathed deeply. He hadn't been back since the night of the body farm. Like many houses he had walked past today, the front door stood ajar, for whatever reason: looters, he guessed, or people just leaving their homes in a blind panic. He was glad; he had no idea where his key had gone in all the excitement.

He walked into the lounge first, taking in the strange bareness of how it had been left. Then he went into the kitchen. Opening the fridge, he was glad to see a light come on. He spotted a bottle of beer in the fridge door, took it out and decided he deserved at least this one treat. He took a bottle-opener from the drawer, flicked off the lid and was about to take a long swig. The lid had come off more easily than he had expected.

Then he looked around.

In that instant he noticed in the mirror hanging in the hallway the reflected image of the walls and doorway out to the living room, the half-visible leg of the trestle table, the corner of the rug on the floor – and suddenly there was a split second of recognition that something was out of place, nothing he could put his finger on, but an awareness of something that did not belong.

And a smell. A presence.

Somebody had been here recently.

Keith went upstairs and now saw what it was he had noticed on the rug, on the walls. A trail of blood here, the smear of a bloodied hand there.

A fugitive looking for shelter. Where else could he have gone, but here? He suddenly shuddered at the thought.

At the top of the last flight of stairs there it was above him, wide open and with the ladder already down and waiting for him to go up.

Keith climbed and pulled himself into the attic.

Chapter Thirty-eight

'Here he comes! Nice and easy does it, Keith. Take your time. Don't want you hurting yourself now, do we… How are you doing, old boy? It feels like it's been a long while, doesn't it?'

Keith said nothing. He just looked at Malcolm, sitting there in his usual chair. No mask this time. Just a pockmarked face, eyes deep in their sockets, blood congealed down one side. In a trembling hand he held a gun, though not in any threatening way.

'You'll have to tell me why I don't kill you here and now, Keith. I wonder why we thought you would be so useful to us…'

Keith made to respond, but Malcolm went on:

'Because you were useful, weren't you? You had that spark to you, that little bit of ego deep within that we helped grow into something beautiful – a messiah complex! And one of the best I've ever seen, too. Caligula the Messiah, a man for the times, a man of the people.'

Malcolm paused. 'Maybe you still believe it, just a little bit? Do you?'

'Maybe I do.'

'Ah! That's the Keith I know and love! Maybe you do, Keith, maybe you do…'

'Why are you here? Why don't you just turn yourself in?'

'Because I have to do something. I have come to take what is mine.'

'There is nothing here belonging to you.'

'Oh but there is, Keith, there is.'

'Go on.'

'It is you, I have returned for. You and your soul, Keith. Another chance to speak, one final fling of the dice. I might just persuade you of what you still have to do.'

'And what is that?'

'Take me back into your head. Let me help you again.'

'You never were in my head. And you're not going to be now.'

'Wasn't I? Really? Let's just think about it, shall we? A modest, straight-laced civil servant living in a lovely part of West London, with a lovely but dull girlfriend, doing a lovely but dull job… Come on, Keith, where do you think all these adventures you've been having came from? Had a swig of beer from the fridge, did you? Good, I thought you'd like one when you got in, thought I'd have one waiting for you. Enjoyed the taste, did you? Excellent!

'Caligula Keith. Caligula Keith.

'Oh, how he runs, how he races through the suburbs on his missions! What a modern-day wonder he is! Ah, the thrill, the desperado thrill of it all!

'Go on then, Keith, where does it all fit in with your life, this great conspiracy? Were you really out there yesterday risking life and limb? Or do you find yourself up here again with me now, just as before? How strange – here you are, after all… Could it really be possible that you just saved the country from an evil plot, or could it be…'

Malcolm leaned forward and whispered with a hiss: 'Could it be that actually you're still half-drunk all the time? Might that not be the more likely answer? What an imagination you have, Keith – wow! What an imagination… Yet all along here you are still, living out your fantasy up in your attic while your empty house festers downstairs. You think you've just gone and got yourself that beer from the fridge? That's because I just told you you did. You haven't been downstairs for weeks now. They've given you up for good. Given up on you, they have… Carter's got someone new in the office to replace you. Karen's still dead. Her stuff's all broken and burnt, down there in the yard. And you didn't just have a ripping time working with the police to solve the greatest conspiracy since the Gunpowder Plot, did you! Come on… What a laugh, Keith, what a completely brilliant confection, the construct of a wild fantasist! Listen to yourself – where have you been living these last few days?

'I'll tell you where – up here, that's where, like you have been doing for weeks now. Weeks and months. What? Don't you believe me? Look around you. Once again you're surprised to see the signs of the truth, Keith. Once again you act as if astonished at the state you've ended up in. Once again… again and again. Each day it's the same, a groundhog day of shocked awakening, the awesome implications of the truth. Well, come off it, my boy. Really, did you truly imagine yourself tied up in that complicated plot, with half of London burning and all the police looking out for you – and you alone saving the day?

'What an imagination. What an imagination…'

'What do you want me to do?' asked Keith, visibly slumping.

'That's better! Now we're talking. Well, for one, you could join me in a drink. Here…' Malcolm reached down to the floor and picked up a nearby bottle of whisky, pouring it into two nearby glasses.

Keith took one. He raised it close to his mouth and sniffed.

'I wasn't alone,' he said. 'Yesterday, when I stopped the attack. Samantha was with me.'

'The policewoman? Are you sure she's not dead again?'

The whisky in Keith's glass flew across the space between them, aimed at the hand holding the gun. As it made contact with Malcolm's skin it fizzed and bubbled. Malcolm shrieked and made to grasp the gun with his other hand, but for a split second he had lost control of his limbs, he hesitated, the gun fell to the ground. Lunging forwards Keith kicked it away, then threw himself at the chair in which Malcolm sat, knocking him out onto the floor, where he writhed in agony at the further disfiguration inflicted upon him.

It was not whisky. Keith knew the smell of real whisky.

'You shit!' Malcolm screamed, lashing out at Keith as he resisted his assailant's attempts to restrain him. They rolled around the attic clasped together in a dance of death. Malcolm reached for the gun, but Keith pulled him back and flung him towards the hatch. Spitting venomous curses, Malcolm brought his fists down onto Keith's face, who held up his hands to defend himself. Malcolm put his face close to Keith's as he bent back his arms in a lock.

'Where are your new friends when you need them the most?' he sneered. 'They'll arrive too late now, they'll find you in a stinking heap up here, a rotting and grinning corpse.'

'Fuck you, Malcolm. You and your fucking games. Coming back here for my soul – you had my soul long ago. You should have pretended Sam was still dead, if you'd wanted to convince me! She'd still be dead, if I was living in your fantasy! But I'm not. Not any more. You're a bastard for coming back.'

With a vehemence that surprised him, Keith wrenched himself out of Malcolm's grip, thrashed his legs with all the energy he could still muster, pushed at his attacker's head with one hand and then rammed his foot onto the hand that was still burning with the acid intended for his own gullet – he felt and saw the skin pulling off the bones, and winced. One more kick, one more punch, and Keith watched Malcolm leaning back towards the gaping hole of the hatch. Back, then further back, then out of sight.

There was a dull thud, then silence.

Complete silence.

Keith dared not look at first. Then he crawled over to the hatch and peered down. Initially, he could not work out how the limbs below had fallen, but then he made out the head twisted below the wrenched-back arms, then the legs on top, all arched back over the lifeless body.

It was over.

CHAPTER THIRTY-NINE

In the following days a strange peace settled over the country, as it readjusted to a sort of normality. There were recriminations, from the attacks on low-life looters and muggers on the streets, to the public declarations in the press and within Parliament. Suddenly there were no more appearances by the Home Secretary, the Minister for Education, the Shadow Foreign Secretary and a large number of various junior ministers, back-benchers and politicians.

The BBC returned to the screens, with an oddly reduced schedule, as it became accustomed to the new circumstances. Some of the Corporation's familiar faces turned up only in the context of newsworthy arrests and trials. At first the news programmes were dominated by pundits who, for once, did not seem to have any answers. There was a feeling of experts finding their way again, blinking in the light of a new reality.

The airports reopened. Slowly the debris from the half-dozen or so planes that didn't make it to a runway was cleared, investigations were opened, debate was aired.

In the weeks that followed, the lid was lifted on the whole affair, and it began to sink in just how many people had been hoodwinked into going along with the plot: Politicians who had been promised this or that, new facilities, extended powers; building contractors sent on wild-goose chases to dig up key roads, putting roadworks into places they weren't needed, digging holes for pipes which were never going to arrive; technicians blackmailed into revealing ways of hacking into transport and infrastructure systems. The list went on. The trials continued.

The railways began to run again. A reduced schedule at first, until all the lines were free of the rogue carriages that had been moved around the system by the plotters. Some of the Underground started to return to normal, people began to go back to work.

The greatest shock had been at Canary Wharf. A few had died, some simply in the crush of panic when the platforms had been cleared. Then the whole district was shut off, the men and women in contamination suits waded in to start the cleaning-up. News seeped out about the intended event, the carnage that had been envisaged. A shocked nation sat up straight and leaned into the television… This event in particular brought home the nature of the revolution that had been planned for the country.

Keith watched it all unfold at home in those first few days. After Malcolm's death, the authorities announced that the plot had at last been comprehensively thwarted, with the last of its ringleaders now dead or in custody. The working routine of the nation finally juddered back to life, and although he was keen to climb back into the rhythm of work himself, Keith was persuaded to extend his holiday for a while longer.

No word had been heard about Karen's whereabouts. She had simply disappeared without trace. Good riddance, thought Keith, though he was puzzled and confounded by her complete and brutal removal from his life. It was odd to be alone again and in such a disconcerting manner. Wherever she had gone, he was sure he would never see her again.

But he was not entirely lonely during these strange few days of aftermath.

The visitors kept coming. Not just officials from the authorities, the military, the police, but family, friends, even just local well-wishers who had seen his face in the papers and on the news. There were even a few who came in quivering admiration for his work as Caligula Keith; these he had to deal with carefully, as their enthusiasm for his undercover 'good works' betrayed a flash of wild-eyed fanaticism.

A visit from his parents actually delighted him for being an antidote to the excessive attention he was receiving. An entire afternoon chatting about various people from their past about whom Keith had no memory or interest, then a 'trip out' to a garden centre and a quick visit to the town centre, where his father could go into every charity shop along the High Street on the perennial lookout for cardigans.

There were a few other 'trips out' which brought Keith back into his new reality. A visit to examine the body farm was as harrowing as he knew it would be, but it was necessary to go through everything he had seen and done here. Many of the bodies had by now been removed, a grisly task with no end in sight for the poor devils in protective suits who were taking them off into special units to be autopsied, investigated, maybe identified.

Other trips took him back to Central London, interviews with various big-wigs, a briefing with the Cabinet and the Metropolitan Police Commissioner, a look through some of the files they now had in their possession. So much more made sense to Keith as he saw the whole conspiracy unfolding in front of his eyes, so much was now in focus.

But one thing was also very clear: his job was done. He had played his role – admirably, but it was over. Things were now in the hands of those above him.

And rightly so, thought Keith.

By the end of the following week, he needed to go back and see again what was happening for himself. He took his usual train into the centre of London and watched the familiar suburbs rolling past: Ickenham; Ruislip; Ruislip Manor; South Harrow; Ealing Common… Although he had spent his time off going into Uxbridge town centre, taking some long strolls out along the canals and rivers near the M25 and pottering around bookshops and in cafés, he had not wanted to venture back to some of those places where everything still felt too raw in his memory.

But today he woke with the urge to look again at the places that had haunted his action-packed dreams throughout the last few nights. Were his memories and experiences now catching up with him, he wondered – did they need to be expunged somehow by going back, by revisiting the sites?

He might not make it all the way across to the east, but he felt the need to see what was going on in and around the Parks and down by Westminster. He had spoken with Samantha the night before and chatted about the situation. She was confident that the centre would soon be back to normal, and that the military shut-down would be eased within a matter of weeks. The system had been more resilient than some had feared, thank god.

It was just how she had described it. Whole swathes of famous parts of the West End still cordoned off and out-of-bounds, several buildings gutted and tied up in scaffolding; parks requisitioned and fenced off, unrecognisable in their new purpose. But the traffic was moving now, and most of the abandoned cars were gone, or delicately placed on the side of the roads with surprisingly understanding notices on them, awaiting retrieval. A polite aftermath to revolution, Keith thought – almost a tangible sense of relief that it had not been worse.

How very British.

Tired, Keith caught the early afternoon train back. He immediately found himself beginning to doze off; clearly he had pushed himself too much this morning – he should have taken it easier. He felt his head nodding involuntarily forwards again and again until a judder of the carriage would jerk him out of his blurry slumber; he would wake for a second or two, glimpsing the cables and pipes running along the dark tunnels outside his window, then drift back into dream.

All the way out of the centre of London, along the familiar Piccadilly Line, station after station passing him by, until someone accidentally caught his elbow or knee, as they sat down in the seat next to him. Then he might look up, spotting the name of the station they were slowly pulling out of: Leicester Square; Piccadilly Circus; Hyde Park Corner; Knightsbridge…

The train, now overground, pulled slowly into the next station. It was with a jolt that Keith realised he was at Barons Court. As they slowed right down to meet the platform, Keith suddenly spotted, among the various passengers-to-be, milling around waiting for his train, none other than Kitchen Woman herself.

Was it her? He was sure of it. Yes, there she was, in a tight-fitting, beige jacket that reached to just below her hips, a short, black skirt that touched her knees and a pair of loose, tan, leather boots that lingered around her calves. She held her two children by their outstretched hands, and was moving with focused intent towards where she was calculating a train door was about to be.

His heart actually jumped.

Why? Was it because she was coming onto his very carriage? Was it because she looked as good as she did from a brief glimpse through several panes of glass each morning? Or was it the sudden intrusion of reality into a dreamy, cocooned unreality he had built up for himself over the past… god knows how long?

She climbed onto the train, disappearing from his view. Then she disappeared for good, not entering his carriage at all, but making her way further down towards the front.

That's it, he thought. She's gone! OK, leave it well alone, then. Let her remain that remote, untouchable, untenable dream. Untainted and beyond reach. Unreciprocated. Unaware, even… *That's* a distant love for you!

But Keith was curious. Of course he was. And this happy serendipity, this single chance he had just been thrown, such an opportunity would not arrive again, surely.

He simply had to see what she was like close up.

He would have to give up his seat, but nobody would mind that, would they?

This was creepy, though, wasn't it? He felt creepy. What if anyone had spotted he was heading off just to peer at someone? What if she noticed, after all?

None of this was likely, Keith decided. Who would really spot him, once he'd headed off to the other carriage. He could have thought he'd seen a friend, that's why he'd headed off. No-one would be any the wiser. And he would finally get to see Kitchen Woman. A kind of closure, that was it…

Closure?

Come off it, Keith – who are you trying to kid? You want to look.

He stood up and left his seat with the burden lifted of not knowing what she actually looked like, but replaced by the guilt of his underhand motive. He felt sullied by it, but pressed on ahead, pushing politely through the crowd and edging out of his carriage into the next.

It took a while to find her, as she had evidently not found a seat here, and had moved on to the next carriage altogether. As he made his way through the following set of pressurised doors, Keith suddenly spotted her. She was sitting almost directly ahead of him. People were crowded around her, standing and leaning against the seats, some reading, others staring blankly ahead. Enthroned amongst them was Kitchen Woman, a young child on her bare knees, another, girl of about five, sitting beside her looking out of the window and chatting away about whatever was flitting through her mind and across her vision. Kitchen Woman listened attentively to her daughter, and every so often raised her legs a little to jolt her younger child rhythmically on her lap, whispering smilingly at them both.

She was slim and elegant, but had slightly puffy cheeks and jowls; her long, dark hair fell over her shoulders, rich and dense. Keith edged a little closer.

Her eyes were tired and dark rings ran around below them where fine wrinkles coalesced. Across her top lip was a moustache that became more noticeable where it reached the crease of her cheeks, at either end of her mouth.

It was like peering at an exhibit in a gallery.

Chapter Forty

The doorbell rang, reminding him that he needed to replace the Mozart-based chimes. It was Samantha.

'Hello, you!' she beamed.

'Hi!' It was the first time he'd seen her on her own since their little trip into Canary Wharf. They'd met for a few meetings here and there with colleagues and officials from Whitehall, but now she stood there on his doorstep, some flowers in her hand, and smiling.

'Back from the dead…' laughed Keith.

'Again! I brought you these,' she answered, 'thought they might brighten up your house. When I saw it last, it all looked pretty bare and empty.'

'Thanks.'

'Not primulas, I'm afraid. Not the right season.'

'Don't worry. I wouldn't want to be reminded.'

'Of our adventure?'

'Of my mother's conversation!' They laughed. He took them from her hands. 'They're perfect. Thank-you. Come on in.'

He closed the door and led her into the kitchen, where he put the flowers into a vase and filled it with water. Placing it on the window sill looking out over the yard, he said:

'I am thinking of going back into work on Monday.'

'Good for you. Feeling ready?'

'I am. It's time to get back into it, and I think they going to need every hand on deck now, so…'

'Nice one. I don't blame you.'

'But I'm also thinking of handing in my notice.'

'Really?' she perched herself on one of the high kitchen chairs. 'Why? You're obviously good at what you do.'

'I don't know, to be honest – but I reckon there's more to be had out of work than what I do. They were talking to me about working higher up, now that I've done what I've done. They said they see a lot more potential in me now, and hope I could contribute to things at a level of… Oh, I don't know – blah, blah! You know what they're like.' He paused to put the kettle on. 'Fancy a tea, or a coffee?'

'A coffee, yes please. But they've got a point. You've got loads to give, especially now. Maybe they could find you a really interesting niche job somewhere else within the Service.'

'Maybe. Maybe not… Milk?'

'Yes please. Perfect, thanks. So what else would you do?'

'Move away. Travel? Work abroad?'

'Really? Gosh, didn't see that coming.'

'Nor did I. Not at all. Sugar?'

'Just one. Cheers. Abroad where?'

'Do you know what?' Keith studied her face as he continued. 'I feel like selling up here, getting away from things so completely that within a few years nobody would hardly recognise me. So, somewhere remote, Africa maybe. Or South America. Set myself up as a different person. Follow a different route entirely, a completely different life.'

'So what are you actually doing by making such big changes? Running away?'

'Probably. Which is why I suppose I won't.'

They moved on into the lounge with their drinks, and she sat on the single sofa, while Keith perched on an upturned box.

'To be honest,' he continued, 'I have been thinking about what I am doing here. I don't have a life left to come home to, and this whole madness has made me wonder what I am actually achieving here.'

'Well, you have achieved something unbelievable, no-one can take that away from you – there's no denying you've saved massive numbers of lives, as well as helping to prevent an attack on the whole state.'

'Fair enough, but…'

'So I guess what I'm saying is, you've every right to feel you've earned a change now. But then, on the other hand, if you've been such a key figure in uncovering the conspiracy, then all your hard work at the Civil Service must have paid off, must have enabled you somehow to apply your knowledge to sniffing things out when they weren't right. Don't you see?'

'I do, I do see.'

'That's great detective work. That's what we look for in the police, especially the kind of stuff I've been involved in these last few years.'

'I know, I know…'

'Don't run away and hide your talents, Keith. Anyway, I for one would miss you.'

'Thanks. I'm only thinking about things, that's all. Just getting stuff off my chest. Bouncing ideas off on you.'

'I appreciate it. I really do.'

'God, I was devastated when they told me you'd died.'

Samantha winced. 'I am so, so sorry to have put you through that. It didn't seem right. I feel awful.'

'I was cut up. Took me by surprise.'

'I'm glad to hear it, though.'

He looked at her with a sideways glance, and they exchanged smiles. The smiles of relief when a disturbing dream is seen for what it is.

'Hey,' he said, with a jolt back to reality, 'you're back now, for good, I hope.'

'I hope so too.'

'Fancy going out somewhere?'

'I do.'

'Let's do it. Let's go out.'

Feeling all his pockets for his spare house key, then finding it in the kitchen on the breakfast bar, Keith realised he had not automatically put it on the docking port. A sign of things to come, he thought, as he pulled his jacket on, saw Samantha out of the front door and closed it behind them.

THE END

Printed in Great Britain
by Amazon

27306487R00169